"You don't get it, do you?"

Cora shook her head. "What's making me nervous is you. International superstar, renowned scientist, sexiest man on the face of the planet— and you're trying to seduce me. One part of my brain keeps screaming yes, while the other part keeps telling me this can't be for real."

While the idea of her saying 'yes' was quickly working its way through his blood, and having a predictable effect on his libido, the sincerity of her doubt rang through. "Why not?"

"Are you kidding? You could have any woman in the world—"

"There's only one I want at the moment."

"See, there it is. Why in the world would you say something like that?"

"Why do I want you? Are you serious?"

"Of course I'm serious. I'm a reasonably attractive, educated woman. And I can't quite figure out why ordinary Cora Prescott has extraordinary Rafael Adriano in hot pursuit."

Dear Reader,

Happy Holidays! Everyone at Harlequin American Romance wishes you joy and cheer at this wonderful time of year.

This month, bestselling author Judy Christenberry inaugurates MAITLAND MATERNITY: TRIPLETS, QUADS & QUINTS, our newest in-line continuity, with *Triplet Secret Babies*. In this exciting series, multiple births lead to remarkable love stories when Maitland Maternity Hospital opens a multiple birth wing. Look for *Quadruplets on the Doorstep* by Tina Leonard next month and *The McCallum Quintuplets* (3 stories in 1 volume) featuring *New York Times* bestselling author Kasey Michaels, Mindy Neff and Mary Anne Wilson in February.

In *The Doctor's Instant Family*, the latest book in Mindy Neff's BACHELORS OF SHOTGUN RIDGE miniseries, a sexy and single M.D. is intrigued by his mysterious new office assistant. Can the small-town doctor convince the single mom to trust him with her secrets—and her heart? Next, temperatures rise when a handsome modern-day swashbuckler offers to be nanny to three little girls in exchange for access to a plain-Jane professor's house in *Her Passionate Pirate* by Neesa Hart. And let us welcome a new author to the Harlequin American Romance family. Kathleen Webb makes her sparkling debut with *Cindrella's Shoe Size*.

Enjoy this month's offerings, and make sure to return each and every month to Harlequin American Romance!

Wishing you happy reading,

Melissa Jeglinski
Associate Senior Editor
Harlequin American Romance

HER PASSIONATE PIRATE

Neesa Hart

TORONTO • NEW YORK • LONDON
AMSTERDAM • PARIS • SYDNEY • HAMBURG
STOCKHOLM • ATHENS • TOKYO • MILAN • MADRID
PRAGUE • WARSAW • BUDAPEST • AUCKLAND

ISBN 0-373-16903-5

HER PASSIONATE PIRATE

Copyright © 2001 by Neesa Hart.

This edition published by arrangement with Harlequin Books S.A.

Visit us at www.eHarlequin.com

Printed in U.S.A.

ABOUT THE AUTHOR

Neesa Hart lives in historic Fredericksburg, Virginia. She publishes contemporary romance under her own name, and historical romance as Mandalyn Kaye. An avid theater buff and professional production manager, she travels across the U.S. producing and stage managing original dramas. Her favorite to date? A children's choir Christmas musical featuring the *Pirates of Penzance*. She loves to hear from her readers, and can be reached at her Web site: http://www.neesahart.com.

Books by Neesa Hart

HARLEQUIN AMERICAN ROMANCE
843—WHO GETS TO MARRY MAX?
903—HER PASSIONATE PIRATE

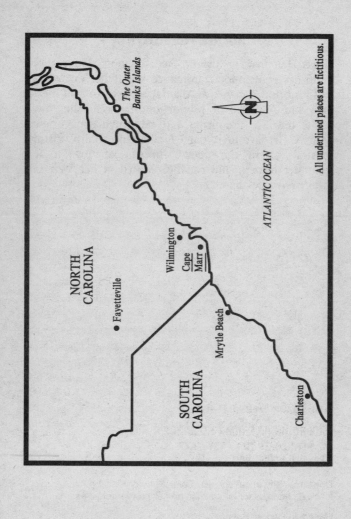

NORTH CAROLINA

• Fayetteville

Wilmington •
Cape •
Marr

The Outer
Banks Islands

N

ATLANTIC OCEAN

Mrytle Beach •

SOUTH CAROLINA

Charleston •

All underlined places are fictitious.

Chapter One

Dearest,

*How I missed you tonight! Father had guests—the
most tedious of gentlemen, and I wished so to look
across the table and find you smiling at me. The winds
were high last night, bringing, as always, thoughts of
you. I lay upon my small bed, willing the currents to
bring you to my side. How my heart longs for you,
dearest. In the night, I strain my ears, hoping against
all reason to hear that most beautiful of sounds—the
slap of your saber against our back stairs as you
mount them in your haste to reach me. I never would
have believed that I could yearn so desperately, nor
ache so much, for the touch of another. But from my
first glimpse of you   with your dashing ways, your fine
physique and your magnificence—I fell completely under your spell. Come quickly, dearest. I need you so.*

Lovingly yours,
Abigail
21 April 1861

Abigail Conrad, with her undiluted admiration for her pirate
lover, was on to something.

Definitely on to something, Cora Prescott decided as she surveyed the man standing at the back of her lecture hall. "Fine physique," indeed.

Deliberately she pulled her gaze from Rafael Adriano's unbelievably magnetic presence and made herself concentrate on her students. "I'm sorry, Ms. Grimes," she said to the college girl who'd just spoken. "What was your question?"

"Well—" Cathleen Grimes leaned forward to press her point "—I wanted to know why you think that the warrior/romantic hero is the definitive women's fantasy."

Turn around and look, Cora thought as she deliberately avoided the temptation to glance at Adriano again. She cleared her throat, instead. "The warrior/romantic embodies what women both want and admire in the opposite sex."

"Like Don Juan?" the student asked.

"Or Robin Hood?" another student added.

Cora nodded. "Precisely. He represents a patriarchal view of the world. He is the king of his own domain. The medieval lord ruled his keep. The duke or earl held responsibility for his entire estate. The Americanized version— heroes like Zorro, Superman or the Lone Ranger—was created to embody the myth of the solitary warrior. He's strong, independent and heroic. But despite this image, he puts aside his warrior instincts for the sake of a woman."

Another of her students leaned back in her chair. "Doesn't that play into the woman-needs-saving mentality? You know, the Cinderella complex?"

"No." Cora shook her head. "In these stories, the woman does the saving. While he may rescue her physically, she rescues him emotionally. The emotional impact of the story is always given more weight than the external plot."

"So redeems him?" the student asked. At that question, Adrian gave Cora a pointed look.

"Yes. Precisely."

Another student offered, "Like the pirate fantasy. He's this corrupted guy, and she comes along and makes him change his wicked ways."

Cathleen Grimes laughed. "Only after he has his wicked way."

The quip sent the students into a round of free conversation and increasingly ribald comments. Adriano shot Cora an amused look and braced his shoulder against the door frame.

"But, Dr. Prescott," one girl said, "I mean, really, isn't that just a bit farfetched?"

"It could be." Cora propped her hip on the edge of her desk. "But that doesn't mean the fantasy isn't still very potent."

"Do you think that explains," asked the same student, "why some women go for that scruffy look—you know, the long hair, three-day beard, that kind of thing?"

Karen O'Neil, one of Cora's brightest students, laughed out loud. "And smelly," she added. "If they're really into the pirate persona, they'd have to smell like they'd been at sea for eighteen months."

Ah, irony, Cora thought as she suppressed the urge to gloat. No way would she let the opportunity to goad Adriano slip through her fingers, not when he'd been a thorn in her flesh for the past several weeks. "That's why it's a fantasy, Ms. O'Neil." She swiveled her laser pointer between her fingers. "Pirates have been romanticized to the point that there are some men who cultivate the look—and there are, undoubtedly, some women who find it attractive."

"Sexy," muttered a student. "They find it sexy."

Cora looked at Adriano. His firm mouth appeared to be twitching at the corner. Deliberately she held his gaze. "They believe it makes them irresistible to women."

"Doesn't it?" Cathleen asked. "I mean, look at that guy who's all over the news lately. What's his name? That archeologist from the Underwater Archeology Unit at the North Carolina Department of Cultural Resources.''

With a loud sigh, another student supplied, ''Rafael Adriano. He's unbelievable.''

He certainly was. Cora saw a sparkle enter the jet-black of his eye. She could almost feel the temperature in the room rising.

Her students lapsed into a casual discussion of his appeal while she watched him. Adriano's name had become almost a household word since his recent discovery of a site believed to be the underwater remains of the *Argo*—the ship of Greek myth. At first only the scientific community had paid much attention to the find.

It hadn't taken long, however, for a few enterprising reporters to look at him and see the most marketable scientist the world had known since Einstein. Like Einstein, he was brilliant, eccentric and groundbreaking. Adriano, however, practically defined sex appeal. He looked more like a pirate than a researcher and almost overnight, he'd become a hotticket item. When his picture appeared on the cover of a magazine, it was a guaranteed sellout. Women everywhere seemed to adore his slight accent, his cultured manners and the edge of barbarism that said all the attention had merely tamed him for a moment. Every talk show, newsmagazine and network in America was clamoring for a piece of him.

But like most scientists she knew, now that the discovery was made, he was ready to move on to a new hunt.

Unfortunately at the moment he was fixated on a project that had reportedly haunted him for much of his accomplished career. He wanted to find the remains of the *Isabela*, a Civil War period clipper that was captained by the successful privateer, Juan Rodriguez del Flores.

And Cora was smack in the middle of his way. She'd hoped her last correspondence with him had been enough to deter him. Obviously she'd been wrong.

His only reaction to the somewhat ribald course of her students' comments was a slight lift of his eyebrows. Cora sensed that the conversation was about to spin dangerously out of her control. Pressing her glasses higher on the bridge of her nose, she dragged her concentration back to her class. Dr. Rafael Adriano had a formidable reputation. And he loved it. If she knew one thing about him, she knew he adored being the center of attention. If he'd thought to disconcert her by arriving unannounced in her classroom, he was about to be sorely disappointed.

"I hear," one of her students was saying, "that Adriano is on the track of some new discovery. Something bigger than the *Argo*."

"Did you see that picture of him in *Time* magazine? He is too hot, girlfriend." The student fanned herself with her spiral notebook.

The other girls laughed.

"I have a friend who saw him give a seminar," one added. "She said he's, like, drop-dead gorgeous. All you have to do is listen to him to get turned on."

"That voice!" Cathleen interjected.

"And the accent," said another girl.

"Can you imagine—" another student leaned over the edge of her desk and dropped her voice "—the sound of that man whispering in your ear?"

"Oh, Lord."

Cora was having trouble containing her amusement as her students chased Adriano's rabbit. "Ladies…" she said, trying to wrest control of the conversation.

They blissfully ignored her. "Gawd. I saw him on CNN the other night. He was talking about some new ship he's looking for. When he started explaining the 'thrill of discovery…'" The student rolled her eyes in mock ecstasy and flopped back in her chair.

Cathleen chuckled. "I'll bet I could think of a few things for him to discover."

Cora used the distraction of the students' ensuing laughter to recapture her advantage. "Okay, ladies." She waved a hand to gain their attention. "Enough. This isn't getting us anywhere with our discussion of pre-Renaissance romantic literature."

"No," one of the girls drawled, "but it's doing a lot for my visualization skills."

"Really?" Cora slanted Rafael a dry look.

"Oh, definitely. I mean, with that eye patch and all... Jeez, Dr. Prescott, you can't say you haven't noticed. The guy is, like, practically the sexiest man alive."

Cora tasted victory. She didn't doubt for a minute that he'd planned to disrupt her class—to catch her off guard with his sudden arrival. It seemed only fair that he should pay the price. "So you think Dr. Adriano is the perfect romantic hero?"

Cathleen rolled her eyes. "Oh, yeah."

"Well, then—" Cora tossed her lecture notes and laser pointer into her open briefcase and shut it with a decisive snap, "—perhaps you'd like to hear him tell you exactly why he chooses to parade about dressed like Long John Silver." She indicated the back of the room.

With a collective murmur of confusion, her students turned to face him. If she hadn't known better, she'd have sworn the color she saw in his face was a blush. "Dr. Adriano," she said, "I'm glad you could make it today. I was half afraid you wouldn't show."

He gave her a knowing look. She'd trapped him like a rat, and he knew it. With thirty students watching him with rapt attention, he had two choices. He could follow her lead and complete her session for the afternoon, or he could look like a fool by turning to leave. Cora waited patiently while he weighed his options.

No surprise, he rose to the occasion. With what she could only define as a look of admiration, he strode toward the front of the room. "You'll have to forgive my tardiness, Dr. Prescott. I was delayed."

"I see. Well—" she indicated her class with a sweep of her arm "—I'm sure you'll have no trouble convincing them to stay a little later. Even if it is Friday afternoon."

From the looks on the girls' faces, he'd have to toss them out of the room before they let him leave. He studied Cora with a lazy insolence that said he knew exactly what she'd done and there'd be hell to pay later. She picked up her briefcase and headed for the door. "You're leaving?" he asked. His voice slid over her nerves like melted butter. In the interviews she'd seen him conduct, she'd noted that he could turn anything, even something simple like standing in the back of her lecture hall, into an erotic exercise.

She refused to be flustered. "Yep. You know how summer school is. Papers to grade. Exams to write."

"I see." He glanced quickly at her class, then back to her. "When can I see you again?"

Damn him. The question was deliberately provocative, and he knew it. By evening, the campus would be abuzz with the news that the reserved Dr. Cora Prescott was somehow involved with Rafael Adriano—America's favorite pirate. "I'm not sure. My schedule is heavy between now and the end of the week."

Her students' heads swung back to look at him. He leaned one hip on the edge of her desk, much as she had done earlier, and said, "Mine is, too. I'll call you later. Don't worry. We'll work it out."

She thought about responding, then decided against it. Anything she said would just make the situation worse. Might as well leave him to deal with the students' questions while she made a strategic retreat to the sanctity of her office. "Fine." She turned to go.

"Dr. Prescott?"

Cora hesitated, then faced him a final time. "Yes?"

"I'm glad I could be here for you."

The rake. Cora gave him a knowing look. "Then welcome to North Carolina, Doctor."

CORA SLIPPED into her office with a quiet sigh of relief and a sense that she'd narrowly prevented disaster. She knew precisely why Rafael Adriano was in town.

He wanted her.

Or rather, he wanted her house. She'd been ignoring his most recent letter for weeks, trying to delay what she knew was the inevitable confrontation. He wasn't about to let a potential lead on the *Isabela* elude him. When she'd discovered an original set of antebellum diaries hidden in the historical seaside house where she lived, his interest had been sparked. According to the news reports, Cora had happened on the diaries during a remodeling project. Initially, because the diaries were written in the form of letters to an unnamed lover, Cora hadn't been able to identify them. After study and carbon dating, however, she'd confirmed that the diaries belonged to Abigail Conrad, the rumored lover of the *Isabela*'s captain. That revelation had put Rafael on Cora's trail like a hound after a fox. Running her to death appeared to be his strategy.

As far as he was concerned, her house sat right on the secret that would lead him to the site of the wreck, and he was determined to have it.

She couldn't think of a worse fate than having him underfoot—especially now, with her three nieces spending the summer with her. The thought of her sister, Lauren, made her frown. Lauren had dropped the girls off three weeks ago on her way to Florida with her married lover. She hadn't called since, and all three of her daughters were showing signs of stress. Kaitlin, the oldest, seemed to stay in a permanent sulk, while Molly and Liza, her younger sisters, were prone to brooding. Cora was nearly at her wit's end, and now Rafael Adriano had shown up to take over her life.

Following his discovery of the *Argo,* he'd become the center of world attention. Cora didn't exactly relish the idea of being in the middle of a global fishbowl. She had too many things on her mind, too many lives to manage, too much work to do authenticating and documenting the diaries, to have him, his research and his ego disrupting her life. So she'd said no.

Unfortunately Rafael Adriano wasn't the kind of guy who took no for an answer.

The door of her office abruptly opened, cutting short her brooding thoughts. "So, Professor—" Cora's graduate assistant, Becky Painter, hurried into the shoebox-size office with two sodas "—what's up with the stud in 203? You've got the whole hall in an uproar."

Cora shot her a dry look. "You mean you don't recognize him?"

"Nope. Believe me, if I'd seen that face and that body together in the same place at the same time, I'd remember."

"You don't get out much, do you, Becky."

"Are you kidding? I'm in the last year of my masters program. Of course I don't get out much. I work for you. I study. I write parts of my thesis. I go to class. I obsess. Sometimes I manage to sleep a little. There's no time for *out* in that syllabus."

Cora laughed. "I guess not. I almost forgot what that was like. I think when I was working on my Ph.D., I slept about nine hours a month." The can of diet soda Becky handed her was coated in tiny shards of ice. Cora wiped it clean with a napkin before setting the can on her neatly organized desk. "The gentleman—and believe me, I apply the term loosely—is Rafael Adriano."

Becky choked on a sip of her soda. "*The* Rafael Adriano?"

"I thought you didn't get out much."

"Jeez, I'd have to live in a hole not to know that name. I do read, you know. He's, like, the hottest thing to hit the ocean since Jacques Cousteau."

"Dr. Adriano is a bit flamboyant."

"And sexy. Now that you mention it, I think I did see a picture of him in some magazine. I remember thinking that if I had time for hormones, I'd really be into this guy." She tipped her head to one side. "What's he in town for, anyway?"

Cora leaned back in her chair. "He wants to conduct some research. He's looking for the site of the USS *Isabela,* and he thinks he can find it here."

"*Isabela?*"

"It's a ship from the Civil War—one of the fastest ever built. Juan Rodriguez del Flores captained it during the early years of the war. There's some evidence to suggest he was a privateer who ran contraband for the Confederate and Union armies."

"Both?"

"Whoever paid cash," Cora assured her. "And when no one paid, he kept the booty for himself and his crew. If Adriano can find his ship and if it's in any kind of decent condition, it might provide some invaluable information to Civil War historians."

"So what's he doing conducting your seminar on women's fiction?"

A tiny smile played at the corner of her mouth. "Floundering, I hope."

"I don't think so." Becky dropped into the chair across from Cora's desk. "He's drawing a crowd. Word is spreading across campus like wildfire, and your class is about to spill into the hall."

"Great. I can't get eighty-percent attendance for a scheduled session, and all he has to do is walk down the hall to have the masses falling at his feet." A clamoring noise from the corridor captured her attention.

"Good grief." Becky glanced over her shoulder. "What's going on out there?"

"I think Blackbeard the archeologist is inciting the natives to riot."

The door of her office was flung open. Rafael, followed by a large group of young women, edged his way in, then shut the door on the din. He gave Cora a disgruntled look. "Nicely played, Professor."

Her only response was a slight inclination of her head. "I thought so." She glanced at Becky. "Becky Painter, meet Rafael Adriano, world-famous archeologist and guest lecturer for women's studies."

Becky stuck out her hand. "Wow. You look taller." Characteristically blunt, Becky glanced at his large frame. "And wider. The picture I saw of you was kind of small."

He looked distinctly amused. He was accustomed, Cora supposed, to having women assess him. He enfolded Becky's hand in his. "I'm delighted to meet you, Ms. Painter."

Her students definitely had a point, Cora mused. That voice ought to be registered as a lethal weapon. He had the slightest hint of a foreign accent that made it just short of devastating. She'd read somewhere that English was his second language. The faint roll of his *r*'s gave his voice a purring quality that was pure sensuality. Cynically she wondered if he practiced that. Becky looked as if she might faint. "Becky, why don't you see what you can do about the crowd in the hallway?"

Without looking at Cora, Becky slowly extracted her hand from his. "I, um, sure. Do you want anything, Dr. Adriano? A drink, maybe?"

That damnable smile played at the corner of his mouth again. He slanted Cora a look, then slowly shook his head. ''No. I'm fine, Ms. Painter. All I need is some time alone with Dr. Prescott.''

Surprise flickered briefly on Becky's expressive features, which then slipped into a mask of blatant curiosity. ''Oh.''

Cora almost groaned out loud. If he stayed much longer, he'd create so much havoc she'd have to spend the next ten years digging her way out of it. ''The hall, Becky. See what you can do about the noise.''

Becky blinked twice, then gave Cora a look that said she'd pursue the subject later. ''Okay—'' she reached for the door handle ''—but let me know if you need anything.'' With a final glance at Rafael, she eased past him. ''Anything at all.''

When the door clicked shut behind her, an uneasy quiet settled on the tiny room. Suddenly the four walls were too confining. Cora turned abruptly to push open the window. ''Why don't you sit down? I can see you obviously didn't read my last letter or you wouldn't be here to—'' With a final groan, the window popped open. A flood of humid air tumbled into the room. She dropped back into her chair. ''You wouldn't be here to harass me.''

His full lips curved into a slight smile. That, coupled with his black eye patch, made him look every inch the rake he was purported to be. ''Is that what you call it?'' he asked.

Cora placed her hands on her desk and drew a sense of calm from the cool wood surface. ''What would you call it?''

''I'm persistent.'' His broad shoulders moved in a casual shrug. ''It makes me good at what I do.'' He paused. ''At everything I do.''

She chose to ignore that. ''Then I'm sorry you came all this way, but I meant what I said in my last letter. I don't have time for you to be digging about in my house this summer. I've got two classes to conduct each session, and my three nieces are here for an extended stay. You needn't have wasted your valuable time making the trip. The answer is still no."

His chuckle lingered in the warm air. "Very impressive, Professor. No wonder your colleagues have such respect for you."

She frowned at him. "I'd appreciate it if you'd at least take this seriously."

"I assure you, I'm very serious," he retorted. "All I meant was that the professor who deftly stuck me with her class full of young women knows how to play a room." He tilted his head to study her. "Jerry didn't prepare me for you."

"Jerry." Inwardly she groaned. Jerry Heath was her department head. He was notorious for stirring up trouble. "You went over my head on this?"

He held up a hand. "It wasn't like that. I've known Jerry professionally for some time. He lent his expertise to a research project for me several years ago. When you denied my request, I called Jerry to find out if a personal visit would further my chances of getting you to change your mind."

"And he told you it would?"

"He told me I should meet you face-to-face." His gaze rested on her mouth. It stayed there long enough to make her aware of dry lips. When he finally met her gaze again, there was an unmistakable sparkle in his dark eye. "I think his exact words were, 'A head-on confrontation with Cora Prescott is an unforgettable experience.'"

"Jerry has a gift for exaggeration."

The look he gave her could have melted glass. "I don't think so. I'm certainly finding it unforgettable."

Cora resisted the urge to loosen the collar of her blouse. A sliver of perspiration trickled down her spine. "Only because I stuck you in a room with a group of hungry college women.''

"You think so?"

"Don't kid yourself. I'm fully aware that you are used to having the world at your feet. The way I see it, this will be an educational experience for you."

"You know how much I want to find the *Isabela*."

"It's good to want things. Builds character."

That damnable smile played at the corner of his mouth again. "I'm very used to getting my own way."

"I can see that."

"And I want this. A lot."

"Disappointment is the key to personal growth."

Something dangerously seductive flared in his gaze—something that reminded her why women reportedly went wild over him. With his looks and his charisma, it was no wonder he had a pirate's reputation. He had a way of looking at a woman that virtually smoldered. "You know—" his expression turned devilish "—I've always admired women with quick tongues."

Cora rolled her eyes. "Does that line usually work for you?"

"Sometimes."

"Well, surprise, Dr. Adriano. This time you've met your match."

"You mean you're not overwhelmed by my persona?"

Was he mocking her? His expression was so serious she couldn't tell. "I will admit that I find the eye patch a bit over the top."

"It's medically necessary," he said. "I lost my eye in a fistfight when I was sixteen."

"I'm not questioning that," she hastened to explain. "I simply think that the, er, look—" she indicated his long hair, the gold hoop in his ear and the patch with a wave of her hand "—is a bit melodramatic."

He laughed, showing a straight line of white teeth. "I like you," he said. "I was hoping I would."

Cora gritted her teeth. "Dr. Adriano—"

"No, really. I feel better about this already."

"I can't tell you how that comforts me," she drawled.

He crossed his long legs so that his ankle rested on his thigh. "A worthy opponent makes any battle more satisfying."

Cora frowned. "Am I supposed to call you a scurvy dog now or something? I left my pirate/English dictionary in my other briefcase."

His lips twitched. "A sharp-tongued woman."

"And an odious egomaniac. What a delightful way to spend an afternoon."

"You know," he said, and she couldn't shake the feeling that he was mocking her, "you might make a good pirate. You've got the wits for it."

"What a relief," Cora said, and took a sip of her soda.

"But I'm not sure you have the guts."

"Excuse me?"

"Hmm." He traced the edge of his patch with a long tanned finger. "'Tis not enough," he said, dropping his voice to a gravelly rumble that she could easily picture coming from Blackbeard himself, "just to wear a patch over yer eye, lassie." He leaned closer. "Ye have tae pick yer teeth with the ribs of a Spanish captain ye knocked off yerself."

Cora stared at him wide-eyed. "I beg your pardon."

He leaned back in his chair. "Captain Pigleg Torstenson wrote that to his grand-daughter in 1783."

"How charming."

His smile was lazy and seductive. "I like to think he was making a general statement about life. It's not enough to simply look the part. You have to have the stomach for it, as well."

He was mocking her, she realized. He thought she was

an intellectual, unadventurous, narrow-minded snob and she'd turned down his request because she lacked vision and foresight. She saw the condemnation and condescension clearly written in his smug expression. "While this little philosophical dissertation is quite charming, Dr. Adriano, I think you should know that I've never liked arrogant men— especially not self-impressed scientists whose only goal is career advancement and public recognition."

That effectively knocked the smile off his lips, but instead of the angry retort she'd expected, she saw his eyebrows lift with marked curiosity. "I'm not arrogant, Professor. I'm simply flagrantly dedicated to my research and cognizant of my considerable talent."

Obnoxious, she told herself. Except that it happened to be true. "Aren't you the man who said you were the most impressive voice in ocean research today?"

His mouth twitched again. Why in hell, she wondered, couldn't she manage to keep her gaze from the firm contours of that mouth? "I might have," he conceded.

"You did. I saw the interview."

"You've been watching my interviews? Should I be flattered?"

"Ha. You've been on every major network for the last few weeks. I'd have to hide in a cave to have missed the sight of you. It seems the whole world is fascinated by the pirate archeologist from the Underwater Archeology Unit."

He sprang his trap by laughing. The sound did funny things to her insides. It was a low, mellow kind of laugh. The kind that said it was used often and well. The kind that ensnared every nerve ending in her body in a web of awareness.

Awareness, she had learned, that was not to be trusted. He'd make her want things if she wasn't careful. He was danger—in huge capital letters. If she had an ounce of intelligence left in her brain, she'd throw him out on the street and make sure he stayed there.

But he tricked her with that laugh. It took the edge off his presence—made him approachable. And likable. Just what she needed—to like the man. She reminded herself that she found his ego insufferable and his love of public spectacle unbelievably annoying.

Amusement danced in his eye. "The match is yours, Professor," he conceded as he leaned forward. His faint scent of fresh air, sea salt and testosterone tickled her nose. "I can see why Jerry is so enchanted with you."

She didn't take the bait. "You are not getting unrestricted access to my house. I've got a life to run."

"That house is more than just your private property." As if his energy for the project physically drove him, he levered himself out of his seat and began pacing her office. "Don't you see? There's no doubt in my mind that if I can find the rest of Abigail Conrad's diaries, I'll have a vital clue to the location of del Flores's ship."

"There may not be any more," Cora pointed out.

He slanted her a telling look. "Didn't you say there are gaps of several months between the volumes you found?" She didn't respond. "Has it been your experience," he pressed, "that journal writers allow months to pass between writings?"

Cora had no answer so she shrugged.

"I'm this close—" his thumb and index finger measured the inch "—are you really going to deny me?"

The sight of him in passionate discourse twisted her stomach. Forcibly she dismissed the thought. Nothing good would come of picturing him in passionate anything. "I'm sorry to disappoint you, Dr. Adriano," she said softly, "but my answer is still no."

His face registered his frustration. He planted his hands on her desk and loomed over her. The sunlight glinted off the tiny hoop in his left ear, and in that moment he looked truly barbarous. Cora tested the description, then rejected it. No, not barbarous. Glorious, perhaps. Her gaze dropped to his long-fingered, bronzed hands. Large. He had large, beautiful hands. Damn him.

"I'm not giving up so easily," he warned her. "You should know that."

She looked at his face. A mistake, that. He was too close, his hard-angled features at eye level with hers and mere inches away. She clenched the edge of her chair and hoped he wouldn't notice. "I'll consider myself warned. But whatever Jerry told you, I seriously doubt you can change my mind. I have to consider—"

She broke off when the door of her office slammed open. Leslie, Cora's baby-sitter of less than six hours, rushed into the office with a harried look in her eyes. Cora abruptly stood, filled with the oddest sensation that she'd been discovered and compromised. "Leslie—" she started.

Leslie frantically shook her head. "I'm sorry, Dr. Prescott. I can't. I thought I could take it, but I can't." Without sparing Rafael a glance, she dropped a wad of keys on Cora's desk. "I just can't take care of them for you."

Cora held out a beseeching hand. "Leslie, I'm sure if we—"

A loud crash sounded from the outer office. High-pitched voices mingled with the distinct sound of a barking dog. "I can't do it. I'm sorry. I quit." The girl fled the room.

Rafael stepped back a scant second before Melody, Cora's large but exuberant collie, vaulted into the room and onto her desk.

"Melody," she chided. "Get down."

"Aunt Cora, Aunt Cora. Don't let her get away." Kaitlin rushed into the room holding a leash. "We chased her all the way from the parking lot."

"Kaitlin," Cora looked at the nine-year-old as she struggled to get the dog off the desk. "What happened? What are you doing here?"

Before the glowering Kaitlin could answer, Jerry Heath ushered six-year-old Molly and four-year-old Liza into the room. Each had liberal splashes of black ink staining their hair, faces and clothes. "They're destroying the copy machine," Jerry announced. "That's what they're doing."

Melody barked in affirmation. With a frustrated oath, Cora pulled on the dog's collar. "Down, Melody. Get down."

She wouldn't budge. Rafael chuckled, then held out his hand to the dog. He whispered a few words, and Melody obediently leaped to the floor where she flopped at his feet. Cora gave him a disgruntled look. "How did you do that?"

"I've had a lot of experience with temperamental females," he said, and sat back in his chair. Melody thumped her tail on the floor.

Exasperated, Cora rubbed her eyes with her thumb and forefinger. She'd been right the first time. He was obnoxious. "Jerry," she said, "what's going on?"

Jerry guided the two girls toward Cora's desk. "As far as I can tell, your nieces decided to help Becky make some copies. Somehow that led to an investigation of the toner cartridge."

Cora's nieces were high-energy kids. Since their arrival three weeks ago, they'd run off six different baby-sitters.

While Cora visibly searched for her patience, Rafael studied her tense expression.

Jerry had mentioned the nieces. At the time Rafael had brushed off his less-than-complimentary description as typical of Jerry's intolerance of childhood antics. Watching the three girls in action, however, Rafael decided that Jerry had underestimated them—just as he'd underestimated Cora. Her nieces had evidently mastered the tag-team approach in dealing with their aunt. Soon they'd have her surrounded. It was beginning to look as if he'd arrived just in time.

The oldest girl, the one Cora had called Kaitlin, immediately staked a position against Jerry's accusations. "That's not what happened, Aunt Cora. It was Leslie's fault."

Cora looked at the next-oldest girl. "Molly, how did you get into the toner?"

Molly pointed at the dog. "We were chasing Melody."

Cora waited. When no additional explanation was forthcoming, she pressed harder. "Why are you all even here? I thought Leslie was taking you to the park today."

Liza spoke up. "We has gonned to the park, but I forgot Benedict Bunny. I wanted to go back and get him."

"And Leslie wouldn't turn around," Molly supplied.

"Liza kept begging," Kaitlin added.

Liza nodded, her eyes wide. "I didn't want to leave him at home."

Kaitlin picked up the thread of the story. "Leslie kept telling Liza to quit crying and she wouldn't."

"I want Benedict Bunny," Liza insisted.

Kaitlin continued, "Leslie got really mad. So she whipped the car around and came here."

"Yeah," Molly said. "She let Melody out of the car before us. When Melody took off running, we had to chase her."

Kaitlin added, "She almost plowed Becky down in the hall. Liza—" she swatted her younger sister with the back of her hand "—was trying to catch up."

"Becky was changing the cartridge," Molly supplied.

Liza, whose face probably looked angelic when it wasn't covered in black ink, nodded adamantly. "I tried to catch it when it fell."

Rafael had to suppress a laugh. Standard operating procedure, he supposed. They'd blame it on the baby. She was less likely to get eaten. If Liza survived, then they knew they were in the clear.

Cora's gaze swung to Jerry once more. "Did you see what happened?"

"No. I heard the noise."

"Is there any damage other than the mess?"

"I don't think so."

"Fine." She glared at Kaitlin. "Take your sisters and go find Becky. Help her clean up all the ink."

"It wasn't our fault," Kaitlin argued.

"We'll talk about it later, Kaitlin."

"But—"

"Now," Cora said.

Kaitlin paused, her expression belligerent. She studied Cora's face for long seconds, then finally relented. "Fine." She wrapped Melody's leash around her hand. "Are you mad 'cause Leslie quit? Because she wasn't very good. I didn't like her."

"Me, neither," Molly said.

"Me, neither," Liza added.

Cora sighed. "I don't know if I'm mad or not. It depends on why she quit. Probably."

Rafael winced. Indecision. Never show children indecision. She'd just lost another major battle on the playing field of child discipline.

The three girls filed out of the room with Melody in tow. Cora pressed three fingers to her forehead in frustration. "Sorry, Jerry," she muttered.

"You've got to do something about them, Cora. They're out of control."

"It was an accident."

"Just like the water cooler last week?" When Cora didn't respond, Jerry met Rafael's gaze across the small room. "I didn't know you'd arrived," he said.

Rafael frowned. Trust Jerry to make it sound as if he'd conspired against Cora. "I just got here."

"Really?" The other man leaned casually against the door frame. "I'm surprised you didn't come by my office."

"I had other things on my mind."

Jerry's gaze shifted to Cora. "So I see. Cora, I see you've met Dr. Adriano. I won't bother with introductions."

Cora slowly lowered herself back into her chair. "No, Jerry, you needn't bother." Her voice held all the warmth of the Arctic Ocean.

Rafael sensed the wisdom of a strategic withdrawal. He'd given Cora something to think about. Later he'd press his point. He pushed himself off her desk, then extended his hand to Jerry. "It's good to see you again, Jerry. Dr. Prescott and I were just finishing."

"Oh?" Jerry's hand was clammy. He gave Rafael a quick handshake, but didn't take his eyes off Cora. "Any decisions?"

"No," Cora said, and did not elaborate.

Rafael followed her lead. "We have a lot to talk about. I didn't expect an answer today."

"Cora—" strained patience laced Jerry's voice "—I'm sure you realize that Dr. Adriano could be an important asset to Rawlings."

"I don't live in a cave, Jerry."

"I realize that. But I was afraid you'd be stubborn about this. Since the diaries—"

"My tenure contract with the college," she said through gritted teeth, "gives me the right to decide the parameters of my research of any historical documents I choose to pursue."

Jerry slid his hands into his vest pockets. "Adriano's in a position to bring us a lot of good publicity. I don't think Willers would be very impressed if you refused to give Adriano a fair chance to state his case."

Bastard, Rafael thought. Jerry had played his ace. Henry Willers, president of the college, was a notorious media hound. Rafael had deliberately kept his correspondence with Cora confidential, knowing that Willers would pressure her to accede. He wanted her cooperation, but not grudgingly. Cora's hands gripped the edge of her desk. "Jerry—"

"Just something to think about," Jerry said amiably.

Cora held Jerry's gaze with barely concealed hostility. "I'll bear that in mind."

"If you want my opinion, with your tenure hearing coming up, this is the kind of thing you should pay attention to."

Rafael had to look away to hide his disgust. He couldn't wait until he got the man alone. What Jerry needed, evidently, was a lesson in academic humility. He could see the anger in Cora's eyes when she addressed Jerry. "Duly noted."

Rafael stood, determined to fend off a full-blown confrontation. "I appreciate your time," he told Cora. "We can finish later?"

She finally tore her gaze from Jerry. "Fine. Now if the two of you will excuse me, I'd like to check on my nieces." She breezed past them and let the door of her office slam behind her.

Chapter Two

*It's her fire I find irresistible. After so many nights
with naught but the cold sea for company, I find such
rapturous warmth in her arms. She may consume me,
but what a blissful demise!*

*Juan Rodriguez del Flores
Captain's Log, 9 December 1860*

Jerry Heath, Rafael decided, was an idiot.

The man had deliberately allowed him to believe that
Cora Prescott was some prudish college professor he could
simply bowl over with a good dose of charm. Rafael had
suspected from Jerry's poorly veiled hostility that he found
Cora threatening. Now that he'd met her, he knew exactly
why. Cora was twice the researcher and a hundred times the
person Jerry Heath would ever be.

"Well," Jerry said, seating himself in Cora's recently va-
cated chair, "what do you think now that you've met the
inimitable Cora Prescott?"

Good question, Rafael thought as he quickly reconciled
his impressions of her with his previous expectations. There
was a wealth of treasure to find beneath her facade, of that
he was sure. But something—or someone—had put that dis-

trustful, slightly wounded look in her eyes. For a man who'd spent a lifetime carefully unearthing priceless antiquities, the challenge of discovering Cora's secret was irresistible. He glared at Jerry. "You set me up, Jerry."

"I did not. I gave you every warning that you didn't know what you were getting into when you decided to take on Cora. She's the stubbornnest woman I've ever known. I'd be surprised if you got past *go* with her."

"Is that why you practically blackmailed her into accepting my offer?"

Jerry bristled. "I don't know what you mean."

Rafael scowled at him. "Playing the tenure card? That was a cheap shot."

"Cora can take care of herself, believe me."

"I don't doubt that."

Jerry nodded. "She'd like to be department head."

And she'd be good at it, Rafael thought. No wonder Jerry seemed intent on keeping her in her place. At his age, he was nearing the end of his academic career. Bright new talent scared him. A woman like Cora Prescott probably left him cowering in the corner. Rafael carefully considered all that Cora had said to him. "She's brilliant."

"She's extremely respected in her field," Jerry acknowledged.

Praise, Rafael realized, but not unqualified. His opinion of Jerry Heath slipped another notch. "So why didn't you tell me about the whole package?"

Jerry swiveled back and forth in the worn leather chair. "I have no idea what you're talking about."

Rafael gave him a knowing look. "Like hell."

"I don't."

"Then you're older than I thought," Rafael said.

Jerry stared at him another few seconds, then understanding dawned in his eyes. He let out a low whistle. "My God. You can't mean you're thinking of seducing Cora Prescott."

Rafael lifted his eyebrows. "Why would you think that?"

"Because I've known you a long time. And I know that look you get. It's the same one you get when you think you're on the cusp of an important find."

"You're being melodramatic."

"Maybe. Still, you'll have to take my word on this. She's not that type of woman. She's not *your* type of woman." Jerry shook his head. "Believe me, other men have tried and failed, and it won't work. She's cold as an iceberg. I'm not entirely certain she's interested in men, if you know what I mean."

Rafael let that pass without comment. He made a practice of not wasting his time on fools.

Jerry reached for the phone on Cora's desk. "Look, why don't you get settled into your hotel, then let Patty and me take you to dinner." He punched a few numbers. "We can talk about old times."

Rafael thought it over. As much as he loathed the idea of an extended stay in Jerry's presence, he genuinely liked Patty Heath. A widely published author and lecturer on ancient Greek culture, Patty could not only provide interesting dinner conversation, but also, he hoped, better insight into Cora Prescott. "I'd love to," he answered.

"Great. Patty's been dying to pick your brain about the *Argo* project." Jerry finished dialing. While he talked to his wife, Rafael mentally recalculated his strategy for gaining Cora Prescott's cooperation.

Even Jerry couldn't be naive enough to think that the aloof mask she wore reflected her true nature. Granted, she had the look down to a science. Tortoiseshell glasses. Hair in a neat French braid. Intelligent eyes set in a classic oval face. She even wore the costume of the conservative academic. Her tailored blouse and simple straight skirt were a timeless style. Most professors wore jeans and T-shirts to class. Cora could have stepped right out of another age.

But that was where it ended. There was absolutely nothing about the woman that didn't scream of undiscovered passion. Or that didn't beg for masculine attention. The less observant of the male species, he supposed, might miss it, but what Rafael saw was an underlying edge of raw sensuality that had him struggling for balance.

Some men, he knew, looked at a woman and saw the sum total of her parts. If the balance sheet didn't tip in their favor, they never bothered to look deeper. He, however, had found that such a superficial examination was generally misleading. Cora Prescott wasn't classically beautiful or even modernly sexy. She'd never make the cover of a men's magazine, but then, he'd always preferred the subtle to the blatant.

In her, he saw something sensual and alluring. A huge part of the appeal, he knew, was her intelligence. He liked that in a lover. But the physical package complemented her mental assets. Perhaps it was the curve of her ear or the way stray tendrils of soft brown hair caressed the nape of her neck. It could be the long sweep of her arm from the juncture of her collarbone to the tips of her slender fingers. The way she moved enticed him. Her waist flared into softly rounded hips. Long shapely legs melded into well-turned ankles. The tailored cut of her blouse had done little to disguise the curves of her breasts. Her clothes floated on her skin like the whisper of a summer breeze.

He had a feeling that when he touched her, it would be like coaxing music from a fine instrument. Cora had the look of a woman who knew her worth. She valued herself too much to waste her energy on men who couldn't appreciate the rare nature of her character and appeal. Like Sleeping Beauty, he mused, she had allowed her passion to remain dormant, rather than squander it on the undeserving.

That idea had him instantly and potently aroused. The realization hit him like a blow to the head. He wanted Cora

Prescott, and he couldn't remember having this strong thirst for possession for anything other than a sunken ship. But Cora was no relic, and his first encounter with her had sent exhilaration pumping through him. It sent his lingering exhaustion from jet lag and the post-*Argo* whirlwind tumbling off into orbit. In its place was a growing hunger for discovery.

He took several long moments to revel in the sensation. With del Flores's ship finally within reach and the tantalizing prospect of unraveling all of Cora Prescott's mysteries, he felt the passion stirring in him, awakening from what had seemed, recently, like an endless slumber.

Slowly his gaze shifted to Jerry, who was just completing his conversation with his wife. Jerry seemed to have no idea just what the world was missing in its ignorant dismissal of Cora Prescott's appeal. An idiot, Rafael mused again. More's the pity.

"Hello." At ten minutes to seven the following evening, in the midst of a torrential downpour, Rafael leaned casually against the frame of the front door to Cora's house while he looked down at a wide-eyed Liza. He'd gleaned what he could from Patty Heath last night, then spent the better part of his day replotting his strategy.

Cora Prescott was turning out to be every bit as elusive and mysterious as he'd suspected.

She was well liked by her colleagues, he'd learned, but kept largely to herself. She seemed to have few close friends in the community, yet everyone spoke of her warmly. People had conflicting ideas about her reticence, but on one point, they all seemed to agree: though they thought she'd been incredibly generous to take in her three nieces for the summer—their mother, rumor had it, was enjoying an extended fling in the Florida Keys with a married real-estate developer—Cora was completely overwhelmed by the responsibility.

Rafael couldn't remember a time when he'd had better news. She had something he needed, and now he had something she needed. With a satisfied smile, he grinned at a bewildered-looking Liza. "Is your aunt home?" he asked.

Becky Painter, who was the ace up his sleeve this evening, peered around his shoulder to greet Liza. "Hey, there, Liza."

Liza smiled at her. "Hi, Becky." Her gaze swung to Rafael's. "I know you. You were in Aunt Cora's office."

"Yes, I was."

"Know how come I know?"

"How come?"

She pointed to his eye patch. "You got that. What is it?"

"It's a bandage for my eye."

She tipped her head to one side. "You got a sore?"

"Yes. I have a sore."

"Oh. Are you a pirate? I have a book about pirates."

He tapped the patch with his index finger. "Does it have pictures of men wearing these?"

"Yes. How come it's black?"

"Eye bandages only come in black." That made Liza frown, as if the thought of black bandages was somehow a grave misfortune. Rafael winked at her. "Shouldn't you be in bed?"

Liza had opened the door to his knock. Her hot-pink pajamas and the ratty-looking stuffed rabbit she clutched told him that Cora was in the middle of the bedtime routine. And if the noise coming from upstairs was any indication, she wasn't having an easy time of it.

In answer to his question, Liza wagged her head from side to side. "I hate bed. I don't like sleeping."

"Really?"

"No. It's boring."

Becky laughed. "Bedtime in this house is a nightmare, Cora told me. She starts at around eight and never gets them down before ten."

"Is that so?" Rafael bent so his face was at eye level with Liza's. "Do you want to know a secret, sweet pea?"

She clutched the worn brown rabbit to her chest and leaned forward. "What?"

"I don't like to go to sleep, either."

Liza held his gaze a few seconds, then stepped aside to let him in. He'd cleared the first hurdle. Liza, at least, seemed to trust him. "I came to see your aunt," he told her.

"She's upstairs. Kaitlin and Molly don't wanna sleep."

"I'm not surprised."

"How come you're all wet?" Liza asked as a sleepy-looking Melody ambled in from the living room. The dog wagged her tail as she watched Rafael, then flumped down at his feet. Mentally he tabulated another point in his column. He had the kids. He had the dog. The aunt was sure to follow.

Becky was shaking out her umbrella. "It's raining outside. Didn't you hear the thunder, Liza?"

"Yeah. That's why I came down here."

Somewhere in that four-year-old mind, there was logic in that statement. "Does your aunt know where you are?"

Liza shrugged. He took that as a no. He was about to ask for the name of her rabbit when he heard Cora's voice from the top of the stairs.

"Liza?"

Liza moved quickly to hide behind Rafael's leg. Cora descended a couple of stairs. "Liza?" She walked down three more, then stopped at the sight of him. "It's you." Then she looked at Becky. "And you. What are you doing here?"

"I met with Jerry and Henry Willers yesterday," he said

carefully. Becky remained silent. "There are some things you and I should discuss." Melody's tail thumped the foyer carpet.

Cora's eyebrows lifted. "I thought we were done."

"Hardly," he muttered. "Things are getting...complicated."

She completed her trip down the stairs. When she reached the foyer, she stepped from the shadows into the light. Rafael got his first good look at her that evening. She wore faded jeans that fit far too well and a well-worn college sweatshirt. Her hair was secured in a ponytail. Heat radiated from her. He could feel the lingering raindrops on his skin beginning to sizzle. He inhaled a great breath of her scent. Baby powder and soap, it was far more seductive than any expensive perfume. "The only thing that's complicated," she said with a distinct snap in her eyes, "is that you won't take no for an answer."

That snap charmed him. "It's what makes me good at my job."

"And obnoxious," she shot back.

He responded with a low whistle. "Do you bite, too?"

That made Becky laugh. "Don't let her fool you, Dr. Adriano. Cora's as even-tempered as they come."

"So I'm the only one who gets under her skin." He gave Cora an appraising look. "I wonder why?"

Her color heightened. "I have an aversion to pushy men."

"And I have an affinity for mouthy women."

Becky stepped between them, laughing. "Okay, okay. This is going nowhere."

Liza clutched her stuffed rabbit closer and announced, "When Molly and Kaitlin and me fight like that, Mama tells us to separate."

Rafael winked at her. Cora muttered, "I think that's an excellent idea."

"You don't understand, Cora," Becky continued. "You aren't even going to believe what Jerry's done. At least Dr. Adriano had the decency to tell you about it first."

Cora frowned. "What's Jerry got to do with this?"

Becky shook her head. "I think we should sit down."

Cora resisted. "Don't you have final exams in a couple of weeks, Becky? Aren't you supposed to be studying?"

Becky shrugged. "I needed a break. This is more interesting, anyway."

Cora glared at Adriano. "Did you talk her into this?"

"She volunteered."

"I'm sure."

"I did." Becky nodded vigorously. "I had to come, Cora. Jerry Heath and Henry Willers called a press conference for Monday morning."

"That soon?" Cora asked.

Becky frowned. "It gets worse. Jerry was so overcome that Dr. Adriano came early, he moved it up to tomorrow."

"Tomorrow's Sunday," Cora pointed out. "No one's attending a press conference on a Sunday."

Becky glanced at Rafael. He had the grace to look uncomfortable. "They will if I'm there," he pointed out.

Becky continued, "Jerry and Willers plan to announce that you've agreed to let Dr. Adriano participate in the Conrad study."

Cora's eyes widened, then she shot an accusing glance at Rafael. "You took the project from me," she accused.

He silently damned Jerry Heath to hell. "It's not what you think."

Becky came to his defense. "I wouldn't have known at all if Dr. Adriano hadn't told me. They're planning to spring it on you tomorrow."

A rumble of thunder sounded overhead, and Liza yelped, then clutched Rafael's leg. He leaned down to pick her up. "Worried?" he asked.

"It's scary," Liza whispered.

"My mother used to say the noise was the sound of angels bowling in heaven."

Another loud rumble followed. Liza buried her face against his neck. "Then why are they so loud?"

"Liza," Cora said. "You're supposed to be upstairs in bed."

Liza peered at her. "He knocked on the door."

Cora ignored that. "Kaitlin said you could sleep in her bed tonight."

"I don't want to go bed."

"Molly and Kaitlin are waiting for you."

Liza's jaw set in a stubborn line. "No. I don't like going to bed." She patted Rafael's chest. "He doesn't, either."

Cora gave him a dry look. "Is that so?"

"I said I didn't like to sleep. I didn't say anything about going to bed." Before Cora could respond, he tickled Liza's ribs. "Tell you what, Liza, will you go to bed if I tell you a story?"

Her look was skeptical. "What kind of story?"

"What kind of stories do you like?"

She seemed to consider it for a long moment. "Can it have a pirate in it?"

"Sure."

"And a dog?"

"Absolutely. A dog named Melody." At the sound of her name, Melody got to her feet, then followed him when he started toward the stairs.

"And ice cream?"

"What flavor?" He shot Cora a silent invitation as he started up the stairs. Cora mumbled something to Becky, then fell into step behind them.

Liza pursed her lips. "I like chocolate."

"Not pickle?"

Liza's face scrunched. "Eeeew."

"What about cabbage?"

"There's no such thing as cabbage ice cream."

"You sure?"

"Sure. That's gross."

He reached the top of the stairs, then met Cora's gaze above Liza's head. Raising a hand, Cora indicated the room to the right of the landing. He headed down the hall. "All right, chocolate. If it has a pirate, a dog and chocolate ice cream, do you promise to go to bed?"

"What if the thunder comes back?"

The storm was nearly over. The thunder already sounded distant. "Then you can get up," he promised.

Liza laid her head against his chest. "Okay."

The door was open and soft light spilled into the hallway. Rafael entered the room to find Molly and Kaitlin having a quiet argument over a book.

"I want to read it," Molly insisted.

"You can't," her sister said. "It's mine."

"Girls," Cora said from the door. "I told you to share the book. Molly, Kaitlin's letting you sleep in her room. Let her have the book back."

Molly hesitated, then released the book. "How come she always gets her way?" she demanded.

Kaitlin glared at Cora. "I don't have to share it if I don't want to. Mama gave it to me. It's mine."

Rafael saw Cora close her eyes in weary acquiescence. She hadn't followed him into the room. Instead, she leaned against the doorjamb. "Fine," she said quietly. "Just quit fighting about it."

He set Liza on the bed and waited for her to scramble beneath the covers next to Molly. When she and the stuffed rabbit were properly settled, he looked at Kaitlin. "Your sister requested a story. Is that all right with you?"

Kaitlin stared at him, wide-eyed. A rumble of thunder had

Liza clutching the covers and pleading with her. "Please, Kaitlin. He said he'd put a pirate in it."

Rafael nodded. "And a dog named Melody."

Melody had followed them upstairs. She now rubbed against his leg. He scratched her ears until she dropped to the floor and thumped her tail on the carpet.

"I'm too old for bedtime stories," Kaitlin informed him carefully.

"Naturally," he concurred. "I'm telling it to Liza. You don't have to listen if you aren't interested."

She hesitated a second longer, then nodded. "Okay."

No wonder, Rafael thought, that she and Cora were having trouble getting along. She liked control as much as her aunt did. He sat on the edge of the bed and started to spin a tale about pirate ships and treasure, chocolate ice cream and a dog named Melody. Liza yawned and rubbed her eyes with her fist. Molly fought her drooping eyelids. Kaitlin sank deeper beneath the covers and watched him, cautiously but intently. When he saw Liza's eyes drift shut and her mouth go slack, he glanced at Molly and Kaitlin. Both were asleep.

He looked at Cora, who still stood by the door. Raising a hand to his lips, he cautioned her to be silent. She nodded and flipped the lights off. The glow of a night-light cast long shadows in the room. Easing off the bed, he walked to the door. Cora stepped aside to let him pass, then pulled the door partially shut as she joined him in the hall.

He gave her a dry look. "Mission accomplished."

"Congratulations," she said. "I'll see what I can do about nominating you for the Nobel peace prize."

He laughed softly as they walked toward the stairs. "Is bedtime always like this?"

"Mostly. The storm made it worse than usual." She hesitated. "They miss their mother. Something like a bad storm makes them miss her more."

He nodded. "When is she coming back for them?"

Cora shrugged. "I wish I knew."

The frustration in her voice made him frown. Cora turned away and would have started down the stairs, but he touched her elbow, halting her progress. "You're very good with them," he assured her.

Her eyebrows lifted. "You're the one who talked them to sleep."

"You're the one who makes them secure. Don't underestimate that."

She studied him for long, inscrutable seconds. "You really didn't know Jerry was going to do this, did you?" she finally asked.

Pleased, he shook his head. "No, I didn't."

"For what it's worth, I believe you. I don't know why. I just do."

"I'm glad."

With a nod, she headed downstairs. "I suppose you'd better fill me in on what exactly Jerry and Henry are planning to announce about my project tomorrow. I'd rather not get ambushed."

WHEN THEY JOINED Becky in Cora's living room, she was setting three mugs of coffee on the table. "You're through already?" she asked. "That's got to be a new record."

Rafael pointed to the ceiling. "They're sleeping."

"It's a miracle." She handed Cora a mug. "Creamed and sugared, just like you take it."

"Thanks." Cora sank into one of the wing chairs.

Becky sat on the couch and cradled her own mug. "Did you want anything in yours, Dr. Adriano?"

He shook his head. "Black is fine. And I wish you'd quit calling me Dr. Adriano. I might forget to answer."

When Becky flushed, Cora gave him a wry look. "What

I want to know is, where was all this charm when you were sending me those pushy letters?''

Rafael laughed and took the seat across from Cora. "You were supposed to read between the lines and find me irresistible.''

Her fingers gripped the arm of her chair. "Well, it worked on Henry Willers, anyway. He obviously couldn't resist you.''

He stifled his frustration when he thought of his earlier confrontation with Jerry and Henry. He'd been just as surprised as Cora to find out they'd already released a statement that he'd joined the project. Just as surprised, and probably angrier. "Look, Cora,'' he said, watching her carefully. She didn't flinch at the liberty he'd taken with her first name. He took that as a good sign. "I had no idea this was going to happen, but we can't change it now. It seems to me that we might as well make the best of a potentially bad situation.''

She hesitated a moment. "I don't suppose there's any chance of talking Henry out of this.''

Becky shook her head. "He already released a written statement. The conference is just a formality.''

"Ugh.'' Cora dropped her head back against the chair. "I should have known.'' She looked at Rafael accusingly. "What did you think was going to happen when you told Jerry I'd refused your request?''

"It never occurred to me that you and I wouldn't come to an understanding,'' he said.

"That's a bit arrogant, don't you think?''

"Maybe.''

"What if we hadn't?''

"I would have respected that.'' He waited for the truth of the statement to sink in. "I asked Jerry for his opinion. If I'd known he'd try to trump you, I would have handled it differently.''

"I can manage Jerry, believe me."

"I don't doubt it." And he didn't. Cora wasn't the type to be cowed by an arrogant SOB like Jerry Heath. "But he can be a real bastard when he wants to be."

Becky laughed. "You could say that."

Rafael nodded. "If it counts for anything, when he and Willers told me about this, I told him he was a pain in the ass."

Cora settled more deeply into her seat. Digging in, he mused. She regarded him with a steady look. "I'm sure he took that well."

Becky snorted. "What a jerk."

She had no idea, Rafael thought. He'd been in a black rage since the confrontation in Willers's office. He'd even threatened to walk off the project, but Jerry had been quick to point out that information had already been issued to the press. If Rafael left and took the prestige of his reputation with him, Jerry would ensure that Cora bore the blame in the eyes of the media and the college. Feeling trapped and hating nothing more than being manipulated and snared, Rafael had conceded, but not without choking several concessions out of Jerry and Henry Willers.

The room had fallen silent, and Cora stared into her coffee mug, frowning intently.

Becky touched Cora's knee. "Cora, I talked to Willers's secretary. She was my roommate last year, you know?" Cora nodded, so Becky continued, "They were going to take the entire project away from you. If Dr. Adriano hadn't intervened, Jerry was just going to make you hand over the diaries to the college. He says you gave the college the rights to any historical records or artifacts you found in this house when you bought it from them."

"I did," Cora muttered. "They wouldn't sell it to me without that clause."

"So at least this way, you get to continue studying them," Becky pointed out.

Cora's short laugh was humorless. "Thank God." She gave him a cold look. "I should be grateful for that, I suppose."

He ground his teeth. He should have slugged Jerry when he had the chance. "You're still in charge of the project," he said. "I insisted on that."

Cora didn't respond. Becky gave Rafael a worried look. "It doesn't have to be that bad, Cora. I know you're frustrated, but I'm sure we can work something out."

Cora took a sip of her coffee. "Becky," she said patiently, too patiently, "do you have any idea what's going to happen when the story gets out that Dr. Adriano is here to join this project?" Becky shook her head.

Cora looked at Rafael and said, "Madness and mayhem."

Rafael decided it was time to tip his hand. "Money and media," he corrected her. "And from what Jerry tells me, you need them both."

"We're not desperate," she insisted.

"You don't even have enough in your research funding to complete your examination of the existing diaries—much less for their preservation and authentication."

Becky nodded. "It's true, Cora."

"I've got some promising leads," Cora protested. "It's—"

Rafael cut her off. "I can guarantee you three million dollars by the end of the week."

Cora choked. "Three million?"

"Oh, my God," Becky said, wide-eyed.

Rafael nodded, satisfied. That kind of grant money was unheard of in Cora's field. She'd probably been hoping for several thousand. "And that's just starters."

Cora stared at him. "What could possibly—"

"The historic record tells us that in the fall of 1861 del

Flores and his ship disappeared. He was last seen when he sailed from Savannah on a reported raid. He was supposed to prevent the French fleet from delivering supplies and munitions. The theory is that he encountered bad weather—maybe a hurricane—off the coast and sank.''

"But you don't think so," Cora said.

"No. I think he loaded the *Isabela* with five years' worth of plunder and headed here, to rendezvous with Abigail. Wherever the *Isabela* is now, it's probably still loaded with del Flores's treasure.''

"Wow," Becky said. "It would be worth millions."

"One of the biggest finds ever," Rafael concurred. "And the cultural significance of those artifacts is unimaginable. Until now, I've had nothing to study but del Flores's own logs and papers. The chance to look at Abigail's work…''

"*If* they had an affair," Becky said. "We don't even know that for sure. She talks about her lover, but she never names him."

"I haven't studied them all," Cora conceded, "but I haven't seen his name."

Rafael wasn't deterred. "I want to compare what Abigail wrote with what I've already discovered about del Flores. If she makes references to her lover that correspond to the dates of his visits, then I can place them together circumstantially."

"What good will that do?" Becky asked.

"It will explain why no one's been able to find the ship off the coast of Savannah," he said quietly. "Because it's farther north. Closer to here."

"And you've got investors willing to stake that hunch?" Cora pressed.

"I've got enough of a reputation that I can raise the money I need."

"Then why help me?" she probed. "With that kind of cash at your disposal, I'm sure you could persuade Jerry and the rest of the college to just hand you total control of the diaries.''

He heard the bitterness in her voice. He couldn't blame her for it. She was right on that account. He had enough clout to wrest the project from her completely, if that was what he wanted. But he didn't merely want access to Cora Prescott's house—he wanted all the privileges that came with having her on his team. ''That's not what I want. I'm no more interested in sacrificing Abigail Conrad to the fortune hunters than you are. I just want the truth.''

''And the ship?''

''I've spent my career looking for the *Isabela*.'' He hesitated. He rarely discussed this. He'd been informed by some very knowledgeable people that he sounded far too intense. Frighteningly intense. ''This is one more piece of the puzzle.''

Cora frowned. ''And that will bring every fortune hunter and relic seeker in the world to Cape Marr, hoping to beat you to the treasure.''

Her tone was pure censure, condemning and condescending. He couldn't keep the irritation from his voice. ''The fact that my research is more accessible to the general public doesn't make it any less valid than yours.''

She gasped. ''I didn't mean—''

''I'm not interested in the treasure,'' he said harshly. ''It's not about that.''

''But you can't deny that its allure would bring chaos. This is a small town. The kind of people who hunt sunken treasure for a living aren't known for their high moral code, you know. I don't think downtown Cape AMR is ready to host the international cutthroat convention.''

''It won't happen. I can stop it from happening.''

''Are you kidding?'' she shot back. ''You draw reporters and attention like honey draws flies.''

''With me,'' he insisted, ''and with my involvement in

the project, you not only get access to my fund-raising team, you get my PR firm, as well. They're very good at keeping reporters out of my hair.''

Becky tucked her feet beneath her legs and looked at Cora. ''It's true, Cora. Don't you remember reading how annoyed the press was because they didn't have access to the *Argo* project until after the ship was raised?''

''Because the Greek military protected the site as a matter of national interest,'' Cora said, then looked at Rafael. ''What are you going to do? Make a phone call to the Joint Chiefs of Staff?''

She wasn't going to back down, he realized, and found himself unaccountably pleased by her candor and resistance. He'd been too long without a challenge. ''Not quite, but I can assure you that my PR people will take the headache out of this.''

Cora shook her head. ''Not if Henry Willers has anything to do with it. The man never saw a camera he didn't like.''

Becky agreed. ''He turns everything into a circus.''

''The secret,'' Rafael said, ''is to make sure you control the press, instead of the other way around. There will be attention. There's no way to avoid it.''

''Lovely,'' Cora muttered.

''But we'll direct it, instead of letting it direct us.'' He paused. ''I already told Willers that after tomorrow he'd better stay the hell out of my business, or I'd make sure he regretted it.''

Cora pulled off her glasses to rub her eyes with her thumb and forefinger. ''God, this is giving me a headache.''

But she wasn't arguing, he noted, and decided to press his advantage. ''I've been looking for the truth about del Flores since I was seventeen years old.'' At her skeptical look, he nodded. ''It's true. I left home because my brother, Zack, and I weren't getting along. I came down here to work my way through college and discovered the del Flores story.

I've been hooked ever since.'' He leveled his gaze at her. ''And if you think about it, I can actually help make all this easier on you. Because of my connections, I can raise the money you need, but because of my family, I can help you with something else.''

''What now? You know the cure for the common cold?''

He laughed. Lord, the woman fascinated him. He found himself increasingly preoccupied with the idea of how all that mental acuity would affect him during sex. Would she approach lovemaking with the same intellectual intensity, or could he coax her to flagrant passion? Or both, he thought, the idea definitely tantalizing. ''Nothing that dramatic,'' he finally assured her. ''But I did some checking today—'' he held up a hand to forestall her interruption ''—and your nieces are running you into the ground.''

''They are not.'' She looked indignant. ''They're just a little…active.''

''Cora, they're hellions,'' Becky said.

Cora gave her a reproving look. ''That's ridiculous.''

''You've gone through three baby-sitters this week alone,'' Becky countered.

Cora squirmed. ''They're having… It's been a difficult adjustment.'' She looked at Rafael. ''My sister is notoriously self-absorbed. They felt as if they got dumped here when she went…when she left. I'd be expecting too much if I thought they wouldn't act out some of that frustration.''

He nodded. ''And it doesn't help any that you've got your course load to handle, the pressure of a major research project looming over your head and the responsibility for the entertainment, care and feeding of three kids. I'm not criticizing you—just sympathizing.''

''If you think harassing me about my nieces is going to win you any points—''

''I'm not harassing you. I'm here to offer you a solution.''

Becky raised an eyebrow. "Boarding school?" she quipped.

Cora frowned at her. Rafael shook his head. "I'm just going to make you an offer you can't refuse."

"I doubt it," Cora retorted.

He ignored her. "You give me access to the house for the next two months, and I'll solve your child-care problem. Two adults and three kids are much better odds than the ones you're playing now."

"You're going to baby-sit? Are you insane?"

"I wouldn't call it baby-sitting," he said. "More like riot control."

"It would never work."

"Sure it would. I'd move in with you and—"

Cora gasped. "Move in?"

"You want to live here?" Becky said.

He nodded. "This is where Abigail lived, where she wrote." He gave Cora a piercing look. "Where she made love with del Flores. I can learn from the atmosphere if I move in."

"Move in, as in your clothes in my closet, your toothbrush in my bathroom?"

The mere thought made his blood pump faster. All he had to do was picture what Cora would look like in the morning—rumpled, warm, addictively soft—to feel himself getting aroused. He could see them stretched languorously amid tangled sheets and scattered pillows, exhausted and sated from an arduous night of sizzling, mind-blowing sex. And it *would* be with her, he knew. It most definitely would be.

He realized that Cora was watching him, saw the heightened color in her face, the awareness in her eyes, and knew she was thinking along similar lines. She didn't want to, but couldn't stop herself. A satisfied smile touched his lips. "I hadn't planned," he said softly, "on sharing a bathroom."

The insinuation that he had definitely planned on sharing other things—like a bedroom—wasn't lost on her. Her color deepened, but she sat perfectly still.

Becky, sweetly oblivious to the undercurrent, was nodding, thoughtful. "You know, Cora. There is the room on the top floor." She looked at Rafael. "It has a separate entrance," she explained.

He knew that already. Cora usually rented the room to a student during the regular term. One of the secretaries in the college administration office had revealed that to him. "Does it?" he asked casually.

"Yes," Becky assured him. "You'd have some privacy that way."

Privacy wasn't what he'd planned, but he and Cora could argue about it later. "I'm sure I would." He kept his tone bland.

Becky turned to Cora. "You haven't rented it for the summer, have you?"

Cora frowned. "Becky—"

"It could work," Becky insisted. "You do need help."

Rafael added, "You'd have more time for research."

Becky had warmed to the idea. "Think about it, Cora. If you didn't have to constantly worry about coordinating schedules and transportation, you could work all day."

"How much time do you lose by not being able to run off to the library for an hour or two because you have to worry about what you're going to do with the girls?" Rafael asked.

"I've worked it out," Cora said tightly.

"And how many times have you been totally immersed in Abigail's writing and had to stop to resolve a sibling crisis?" he went on.

"That's not—"

"There are three of them and one of you." He pressed

his hands to his thighs and leaned forward to drive home his point. "You need help. And I can give it to you."

"By living with me?"

"I don't have to." He watched her closely. "I could live in town and come by during the days, but it suits my purposes better to be here, and it helps you more if I am. We both win."

She shook her head. "I don't think it's a good idea."

"I do," Becky said.

"It's an excellent idea," Rafael insisted. "I could be there during the day while you're tied up in classes. And face it, you've got to do something with the girls before they drive you crazy."

"Something like turn them over to you? What could you possibly know about three little girls?"

"I'm the second oldest of thirteen children. I have nine sisters—all younger. I know a lot about girls." He leaned closer. "Of all ages."

Cora snorted. "You know, if you ever decide to give up ocean archeology, you might want to consider stand-up comedy. You've got a comeback for just about everything, don't you."

Becky looked at Cora. "This is the perfect solution, Cora. You know it is."

She visibly wavered, then looked at Rafael. "This is exactly why I said no to your first letter," she told him. "I didn't want this kind of disruption."

"It'll work out, Cora. You'll see," Becky assured her. "In the long run, if he's handling the media, you'll have more time for the diaries. Everyone wins."

He saw her indecision and realized he was holding his breath. Finally she sighed, a weary sigh of surrender. "Since there's no reasonable way to stop this now," she told him, "then I at least want your promise on one thing." She paused. "I haven't had the chance to fully examine the diaries, but they're…intensely personal. I'd prefer not to see Abigail's private thoughts printed for public consumption without my consent.''

Rafael felt a surge of satisfaction. She had a strong desire, he realized, to protect Abigail's privacy. Dared he hope that she felt a connection to Abigail and del Flores similar to his own? ''Fine,'' he agreed.

She held his gaze a moment longer, then dropped her head into her hands. ''Oh, God,'' she groaned. ''What have I done?''

Chapter Three

She always charms me, this passionate, consummate lady of mine. How they misread her, I'll never know. The lot of fools sees only what they look for. I'm grateful, really. The world may see her proper outward appearance, but I, alone, have seen the fire beneath the ice.

Juan Rodriguez del Flores
Captain's Log, 10 April 1861

"Dr. Prescott," the wiry-looking man in the front row of the university auditorium clutched his notepad with journalistic fervor, "why the change in policy? Sources say you've turned down over a dozen other joint projects on the Conrad diaries."

Cora could practically feel Jerry gloating as she faced the roomful of inquisitors the following morning. He sat behind her on the dais, flanked by Henry Willers and the chairman of the Rawlings College board of trustees. Rafael and Becky had left her home at two o'clock that morning. After too little sleep, Jerry's phone call had awakened her. He'd informed her of the press conference in a gratingly cheerful voice that had Cora wanting to spit nails. By the time she'd gotten the girls ready—amid Kaitlin's complaining, Molly's incessant questions and Liza's insistence that Benedict Bunny come along—Cora's mood had disintegrated from bad to rotten. She had a pounding headache and a serious inclination to tear Jerry's head off.

Summoning her dignity, she glanced at her nieces where they sat in the front row with Becky. They'd seen enough episodes, she reminded herself, of their mother, sans dignity, to last them a lifetime. They didn't need to see it from her.

The only person conspicuously absent from this circus was Rafael. He was late, and when she got the chance, she'd kill him for it.

Cora gripped the edge of the podium and forced herself to concentrate on the question. "My priority," she told the young reporter, "has always been to conduct my study of the Conrad diaries in a manner that will glean the most information in the most responsible manner. On consideration of Dr. Adriano's proposal, I decided—"

"—that she can't live without me," came his low drawl from the wings of the stage. He flashed her a bright smile as he strode toward the podium.

Predictably his arrival caused a flurry of interest. Cameras popped. Reporters began hurling questions at the stage. A microphone, suddenly adjusted too high, squealed feedback into the house. Rafael seemed oblivious to the commotion as he walked toward Cora in long, ground-eating strides. He stopped when he reached her.

"You're late," she said in a taut whisper.

He gave her a heated look "Miss me?"

Cora clenched her teeth. "You're creating a spectacle." From the corner of her eye, she saw Liza smile broadly at him and give him a slight wave. The innocent act left Cora feeling oddly betrayed.

He bent his head closer. "The better to dazzle you with," he retorted with infuriating cheer. "Watch and learn."

Cora glared at him. He gave her a cocky grin, then faced his audience with aplomb. For the next several minutes he volleyed their questions, expounded on his research goals, gave eloquent testimony to her work with Abigail's diaries and generally charmed the audience's collective socks off.

He flirted, flaunted and flashed his million-dollar smile until he had them eating out of his hand. Cora watched, torn between amusement and irritation. Even her three nieces sat uncharacteristically still during the discourse. Several times Becky sent her telling looks. No wonder, she thought, that she'd had to work so hard to dig beneath the charismatic mantle he wore to glimpse the passionate man she'd seen last night. His armor was so thick he seemed undaunted by the occasionally blatant accusations that came his way from the handful of reporters who seemed determined to resist his charm. When one asked if he deliberately courted wealthy history buffs and thrill seekers for access to their money, he smiled and said with disarming nonchalance, "Whom would you suggest I court?"

And the crowd laughed appreciatively. Even Henry Willers, whose notoriously sour expression was the constant fodder of cartoons in the student paper, chuckled.

Another reporter captured his attention by asking, "Coming off the *Argo* find, isn't Cape Marr going to be anticlimactic?"

Rafael nodded. "I certainly hope so. You can understand how an expedition of that sort can be exhausting."

"Of course," the man persisted. "But your career is peaking, and our readers would like to know why you'd choose to invest your time on something as seemingly innocuous as the Conrad diaries."

"The del Flores story has been a career-long interest of mine. I'm eager to work with Dr. Prescott and learn more."

"Any reason you can give us," yelled a woman from the

back, "for why you haven't been able to find del Flores's ship yet?

From the corner of her eye, Cora saw Rafael tense. He seemed to carefully consider the question, but she sensed a fine tremor of energy in him. In a deceptively casual move, he propped one arm on the podium and leaned forward. "Sometimes," he said softly, "the sea is a tantalizing adversary."

An unnatural hush seemed to fall on the room as they waited for him to continue. "In some ways," he went on, "exploring the ocean's mysteries is like courting a woman. It can be elusive and mysterious. It's mercurial and unpredictable."

Cora could almost feel the audience falling under his spell. And who could blame them? He was weaving a delicate wave of evocative images designed to entice and fascinate. She resisted the urge to wipe her suddenly damp palms on her skirt.

Rafael seemed lost in thought now. He absently stroked the outer edge of his eye patch as he continued, "The ocean is the source of life for the world. The mother of the earth, if you will. In her womb, she still carries the remnants of the earliest forms of life."

Cora swallowed so hard it was audible. If he noticed, he didn't look at her. "It's full of secrets that it hides beneath a calm surface. Like a woman, the ocean can be as warm as a tropical breeze or as cold as an Arctic current." A suspiciously strangled cough escaped her.

"Something about that fascinates me," he said. "I especially like to find warm currents of water where the weather pattern demands frigid temperatures. The sea is a paradox. Always changing, always moving. You can never predict what the ocean will do. She can be calm as a breezeless day one minute, and catch you in a violent storm the next. She's fathoms deep. Passionate. Alluring." He rolled the last word off the tip of his tongue. "I love the mystery, and I love the challenge."

He glanced momentarily at Cora. Their gazes met. Her body temperature went up a notch. He flashed her a slight smile that said he knew exactly what she was thinking, then turned back to his audience. "Nothing compares," he drawled, "to that brief moment of mindless euphoria that always follows the climax of an expedition."

The crowd sat in stunned silence. Cora resisted the urge to strangle him. A fine sheen of sweat had beaded her forehead, and as much as she'd like to blame it on the stage lighting, she suspected it owed more to an increased pulse rate. Damn the man, she thought irritably.

As rumbles began in the audience, one reporter, a strikingly attractive woman in a lipstick-red tailored suit, managed to shoulder her way through the crowd of photographers near the edge of the stage. She had dark hair and an olive complexion that gave her an exotic look. "Dr. Adriano," she said, and Cora saw an unmistakable smirk on her full mouth, "while that's all fine and good as the reason for your, uh, passion about your work, we'd still like to know why you've been looking for del Flores's ship specifically for the past twenty years."

Amusement danced in Rafael's eye as he met the woman's gaze. "Some lovers are harder than others to catch."

While the crowd laughed, the woman shook her head at him, her expression slightly mocking. There was an obvious history here, Cora noted. She just couldn't determine its dynamics. The reporter pressed, "Then can we assume that you're expecting to find some new information in the Conrad diaries that might shed light on the disappearance of del Flores's ship?"

Rafael straightened from his languid pose and crossed

both arms over his broad chest. "Hello, Elena," he said with obvious warmth.

She acknowledged his greeting with a slight tilt of her head. "Are you expecting to find something in Abigail Conrad's diaries that will shed new light on del Flores's ship?" she persisted.

His challenging stance didn't alter, and from the corner of her eye, Cora thought she saw his jaw tense. "Direct as usual," he said.

"While you're just as elusive." The woman pressed closer to the platform. "Aren't you really here because you believe that something in those diaries will lead you to the *Isabela?*"

Cora held her breath. He nodded, his expression thoughtful. "There's always a chance," he said carefully, "of an unexpected discovery. If Abigail Conrad was intimately acquainted with del Flores, it's my hope that her writings will help me understand the man better. Beyond that, I have no expectations."

"Really?" the reporter asked, her tone skeptical.

Rafael's nod was short. "Really."

An unnatural silence had settled on the crowd as they watched the interplay. Cora glanced at her nieces and noted that Liza seemed to have grown restless. She was resisting Becky's efforts to keep her in her seat. Clutching Benedict Bunny in one hand, she squirmed against Becky's restraining arm and tried to wriggle free. Elena, unaware of the movement behind her, forged ahead. "But there could be direct information about the wreck," she countered. "Couldn't there?"

"It's possible, but highly unlikely. As Dr. Prescott explained, the Conrad diaries predate del Flores's disappearance by several years."

Elena lifted her dark eyebrows. "But there could be more diaries?"

He shrugged. "I'm sure there could be. Dr. Prescott's team has already conducted a search, however."

"But you haven't searched yourself?"

"Not yet," he conceded.

Elena seemed to sense she had gained the advantage. "And weren't you in the middle of another project when you left Chapel Hill?"

"I was considering several options, but none piqued my interest." His tone had taken on a slight edge as the verbal confrontation escalated.

Liza, Cora noted with another glance at the front row, was now out of her seat. She and Molly appeared to have a brief argument. Liza pointed to the stage. Molly shook her head emphatically. Kaitlin looked on, her gaze speculative.

Elena ignored the rapidly elevating noise behind her and asked another question. "So you're going to spend valuable research time waiting for Dr. Prescott to tell you what's in the diaries just to learn a little about del Flores? Come on, Dr. Adriano, you're the leading expert on the man and his career. No one's going to believe you're here for nothing more than a glimpse of his love life."

"That's up to them, I suppose," he retorted.

Elena shook her head. "I think you believe there's something in Dr. Prescott's house, or at least in the Conrad diaries, that's going to help you find del Flores's ship." There was a collective rumble in the audience.

Rafael leveled a piercing look at the reporter. "Why in the world would you think that?"

"Because," she said, clearly undaunted, "you could have chosen to pursue another project while Dr. Prescott studied the diaries. If you weren't hoping to find something she might miss, why else would you be in that house?"

Cora felt the situation begin to slide into a dangerous, out-of-control spin. What was it he'd said? We'll direct them, instead of letting them direct us. Too late for that strategy obviously.

She glanced at her nieces again and saw that Liza was making her way toward the stage, having eluded Becky's grasp. Kaitlin now had Becky's attention as she distracted her from Liza's behavior. Dragging Benedict Bunny behind her, Liza looked for all the world like a miniature avenging caveman with a club. Cora could only hope that the little girl would succeed in knocking the reporter off her feet before this went too far.

Cora brought her gaze back to Rafael. The scar that ran from his hairline to the edge of his patch had whitened, giving the only indication of his rising tension. She had a sudden image of Juan Rodriguez del Flores damning caution and setting a course for the outer banks where he could rendezvous with Abigail. Abigail Conrad, Cora thought, who had flaunted convention and bravely conducted a forbidden affair with her pirate lover.

Having spent so many weeks immersed in Abigail's writing, Cora, who was known for her formidable self-control and dignity, decided that she owed Abigail a worthy show of élan. Liza was now a few steps from Elena, and in the face of certain disaster, Cora nudged Rafael away from the microphone and faced the reporter with a bright smile. "Actually, you're reading this entirely wrong," she told her.

Elena gave her a shrewd look. "Am I?"

"Yes." Cora glanced at Rafael, then back at the crowd. Liza moved into place behind Elena, but froze when she realized her aunt was speaking. Cora gave Liza a censorious look as she continued, "Dr. Adriano, as you all know, has just completed an extensive excavation project in Greece. He and my colleague, Dr. Jerry Heath, are old acquaintances, and when Dr. Heath mentioned the Conrad diaries, Dr. Adriano felt that the nature of the project would provide a welcome respite from the pace of the last several months."

"He's on vacation?" Elena asked, her voice skeptical.

"Does he ever go on vacation?" Cora said dryly. The crowd gratified her by laughing. She continued, "And for the record, my early examination of the diaries indicates that they are quite, er, specific about the nature of Abigail's affair with her lover."

"Is del Flores mentioned by name?" Elena asked.

"I don't know yet," Cora answered truthfully. "I haven't examined them all, but Abigail's writing is a bit cryptic and I won't really have a firm grasp of it until I study it further. In any case, the five volumes we found are dated years before del Flores's disappearance. They couldn't possibly contain information about the wreck."

"Then if you're going to be studying the diaries," Elena persisted, "and you don't think they contain any information about the ship, why is Dr. Adriano going to be living in your house?"

Liza seemed to have lost interest again and was slowly raising Benedict Bunny over her head. Elena's attention remained on Cora. "Couldn't you have coordinated your research if he'd remained in Chapel Hill?"

"Well," Cora said, "not exactly."

The reporter frowned. "Why not?"

She cleared her throat. "Because he's going to be my nanny."

Liza seconded the announcement by whacking the reporter in the behind with Benedict Bunny.

"YOUR NANNY." Jerry snorted. "God, Cora, what were you thinking?"

They were in the large conference room adjacent to Henry Willers's office. The elegant room, with its blue carpet, cherry and leather furniture and twin sets of French doors leading to the terrace, seemed like an oasis of calm after the roiling chaos in the outer office. Following Cora's announcement, they'd fled the stage amid a renewed flurry of questions. Reporters now cluttered Henry's office where they were grabbing press kits and releases from his secretary. Several were insistently demanding interviews. To Cora's relief, Becky had managed to round up her three nieces and was keeping them momentarily corralled in Cora's office.

Cora flicked a speck of lint from her sage-green suit and mused, absently, if Elena whoever-she-was had ever been assaulted before by a stuffed rabbit. Cora met Jerry's hostile gaze and wondered why no one else seemed to see the humor in this situation. "What should I have said, Jerry? That we hired him because he had nice legs?"

Henry gave her a withering look. "I don't think there's anything funny about this."

"I wasn't offended," Rafael assured him. He was leaning back in one of the leather chairs, watching her with a look of amusement. He hadn't spoken since Henry Willers had hurried them all off the stage, then cloistered them in the conference room.

Jerry grunted. "You should have been."

"Damn right you should have been," Henry Willers agreed.

Colleen O'Shannon, chairman of the board of trustees, gave Cora a wry look. "Personally I thought it was brilliant. Talk about a diversion." A rich chuckle burbled from her throat. "Your nanny! I wish I'd thought of that."

"Thanks, Colleen," Cora muttered.

Henry Willers continued his tirade. "We had an opportunity to place Rawlings College among the top research facilities in the country with this project, Cora."

"If you hadn't been so damned stubborn about it," Jerry added, "we would have had more time to plan this. But you wouldn't agree to share the spotlight."

Henry nodded and placed his plump hands on the girth of his belly. "Do you have any idea what this could have meant to us financially?"

"We've lost millions," Jerry accused. "Millions."

She gritted her teeth. "You're blowing this out of proportion."

"I agree," Rafael said, surging from his chair in a sudden burst of energy. "You know, Jerry, I never liked you, but I at least respected your integrity. Now I'm not so sure."

Jerry's face paled. "How dare you!"

"The Conrad diaries are Cora's project. I made that clear to you yesterday."

Henry paled. "There's no reason to get upset."

Rafael glared at him. "Cora is the project director. Period. And she did exactly what any responsible researcher would have done in her position. She could have released the diaries early, possibly sacrificing whatever information we might get from them, or she could stand up to the pressure you were putting on her and take her time deciding how to proceed." Rafael leaned over the conference table to glower at Jerry. "And let's at least be honest. You're not concerned about the research or the money or the college. You're concerned about yourself. You want credit for whatever comes out of this project."

Jerry's eyes glittered with rage. "You're accusing me of being a glory hound."

"Now, now." Henry Willers stepped between them. "This is getting us nowhere." He looked at Rafael. "I explained to you yesterday, Dr. Adriano, that this project and this college were in serious financial trouble before you got here. While I'll admit that Jerry and I proceeded without your express permission, neither of us imagined that you would have agreed to play second chair to Dr. Prescott's competent if, er, methodical pace."

Rafael's expression turned harsh. "Just because Jerry is threatened by her competence doesn't mean that I am."

Jerry leaped up from his chair. "I don't have to take this."

"Jerry," Colleen snapped, "haven't you caused enough trouble?"

Henry mopped his forehead with his handkerchief. "I'm sure that if we just put our heads together, we can come up with a solution. Nothing happened today that can't be easily fixed. We'll just release another statement—"

"Are you out of your mind?" Cora asked. "If you say anything else, all you're going to do is increase the speculation that Dr. Adriano is here to find that ship."

"Well, he is," Jerry sneered, "isn't he?"

Rafael glared at him so hard that he finally dropped back into his chair. Cora continued, "Don't either of you know what's going to happen when word leaks that Abigail's diaries or the house itself might contain information about the *Isabela?*" She ignored the suddenly speculative look Rafael shot her way. "These aren't nice people, Henry. We're talking about millions of dollars in unclaimed gold."

Colleen coughed into her fist. "I think the trustees should have been informed of this earlier," she asserted. "This could have terrible repercussions."

Jerry snorted. "Don't be melodramatic." He glared at Cora. "Cora's exaggerating."

"I don't think so," Rafael countered.

Henry wiped a hand over his balding head. "The important thing is for us to decide exactly what we want to say to the press. They're clamoring for answers right now, and my secretary isn't going to be able to keep them out of here forever."

"Maybe that little brat could beat them all away with her rabbit," Jerry said derisively.

Cora shot daggers at him. "Shut up, Jerry."

"Then what do you suggest we do?" he retaliated. "Stick with the nanny story?"

Rafael laughed. "Might as well. It's not that far from the truth."

Henry opened his mouth to respond, but the door flew open and his stricken secretary gave him an apologetic look. "I'm sorry," she told them. "I'm sorry, but I can't—"

Like water through a breached dam, a crowd of reporters began flooding into the room. Cora shielded her eyes from the glare of a television camera. She felt a strong hand close on hers and pull her to her feet. "Follow me," Rafael said into her ear. He faced the crowd. "One at a time," he yelled. "Henry Willers can give you complete details of the project." He pointed to Henry, who stood on the far end of the conference room. Collectively the crowd turned its attention to the beleaguered president. Rafael used the opportunity to guide Cora along the perimeter of the room. She caught a glimpse of Henry's panicked expression an instant before Rafael slid open one of the French doors and slipped outside. Cora hesitated, but as the noise in the room grew, she accepted his outstretched hand and followed him to safety.

Rafael led them swiftly across the marble terrace, through a narrow breezeway and toward the seldom-used gates of the college. "Where are we going?" she asked.

He pushed open the rusted gates with a strong kick of his foot. "Anywhere but here."

"I thought you thrived on this kind of thing." Deliberately she dropped her voice to imitate his drawl. "'Watch and learn,' you said. 'Follow my lead,' you said."

He shot her a wry grin as he shut the gates behind them. "Didn't anyone ever tell you not to believe everything you hear from a strange man?"

"Ha." They wended their way through a grove of trees.

"You're supposed to be the expert at handling these people. Liza did better than you did."

"Elena took me off guard." He checked over his shoulder again, then steered her toward a large maple.

"I'll bet. You weren't at all distracted by the fact that you could see down her blouse when you leaned over the podium, were you?"

He laughed. "Would it do me any good to say I didn't notice?" He guided her to the far side of the tree so they were completely shielded from view.

"No." She leaned against the trunk and gave him a disgruntled frown.

He braced one hand next to her head and bent close. "Then would it do me any good to tell you that Elena happens to be my sister, and that if I'd known she was going to show up, I'd have hidden backstage until the entire thing was over?"

Cora stared at him. "She's your sister?"

"Did I happen to mention that I have nine of them?"

"Do all of your siblings attack you in public like that?"

"Some more than others," he confessed with a wink. "But she wasn't attacking. She was just doing her job."

"And trying to make my life miserable."

"No, she wasn't. It's not Elena's fault that the roomful of half-wits didn't figure out what was going on." He slanted her a grin. "Although I'd wager even she wasn't expecting the rabbit."

"Bunny," Cora muttered.

"What?"

"It's a bunny. Benedict Bunny."

"I'll have to thank him the next time I see Liza. I can't remember the last time I had such an ardent defender."

"This is going to be awful, you know."

"I can control it, Cora. You have to believe me."

She rolled her eyes. "Is seducing a pack of female reporters with that sea-is-like-a-woman bit part of the plan? I mean, did you actually rehearse that?''

He blinked, his expression the picture of innocent bewilderment. ''I have no idea what you're talking about.''

She shot him a wry look. ''For the record, you're a rotten liar. The sea—'' her voice had dropped an octave ''—is dangerous and elusive. Unpredictable. I can't wait to have my hands on her.''

His mouth twitched. ''I did not say I wanted my hands on her.''

''You thought it.''

With a quick step forward, he trapped her against the tree. ''Were you thinking it, too?'' he challenged.

Her breath was short. ''What if I was?''

He traced a finger along the lapel of her jacket. ''If you were—'' his voice had lowered to a silky purr ''—were you wondering what my hands would feel like?''

Cora swallowed. ''I have a pulse, you know. I don't know what Jerry told you, but—''

He interrupted her by tucking a windblown strand of hair behind her ear. ''Jerry's an ass. I knew it the day I met you.''

''We can agree on that at least.''

''But little else?''

She searched his expression. ''Why are you here?''

His smile was lazy. ''Right now, at this moment, I'm here because I'm with a woman I want.''

Cora sent a silent command to the butterflies in her stomach to cease and desist. ''Stop it,'' she told him. ''I just want you to tell me the truth.''

His eyebrows lifted. ''That I'm attracted to you? You need me to say that?''

Cora shook her head. ''Not that.'' She didn't begin to have the fortitude to talk about that, not when her pulse was still running full throttle. ''I want you to quit giving me the same line of rhetoric you dish out for your investors and your fans and the media, and just tell me the truth.''

He tensed. ''Specifically?''

''Oh, for God's sake, give me a little credit. The rest of the world might fall for that polished act of yours, but I don't.''

''If it makes you feel any better, I've never given that speech before.''

She searched his gaze. ''Who are you?'' she asked softly.

''I'm just like you, Cora. I don't merely want to learn about Abigail and del Flores. I want to *know* them.''

She searched his gaze. When she spoke again, her voice had taken on a husky tone. ''Why?''

His gaze turned wary. ''What do you mean?''

''Why this ship, these two people?''

''I've been interested in del Flores for twenty years.''

''Why?'' she said again.

''Because I find the story fascinating, and because the *Isabela* has eluded me.'' His gaze moved to a spot beyond her shoulder. There was a wariness about him she'd never seen before. ''Because it's there,'' he finally said, ''waiting for me.''

Her eyes narrowed. There was more to this story. He was hiding something—or maybe protecting something. She couldn't tell, but the brash veneer had momentarily slipped off, and she found herself fascinated by the man underneath. When she said nothing, he looked at her again, his ready smile chasing away the momentary vulnerability. ''What are you thinking, Dr. Prescott?''

Cora raised her hand to trace the edge of his eye patch. He didn't flinch. ''I think,'' she said softly, ''that I believe you.'' Her finger found the scar and she followed it to his hairline. ''Did you know that the first time I saw you talk about the *Isabela* was when you told a TV reporter that you weren't obsessed with finding it?''

He captured her hand. "Cora—"

She interrupted him. "Tell me the truth," she prompted again. "There are no reporters now. Just you and me." She gave him a small smile. "So woo me."

Other than the tightening of his hold on her hand, he showed no outward signs of reaction. "I want you to help me learn who Abigail Conrad was," he said with careful precision. "I want to tell you what I'm looking for, and then I want you to help me see del Flores as she saw him. You know Abigail better than I do."

"And you know del Flores," she said.

"Yes."

"Why can't you wait until I'm finished with my work?"

"There's more to see than the diaries," he explained. "There's the feel of the house. The way it looks at night. There's something about being right there where Abigail and del Flores met and talked and probably made love that will tell me more than anything you could ever show me in print."

He threw his head back and the sun glinted off his earring. "In his captain's logs, del Flores makes veiled references to the diaries several times in some of the correspondence I've found. He even mentions in one entry that he'd warned his lover to hide them."

"You have no proof that Abigail Conrad was that lover. The man traveled all over the eastern United States. Why Abigail?"

"She was a colonel's daughter. The connection and information she could provide del Flores would be invaluable. He was wanted by the Union and Confederate governments at the time. Surely you can see why Abigail could be so helpful to him."

"And you believe he pursued her for information about her father?"

He pressed her hand flat against his chest. "Do you?"

Cora stared at him for long seconds. "No," she admitted, "I don't."

He acknowledged her confession with a slight nod. "I didn't think so."

"What about the ship?" she asked. "What are we going to do about that?"

"I have the clout and the resources to protect everything we're doing, Cora. You just have to trust me."

That brought another smile to her lips. "If I didn't trust you, I wouldn't even let you near my house or my nieces. I don't give a damn what Henry Willers wants."

"You're sure? It's not too late to change your mind."

She laughed. "Are you kidding? I just told CNN that you're going to be my nanny."

"A stroke of genius, I might add." He moved his thumb over the back of her knuckles. His heart beat a comforting rhythm under her palm. "I meant what I said, Cora. If you decide you want me off this project, I'll support you. Hell, I'll even agree to finance you if you want."

She released a long breath. "I don't want you off. I think we can do more together than I could do by myself."

"I'm counting on that." She didn't think she imagined the slight heat in his gaze. "And the girls?" he continued. "When Elena asks again, I'd like to know what to tell her."

"You don't think we can just refer her to Liza?"

He laughed. "Benedict Bunny's power is in a surprise attack."

Cora nodded. "Then tell her, and anybody else you want, that you'll be living in my home for the duration of the project."

"You're sure?" The look he gave her was so intense, so darkly probing, that she felt as if he was watching her thoughts unfold inside her head. He was asking for more, and she knew it.

Her fingers fluttered. "I trust you," she said finally. "Academically and…personally.'' She rubbed her fingertips on his shirt. ''I'm sorry I misjudged you.''

His expression turned to satisfaction. ''What changed your mind?''

''Instinct,'' she replied. ''The same instinct that tells me Abigail has more secrets to reveal. I want to find them. I want to share them with someone who's going to protect them the way I would.''

''I will,'' he vowed.

''I know. And before this morning, I was going to say that I didn't think you had a real grasp of what you were getting into with the girls…''

''But?''

''I met your sister.'' She smiled slightly. ''And I watched your reaction when Benedict Bunny had his way with her.''

He laughed at that. ''Don't judge Elena too harshly. You'd actually like her if you got to know her.''

''If you say so.''

''She reminds me of you.''

''Am I supposed to be flattered?''

He interlaced their fingers and lowered her hand from his chest. ''As a matter of fact, you are. Elena's determined and talented and smart as a whip. She's one of the few people I know who can get the better of me.''

''Well, if she was half as, er, precocious as a child, then I don't think you'll have any trouble coping with Kaitlin and Molly and Liza.''

He grinned at that. ''Thanks for the vote of confidence.''

''We'll just have to see how it goes. I'm not sure they'll accept you any better than they have the others.''

''I'll risk it.''

She nodded. ''I've already promised to take them to the beach tomorrow. Why don't you come with us? It'll give you a chance to bond with them a little. Maybe they'll respond better if I'm there.''

"Perfect," he said, and she couldn't keep from staring at the way his lips formed the word. His thumb was tracing lazy circles on her palm. Heat radiated up her arm and made her skin tingle. "I'll bring my bags in the morning."

"Tomorrow night," she continued, ignoring the renewed flutter in her stomach when she thought of him sleeping under her roof, "I'll show you what I've already discovered about Abigail."

"You care for her, don't you?"

She nodded, not bothering to deny that she'd developed an odd affection for a woman who'd been dead for a century. Somehow she knew that he would understand. "The house—it's always spoken to me. When I found the diaries, the connection got even stronger. I think that Abigail was a strong woman, but del Flores made her vulnerable. I'd feel like I was violating her if I let her get exploited."

"I'm glad you feel that way."

"Anyone else would think I'm crazy."

Another grin. "Takes one to know one."

"You feel it, too. Don't you?"

"Why do you think I've spent almost twenty years looking for del Flores?" He laid a hand against her cheek. Again her skin tingled from his warmth. "So we're agreed about the research and the girls. What about the rest, Cora?" He traced the whorl of her ear with a callused fingertip. "What about you and me?"

"There is no you and me," she said.

"There will be."

"You sound sure."

"Aren't you?"

Unable to deny it, she took the coward's way out and tried to retreat behind a quip. "It's the long hair and the patch, I guess. What woman could resist—"

He seemed to lose patience with her then. "Tell me later," he said, "and kiss me now." He pulled her into his arms and covered her mouth in a kiss rife with hunger, heated with need and filled with enough passion to make a pirate proud.

Cora gasped, momentarily stunned by the onslaught, but passion sparked and flared seconds later. One of her arms snaked around his neck, and Rafael spread a large hand at the small of her back to fully align her curves to his hard lines. His warm, tangy scent made her head spin.

He whispered her name as he deepened the kiss, and she absorbed the incredible, intoxicating sound as he tasted her. When he finally tore his mouth free, she dropped her head to his chest with a slight moan. She closed her eyes momentarily, waiting for a sense of reality to return. Slowly he trailed his fingertips down her cheek and along her jaw until he gently tipped her chin up to face him. ''Cora,'' he said. She forced her eyes open. He was watching her. He rubbed the pad of his thumb over her moist lips. ''Tell me you feel it.''

She blinked. He pressed his thumb against her lower lip. ''Tell me,'' he said again.

She shivered. With a soft smile, he enfolded her in his embrace and gallantly let her off the hook. ''Never mind.'' He kissed the top of her head. ''We have plenty of time.''

Chapter Four

Dearest,

I had to write you tonight! You'll never know how very hard I laughed this afternoon when that horrid Mr. C. called on Father. You know him—the gentleman with the puce evening jacket and satin trousers? He's been feeling quite puffed up and conceited since the Governor appointed him to a post in the capital. You'd think the man was completely unaware that in wartime, the Governor's choices are so limited. All the true leaders are out in the battlefield—but I refuse to dwell on that now.

What I wanted to tell you was what Mr. C. told Father about me. Last week, he went so far as to make advances to me at J.M.'s cotillion. Now, stop frowning, darling. You know I have eyes for no one but you, and you are quite free to defend my honor on your next visit. Anyway, I gave him quite the set-down, you'll be happy to know. I informed him in no uncertain terms that my affections were otherwise engaged, and even if they weren't, I would never consider a suit from him. Well, he announced to Father this afternoon that he'd best take me in hand, and soon, lest I embarrass the Conrads with my "headstrong and outspoken ways."

*Father told him that, unlike Mr. C. himself, I at least
had something of value to say. Mr. C. blustered and
blubbered his way from the house—furious over the
insult.*

*I wonder if I should confess now that you taught me
the art of pugilism on your last visit?*

Lovingly yours,
Abigail
19 August 1860

The following morning Cora carefully searched her reflection in the mirror. At least she wasn't showing any outward signs of insanity. Except for the dark circles under her eyes, she really didn't look all that different. Still, something had to be misfiring in her brain or she never would have agreed to this. Maybe it had been the stress of the past few weeks. Maybe, she admitted, it had been the way her blood had heated when Rafael touched her. He'd woven a spell of seduction and charm, and she'd tumbled right into his trap.

Sensible, practical, predictable Cora Prescott had tumbled like a rabbit down a hole. She frowned as she applied a thin layer of lipstick. The seductive way he'd looked at her when he'd talked about Abigail and del Flores— that had been her demise. All she had to do was remember the rough sound of his voice whispering, "Tell me," and her stomach fluttered.

By two this morning, when she still lay sleepless, she'd given up trying to pass off the sensation as indigestion.

Muttering in frustration, Cora put the finishing touches on her makeup, then stalked out of the bathroom.

Who was she trying to fool? What had her wound up tighter than a Swiss clock was the memory of that kiss. It made her shiver, despite the summer heat. No wonder the man had a reputation as a rake.

Every inch of her flesh felt strangely sensitized this morning, as if he'd left an indelible imprint on her skin. As she pulled on her clothes, the heightened awareness gave her goose bumps. Worse, she felt as though the rational side of her brain—the one she listened to most often—had betrayed her by remaining stubbornly silent during that kiss. Where were the warning bells? Where was the voice of reason? Where the hell, she thought irritably, was her reputedly unflappable common sense?

Moving in with her.

Sharing the secrets of Abigail's intimate, sensual, stirringly personal diaries.

The very idea set off a bevy of longings she ruthlessly tried to suppress. When they'd parted yesterday, he'd assured her that he would handle the media fallout from the press conference. True to his word, her phone had rung only once that afternoon. She'd been shamefully relieved when she'd called his hotel and gotten his voice mail—she, who never cowered from anything and hadn't avoided a confrontation since her last fight with her father on her twelfth birthday. Leaving Rafael a message about when to meet her and the girls this morning, she'd hung up and briefly considered whether or not she'd lost her mind. The rest of the afternoon had given her ample time to consider the rashness of her decision. And what it would be like to have him underfoot.

Calling herself a thousand times a fool, she'd deliberately avoided thinking about the practical considerations of their arrangement by burying herself in activity. Her nieces had been in unusually high spirits after learning she wasn't angry about Benedict Bunny's assault on Rafael's sister. Cora told herself that she hadn't mentioned Rafael's new role in their lives in order to maintain the rare good mood. The four of them had gone out to dinner, done a little shopping, which included new shorts for them and new pajamas for herself. She refused to speculate on why she felt the sudden need for sleeping attire that looked somewhat more respectable than her usual oversize T-shirt.

She also hadn't allowed herself to question why she'd purchased new sheets and towels for the guest apartment. Generally her tenants supplied their own linens, but she'd guessed that Rafael had not brought towels and bed linens with him to Cape Marr. That didn't explain why she'd splurged on burgundy sheets. In Egyptian cotton. Or why she'd gotten goose bumps when she'd spread them on the bed and pictured him lying on them. His skin would look luxuriously dark against the blood-red cotton. And he probably didn't even own pajamas.

That thought made her fingers tremble as she buttoned her shirt. Taking herself firmly in hand, she squared her shoulders and pulled open the door. As she headed for the stairs, she caught a glimpse of herself in the hall mirror. She pressed her fingers to her lips. What had her stomach in knots this morning wasn't nervousness, she admitted, it was anticipation. She wanted to see him.

To touch him.

To have him touch her.

She wanted to throw caution out the window of the third floor, where a bed with newly made burgundy sheets lay waiting, and find out why Abigail had risked everything for passion.

Cora shivered and shut her eyes. She really was losing her mind. There was no doubt. Why else had she been able to calmly set aside every reservation and practicality that told her this was a bad idea?

Deep in the night she'd searched for her ever-present common sense, which had tried in vain to argue that Rafael wanted to use her. His interest in her stemmed from his obsession with finding del Flores. Only she, and her ability to control his access to Abigail's diaries and the secrets of her home, stood in his way. If he needed to seduce her to gain access, he seemed willing to do so.

It should have made sense. She was not, after all, his kind of woman. She'd seen him in pictures and interviews flanked by stunning, glamorous women who perfectly matched his beauty and charisma. Supermodels and movie stars—they were what he needed and, if the rumors were true, preferred. Bookish, too-serious Cora Prescott didn't compare.

But she had refused to listen.

Now, she lowered her hand from her mouth as she stared at her reflection in the hall mirror. She couldn't even remember the last time she'd looked in a mirror for any reason other than a practicality. She used mirrors to apply cosmetics or tweeze her eyebrows or check to see if she had something in her eye, not to wonder if she could measure up to the other women in some man's life. It seemed so…belittling, and she was ashamed of herself for even letting her mind go there.

So her face was a little too square and her breasts were smallish. So her hips were a bit wider than fashion decreed acceptable, and her hair was an indistinguishable shade of reddish-blond. She was not about to succumb to the kind of constant fear and anxiety about her appearance and self-worth that had destroyed her mother and was rapidly destroying her sister, Lauren, too. Either he accepted her on her own terms or he didn't. And if he didn't, then they could certainly establish a professional relationship that might still be advantageous to them both.

Deep inside, though, where Cora had locked away unfulfilled dreams, roads never traveled and bridges never crossed, the doors were starting to rattle. Something in her was demanding freedom—freedom to make a colossal mistake or to answer a consuming desire without fear of the consequences. Rafael had a wanderer's spirit, a Gypsy's heart and a pirate's passion, and the combination danced tantalizingly before her like an invitation to bliss. Temptation pulled at her, beckoning seductively toward uncharted waters.

She prided herself on her self-restraint and common sense. Rafael was offering her a trip into glorious instability. Immersed as she'd been in Abigail's diaries, reading of the woman's passionate affair with del Flores, of the risks she took to unite with her lover, Cora had begun to feel long-suppressed needs fluttering to the surface.

It was almost as if Rafael had tripped a hidden trigger deep in her soul. A part of her said she'd regret it later, though she'd begun to suspect that the fear of regret—and all the unfulfilled longings and forsaken dreams that came with it—was a worse fate than regret itself.

As if the thought shocked her, she blinked at her reflection. "Get a grip, Cora," she muttered as she tucked a strand of pale hair behind her ear. She shook her head to clear it, and the noise from the kitchen told her that Kaitlin, Molly and Liza were, with any luck, finishing their breakfast. The familiar voice of duty calling gave her a measure of comfort.

She breezed into the kitchen to find Molly feeding Melody strips of bacon. "Is everybody almost ready?" Cora asked.

Kaitlin shot her a wary look. "Why are we going to the beach?"

"I thought maybe you'd like to drive down the coast and get out of town for a while. We haven't had much time to do that since you've been here."

Molly looked at her inquisitively. "Can we go in the water?"

"Yes. I packed your swimsuits in the bag."

Kaitlin continued to look sullen while she played with her cereal. "I don't want to go. I want to stay here."

Cora suppressed a sigh and braced one shoulder against the doorjamb. "It'll do us all good to get some fresh air."

"I want to swim in the ocean," Liza chimed in.

Kaitlin glared at her. Molly looked anxiously at her older sister, but said nothing. Cora waited for an outburst. Finally Kaitlin looked at her. "I want to call Mama. I want to talk to her."

Damn Lauren, Cora thought. "I know, sweetie. I don't have a phone number for her."

"She said she'd call and give us one," Kaitlin insisted.

And typical Lauren, she'd neglected to do so. Cora nodded. "I know."

Kaitlin dropped her spoon to the table and pushed her chair back. "Then why hasn't she?"

"I'm sure she's just busy."

"She is not," Kaitlin said angrily. "She just doesn't care. The only thing she cares about is George."

"Kaitlin—" Cora held out a hand.

"I'm going upstairs," Kaitlin announced. "And I'm not going to the beach. It's dumb." She ran out of the room, leaving a stricken-looking Liza and Molly staring at Cora for guidance.

Cora managed a tight smile. "I'll go talk to her. Molly, why don't you put the dishes in the sink?"

Liza clutched Benedict Bunny closer to her chest. "Can we still go to the water, Aunt Cora?"

"Yes. We're going."

"Without Kaitlin?" Molly asked, dumping two bowls in the sink.

"Kaitlin's going, too."

"She doesn't want to," Molly said.

"Maybe I can get her to change her mind."

Liza looked at her wide-eyed, as if that seemed like the

gravest of impossibilities. Cora gently ruffled her hair. "Don't worry," she said. "You and Molly get dressed, and we'll be at the beach before you know it."

"Can I wear my new orange shorts?" Liza asked.

"Sure."

Molly looked over her shoulder. "Me, too?"

"You, too." Cora added as she turned for the door. "I'll talk to Kaitlin."

She was halfway up the stairs when she heard the knock at her front door. A quick glance through the transom revealed the top of Rafael's dark head. "I'll get it," Liza yelled as she ran from the kitchen. Cora deliberately headed up the stairs, leaving Rafael on his own with Liza and Molly.

She heard Liza's exuberant greeting as she turned the corner toward Kaitlin's room. Her knock yielded no answer. She waited several long seconds, then tried again.

"Go away," Kaitlin muttered from inside the room.

Cora gathered her calm and gently pushed the door open. "Hi."

Kaitlin was lying on her bed, clutching a pillow to her chest. When Cora entered the room, she turned away to face the wall. "I told you to go away," she said sullenly.

"I heard you."

"Then what are you doing in here? This is my room."

Without comment, Cora made her way across the room and sat on the edge of the bed. Kaitlin scooted as far from her as possible, until she was practically pressed to the wall. Cora remembered too many times when she'd felt like that, wanted to disappear. She'd resented her own mother's semi-desertions just as Kaitlin resented Lauren's. "You know what, Kaitlin?" she asked quietly.

Her niece didn't answer. Cora forged ahead. "I think it's really rotten that your mother hasn't called. And if I were you, I'd be mad, too."

The child visibly stilled. Cora laid a tentative hand on her back and began a slow soothing stroke. Briefly she considered the wisdom of what she was about to say. It seemed disloyal to criticize Lauren to her own children, but Kaitlin was old enough to know if she was being patronized. Cora had too many memories of simply wishing that someone cared enough to tell her the truth to ignore her niece's need for empathy. "Did you know that when I was about your age, my mother used to do the same thing?" No answer. "She'd leave me and your mother with my father or another relative and go on a trip somewhere without us. Sometimes we didn't hear from her for weeks."

Several seconds ticked by. "Were you mad?" Kaitlin asked.

"Usually. And it hurt my feelings. It wasn't a very nice thing to do."

Kaitlin still didn't look at her. "Molly and Liza get really upset."

"Mmm. I'm sure they do."

"What did you say when you saw your mother again?"

"I used to think about that while she was away. I'd think of all the questions I wanted to ask her about where she'd been and who she'd been with."

"My mother is with George."

Cora ignored that. If she talked about Lauren's affair with George, she'd probably reveal more than she should. "But when she got back," she continued, "I never asked her anything."

A teary-eyed Kaitlin turned to face her. "Why not?"

"I don't know." Cora shrugged. "Maybe I thought she wouldn't tell me. Maybe I didn't want to know what she had to say. We'd just go home and wait until the next time she went away."

Kaitlin wiped a hand over her flushed cheeks to clear

away her lingering tears. "It's mean," she whispered, as if confessing a dreadful sin.

Cora couldn't agree more. "It *is* mean. People shouldn't make promises they don't intend to keep." She thought about trying to apologize for Lauren's behavior, but didn't see the value. "And I'm sorry it makes you feel bad."

"Why does she do it?"

Good question, Cora thought. "Maybe because her own mother used to do it, so she never learned any better."

"You wouldn't do that," Kaitlin said. "You always call us, even when you're only out for a little while."

Cora nodded. "I know."

Kaitlin sat up on the bed. "She makes me really mad, Aunt Cora."

"She makes me mad, too," Cora confessed.

Kaitlin drew a shaky breath and set aside her pillow. "Molly and Liza really want to go to the beach today, don't they?"

"Yes, but Dr. Adriano is here. He was going to go with us. If you really want to stay home, then he can take Molly and Liza, and I'll stay here with you."

Wide-eyed, Kaitlin asked, "You would?"

"Sure." Cora knew the concept of an adult putting aside her personal wishes on a child's behalf was alien to Kaitlin. Lauren would never dream of changing her plans to accommodate her children. "Do you want me to?"

Kaitlin thought it over, then shook her head. "No, I'll go."

"You're sure? You don't have to."

"I know." She scooted to the side of the bed to sit next to Cora. "Aunt Cora?"

"What?"

"Dr. Adriano told us we could call him Rafael."

"He did?"

"Yes. Can we?"

"If he said so."

"Mama makes us call George 'Uncle' George."

Cora frowned. "Ugh."

Her expression made Kaitlin laugh. "I don't like it, either."

"What's George like?"

"He's okay. He's not mean or anything." She held her arms out in front of her stomach. "But he's kind of fat. And he doesn't have much hair."

"Really?"

"Yes. I don't know why Mama likes him."

Because George, Cora thought cynically, owned a villa in the south of France and Lord knew what else. "There's more to liking a person than what they look like," she said carefully.

"I know." Kaitlin flashed her a broad grin. "But you know what else?"

"What?"

"I think Rafael is very handsome."

That made Cora laugh. "You do?"

"Yes. Don't you?"

She hesitated, then nodded. "Yes, I do."

"He's way better-looking than any man Mama's ever dated."

"Really?" she said.

"Yeah, sure." Kaitlin rubbed her hands on her thighs. "If Mama saw him, she'd have a fit."

That was probably true, Cora mused. "Maybe," she said aloud.

Kaitlin pushed her bangs off her flushed face with a slight sigh. "I guess I gotta get dressed."

Cora took that as her cue. She rose to leave the room. "Liza and Molly are wearing shorts. We're going to be outdoors a lot. You'd probably be more comfortable if you wore shorts, too."

Kaitlin stared at her. "Mama never tells me what to wear."

Cora filed that piece of information in her growing dossier of Lauren's faults. She doubted her sister was interested enough in the comfort of her children to even consider something so trivial. Their woeful lack of appropriate summer clothing had borne testimony to that. "Neither am I," she assured Kaitlin. "I just thought you'd like to know."

Kaitlin nodded. "I think I'll wear the new purple shorts you bought me last night."

"Good idea. I like the way they look on you."

Kaitlin smiled and said, "Me, too."

The smile, the first Cora had seen since the girls arrived, made her feel as if she'd successfully negotiated a Middle East peace agreement. She tucked the victory close to her heart and said, "See you downstairs," as she withdrew from the room.

She found Liza and Molly seated in the kitchen, listening with rapt attention to a tale Rafael was spinning about pirates and treasure hunts. He looked potent, she admitted, and decided to cut herself a little slack for falling under his spell. What woman wouldn't? Clad in a blue shirt and faded jeans that hugged every muscular angle, with his hair pulled back in a clip, he was breathtakingly sexy. Her stomach clenched.

Liza was clutching Benedict Bunny so tightly he looked like his head might pop off. "Sorry to interrupt," Cora said smoothly, "but you girls better get dressed. We're leaving soon."

Rafael greeted her with a broad smile that made her heart skip a beat. "We were in the middle of a story."

She flashed him a look. "I see."

"Is Kaitlin going?" Liza asked.

"Yes," Cora told them. "So hurry. Get dressed."

Molly gave Rafael a pleading look. "Can you finish the story later?" she asked.

"Absolutely," he assured her. That sent the two girls scurrying from the chairs and out of the room. Liza dragged Benedict Bunny by one ear.

The door swung shut behind them, leaving the kitchen unnaturally quiet. Rafael braced his hip against the counter and regarded her with a steady look. "Good morning," he whispered.

Cripes, she thought, how did he manage to wrap that voice around two simple words and make them sound like a seduction? "Hi." She went to the sink to finish loading the dishwasher. She felt a strong need to occupy her hands before they got her into trouble. "How was your afternoon with the press?"

His laugh was a butter-smooth chuckle. "It wasn't so bad. At least, I think I persuaded most of them that this isn't about the *Isabela*. That should keep them off our backs."

"I hope so. I want to protect the girls from—" She stopped as he advanced toward her. "What are you doing?" she asked warily.

He settled both hands on her waist and toppled her against him with a brief pull. "I want to test something."

"Test—" The rest of her question was cut off when he covered her mouth with his. The kiss was thorough and leisurely, lacking all the urgency of yesterday. He mapped her mouth with his own, learning its curves, experimenting with pressure and taste. A tingling sensation started at her toes and tickled its way to her hairline. By the time he lifted his head, she felt a little dizzy. Her hands had found their way around his shoulders and lay linked beneath his glossy hair where it was clipped at his nape.

Rafael gave her a slow, lazy smile, then rubbed his nose against hers. "Good," he muttered. "I was afraid I had imagined it." He kissed her again, softly this time. "You taste just as good this morning."

Cora took a step back and tried to steady her nerves. "Um, about that—"

He grinned. "Yes?"

"Now that I've had a chance to really consider this, I realize that we didn't have a lot of time yesterday to lay out the details of this arrangement. I think it would be prudent—"

"I hate that word." He used a long, bronzed index finger to twine a tendril of her hair into a soft curl.

"Prudent?"

He nodded.

She should have known. She pushed his hand away from her face. The heat of it was distracting her. "Maybe you do, but surely you can see why we need a few ground rules here."

The teasing sparkle left his eye. "Uh-oh."

"Could you take this seriously, please?"

"You have no idea," he drawled, "how seriously I'm taking this."

Cora frowned. "All I'm saying is that I told you yesterday that I think the girls are going to have a hard time adjusting to you. They're used to their mother having a man around, and his presence generally means that Lauren ignores them. They are not used to having a male role model. I believe the transition will be easier if you and I make a concerted effort to show them that they don't have to compete with you for my attention."

"Will they?" he asked with a raised eyebrow.

"Of course not. Since Lauren brought them here, it's been my top priority to give them a little stability—someone they can count on."

"And that means?"

He was watching her with a disarmingly frank stare. "That means," she said, drawing a deep breath, "that I think they'd feel threatened if they thought you and I were romantically involved.''

The angles of his face shifted into a determined look. ''It's good for children to see adults in a caring, nurturing relationship.''

''Well, these three children happen to have often seen their mother involved in unbalanced, one-sided destructive affairs. I'm not sure they'll be able to tell the difference.''

''Then we'll show them,'' he said.

''It's not that easy,'' she countered.

''Of course it is. There's no reason they have to feel excluded simply because you and I are...together.''

His meaningful pause raised goose bumps on her flesh. ''I just don't see how—''

''Trust me,'' he muttered, and took a step forward. ''We'll make it work.''

That was easy for him to say, she thought, feeling disgruntled and frustratingly trumped. He'd be sleeping upstairs while she tossed and turned all night remembering what his kiss felt like. She drew a calming breath. ''It won't work,'' she said.

''Cora—'' he leaned forward so his face was level with hers ''—I thought we settled this yesterday.''

''No, we didn't. You kissed me and I—'' She stopped.

''You forgot,'' he said. He sounded so arrogant she almost laughed.

She shook her head. ''It's not that I'm trying to deny anything,'' she admitted against her better judgment. ''It's just that—''

He interrupted her by placing a large hand on her shoulder. ''That you don't want to admit to anyone that we're going to be lovers.''

He sounded so sure. She closed her eyes and swallowed. ''It's not that.''

''Then what is it? Precisely?''

"I just want you to realize that this…arrangement is going to be a lot more difficult than you think. Living with three children has certain, um, challenges."

He laughed. It shredded her nerves like sandpaper on balsa wood. "Where did you get the idea," he asked quietly, "that children aren't perfectly capable of distinguishing between healthy adult affection and a dysfunctional relationship?" His gaze narrowed. "Your sister's a real piece of work, isn't she."

"You could say that." She resisted the urge to push his hand away. "Look, I'm not talking about coordinating an amphibious landing, you know. This doesn't have to be complicated. We're both reasonable adults. And while I agree that it's inevitable that our proximity is going to have something of an effect—"

"Something of an effect? You mean like plastic explosives cause a little damage?"

She squared her jaw and continued, "I don't see why we can't simply agree that the girls have to come first, and if that means a suspension of our personal, er, wants, well, there's no reason to let this situation go to our heads."

"Then I have bad news for you," he announced. "Because you're so far into my head, I'm consumed."

She was saved a response by the sound of Liza's ear-splitting wail and Molly's yelling, "Aunt Cora, Aunt Cora! Come quick!"

After a startled instant she broke away from Rafael. With him hard on her heels, Cora mounted the stairs two at a time. From the sound of Liza's sobs, she was certain the child had mortally wounded herself. She followed the noise to the bedroom at the end of the hall. Kaitlin stood near the door, her expression wary, while Molly restrained a screaming Liza. Cora stopped so abruptly that Rafael slammed into her. She would have fallen had he failed to catch her.

"What's wrong?" he said.

At the same instant Cora asked, "Liza, are you all right?" She raced across the room to examine the child. No signs of blood, she noted as she ran her hands up and down the shaking girl's limbs. "Are you hurt?"

Liza shook her head and tried to suck in a breath between sobs. Molly came to her aid. "It's Benedict Bunny. He fell down the hole."

In the aftermath of her adrenaline rush, Cora now felt boneless. "Benedict Bunny," she repeated.

Liza pointed to a gaping crater in the plaster wall. "He felled down the hole. You have to get him out. You have to."

Cora shuddered as reason returned. She glanced at Kaitlin, who seemed to be the calmest of the bunch. "What are you three doing in here? I keep this door locked."

Kaitlin's expression turned wary. "It's not my fault. I heard Liza screaming."

Rafael had entered the room and gone to examine the damaged wall. The hole was about three feet off the floor, and approximately two feet square. Cora had examined the opening when she'd purchased the house and again when she was searching for the rest of Abigail's diaries. It appeared to be the remains of a shaft—perhaps a refuse chute—that had been filled and closed over when future innovations made its purpose obsolete. "This is deep," he said over his shoulder. "How did it get here?"

Cora wiped at Liza's tears with her palm. "When I bought the house, it was already in disrepair. I've been working on it for years, and I just haven't gotten this far yet. Since there's so much water damage, I always keep the door locked." She looked at Molly. "I don't want anyone getting hurt."

Molly's lips started to tremble. "We just wanted to know what was in here," she said.

"How did you get the key?" Cora pressed.

Molly bit her lower lip. "I found it." Cora waited. "In your desk drawer," Molly continued.

"You took it from my desk, Mol?"

"I'm sorry, Aunt Cora. I am. I just wanted to know what was in here."

Liza pulled away from Cora and ran across the uneven floorboards to Rafael. "Benedict Bunny," she said. "I want Benedict Bunny."

Rafael leaned into the cracked wall for a close look. "I don't see him."

"He's in there. I dropped him."

Cora decided she didn't even want the harrowing details of how Liza had come to drop Benedict Bunny into a hole that was almost higher than she was tall. The image of her tumbling into the cracked plaster made her feel queasy.

Liza tugged on Rafael's jeans. "Can you get him out?" Her small face mirrored her anguish.

He gave her a reassuring wink. "Aye, missy," he said in a pirate's brogue. "We pirates pride ourselves on recovering lost treasure."

At his teasing, Liza's expression turned slightly hopeful. "Really?"

"Really," he assured her in a normal voice. He looked at Cora again. "Do you have a flashlight?"

Kaitlin volunteered. "There's one in the kitchen. I'll get it." She raced out of the room.

Rafael stuck his arm into the hole and gingerly searched the dark cavern. "I'll need a coat hanger, too," he said. "I think I can just touch him with my fingertips."

Molly eagerly offered, "I have one in my room. I'll be right back."

Cora walked over to the wall and scooped Liza into her arms. "It's all right, sweetie," she assured her. "We'll get him out."

Liza buried her tear-streaked face in Cora's neck. "I'm sorry, Aunt Cora. I'm sorry."

"It's okay."

Kaitlin and Molly returned with the requested items. The room had the tense, silent feel of an operating room as Rafael peered down the hole with the flashlight.

"Is he downed there?" Liza asked, her voice wobbling. "Can you see him?"

"Yes," Rafael told her. "He's right where I thought he was."

"Can I see?" Molly asked.

Cora shook her head. "That wall could be dangerous, Mol. I don't want you to get hurt if the plaster gives way."

Rafael nodded as he reached for the coat hanger. "Good advice. And next time—" he gave Molly a gentle look "—maybe you'll listen to your aunt when she tells you to stay away from certain things."

Looking sheepish, Molly nodded. With a few deft twists of his wrist, Rafael molded the coat hanger into a long hook. "The difference between men and animals," he told Cora with a wry smile. "The ability to make tools from coat hangers."

She chuckled. "Another scientific mystery solved."

Using the coat hanger to extend his reach, he slid his arm back into the hole and gingerly maneuvered the hook. After several tense seconds he began to withdraw from the hole. Hanging by his ears on the end of the hanger was a dusty but otherwise whole Benedict Bunny.

Liza gave a shriek of joy when the rabbit appeared. "You got him!"

Molly breathed an audible sigh of relief. "Whew."

Rafael eased the toy off the hook and handed it to Liza. "Here you go, sweat pea. He's a little dirty, but I think he'll make it."

Liza clutched the stuffed toy to her chest like a cherished

friend and beamed at Rafael. "Thank you," she said, her eyes filled with adoration. Then, in a dramatic voice that sounded so much like her mother that Cora almost laughed, the child added, "I would have just died if he'd been gonned forever."

Chapter Five

Dearest,

My days seem to grow longer, and the nights, longer still. Though I fear you'll think me indelicate for saying so—I have a deep hunger for your presence. I wish so that Father could understand the man you truly are. Had he seen your heart, as I have, I know he would love you just as much.

Lovingly,
Abigail
9 March 1861

From the corner of his eye, Rafael watched Cora fidget. After he'd played hero for the day and retrieved Benedict Bunny, Cora had hurried the girls to their rooms to change. The five of them had driven down the coast to Fort Fisher, where Cora was boring her nieces almost to death with Civil War history. Hell, he even *liked* Civil War history, and he was bored. Twenty minutes ago he'd tuned out her informative lecture and focused on the woman. Everything about her, from the way her lips moved to the way she nervously rubbed her fingers together when she was agitated, enchanted him. She was in constant motion, he had noticed, like the surface waters of a volcanic crater. The energy and fire that lay just beneath her smooth surface caused tiny eruptions, waiting, brewing, until the moment of release.

The thought made his groin tighten.

Yesterday, when she'd stood in the shade of the tree and looked at him with that delicately probing expression, he'd admitted to himself that he wanted her so much that the hunger was clawing at him. His imagination told him that this was exactly what it must have been like for del Flores the first time he met Abigail. There was something heady, something arousing, something addictive about the idea that he could unleash feelings in her that no other man had.

He had no idea why he was so certain of her inexperience.

The word made him frown. It wasn't inexperience, precisely. Cora Prescott was a warm, intelligent, vibrant woman, who'd had, no doubt, her share of lovers. But his gut told him that no one had ever truly tapped the passion buried within her. She was, he mused poetically, like a rare instrument: capable of breathtaking music when handled with skill and finesse. And he desperately wanted to free her.

Even the *idea* that she'd been waiting for him was a powerful aphrodisiac. As he watched her now, he took careful note of her movements, wanting to burn on his brain all the things that made her so alluring. Unable to sleep last night, he'd lain awake and probed his conscience, hoping the exercise would calm his ardor.

And if he wasn't such a cad, he thought ruefully, it should have. Cora was the kind of woman who deserved much more than he could offer. Like Abigail Conrad, she would give her heart without strings or reservations or fear.

And like del Flores, he would probably break it. He could give her many things. Including incredible sex. That might be arrogant, but he had no doubts about it at all. He'd been with enough women to know exactly how they responded to him. And having kissed Cora, he could only imagine what it would be like when he coaxed that rapturous look onto her expressive face.

She'd humble him in that moment.

He knew that.

The first time she looked at him in the height of her climax, her skin would be flushed, her eyes would be feverish and bright, and the impact would bring him to his figurative knees. And until the emotion ran its course—not a foreseeable circumstance with her scent still lingering in his nostrils and the imprint of her fingers on his nape—she'd own him.

But experience told him that once the power faded, once the fire was released and the ardor cooled, she would realize that he was not the kind of man a woman built forevers on. The headiness of it would pass. And before the feeling grew stale, before he looked at her one day and saw disappointment in her eyes, he'd leave.

Like del Flores had left Abigail. He'd leave because he didn't have the courage to see that expression on her face.

And Cora would be better off because he'd left her. A bitter voice reminded him that she'd be better off if he never touched her at all, but he wasn't decent enough to heed it. Soon, too soon, she'd know it, too.

He dragged his attention from the dismal thought to watch Liza, who was shifting from one foot to the other as her gaze wandered around the stone interior of the fort's history center. Looking for an escape route, no doubt. Cora launched into an explanation of the complexities of nineteenth-century weaponry, and Rafael decided it was past time he took matters into his own hands.

He approached Cora from behind and slid an arm around her waist, effectively terminating her lecture on maritime strategy. She gave him a sharp look as she tried to worm away from his grasp. "What are you doing?"

He held fast. "It's summertime, Professor. Time to let class out."

She glared at him. "I thought that we may as well include the fort in our trip today since—"

"Since there's a law against fun without fetter?" Her lips turned into a delicious frown—one that had him aching to kiss her again. He laughed softly. "Come on, Cora. Lighten up."

Something flared in her gaze. It looked an awful lot like hurt, and he watched it for a fleeting second until it disappeared behind her usual resolve. She glanced at the girls. "You're bored, aren't you."

Molly reached for Cora's hand. "Can we go to the beach now?"

"I wanna swim," Liza announced while Molly nodded vigorously.

Cora gave up with a resigned sigh. "When I was your age, I liked this stuff."

Rafael pressed his lips to her ear and whispered, "If it makes you feel any better, I'll let you finish the lecture tonight after they're in bed."

She pushed his hand from her waist with an unsubtle shove and stepped away from him. "Okay." She handed Kaitlin the oversize tote bag she had hanging on her shoulder. "Your swimsuits are in here. There's a changing area down the path at the edge of the beach. Last one ready to get in the water has to do dishes after dinner tonight."

With a collective squeal of delight, the girls took off.

"Wait for us before you get wet," Rafael called after them.

"We will," Kaitlin said.

The three girls crowded through the swinging door. He and Cora followed at a more leisurely pace. "Bring your suit?" he asked.

She shook her head. "Are you kidding? With my complexion, I burn sitting in the shade. If I sat on the beach, you'd have to soak me in ice for the rest of the night.''

Not, he admitted, an entirely bad idea. He slid his hands into his jean pockets to keep from touching her again. Easy, he warned himself. He needed to take things easy.

They walked in comfortable silence toward the changing area. Rafael stayed a half step behind her so he could watch the sway of her hips, neatly outlined in khaki shorts. She looked soft, and subtle—not at all his usual type. Yet he was rapidly finding that no matter what she wore, she managed to elicit the familiar tug at his gut. When he'd first met her, she'd worn her professorial uniform—a tailored skirt and blouse that he'd found irresistibly sexy. Yesterday's press conference had found her in a no-nonsense business suit. The slit in the back of the skirt had exposed just enough shapely leg to tantalize him. He'd decided, then, that Cora had a knack for driving him to new heights of frustration.

Then there was this morning. She'd walked into her kitchen and sent him straight to the moon. She'd looked fresh and inviting. Her hair was pulled into a loose ponytail. All day, he'd wanted to run his fingers through that thick shank of strawberry-blond hair. It irrationally irritated him that she managed to look so wickedly tempting clad in shorts and a simple sleeveless shirt that should have looked plain, but somehow didn't—probably, he decided as he studied it now, because the way it outlined her breasts fell so easily on the eye.

He was glad he'd had the foresight to hire a couple of college kids to move his few suitcases from his hotel to Cora's house today. Though he traveled light—a lesson learned after years on ocean expeditions—he still didn't want to be hustling the luggage tonight after the girls were asleep. He had other plans.

"I don't think it will," he heard Cora say in a distant part of his brain. "Do you?"

Rafael looked at her blankly as he realized with some chagrin that he'd been concentrating so hard on studying her, he'd failed to listen to her. If she had the first clue what he was thinking, she'd slug him. "I'm sorry?" he said.

She frowned. "Have you been listening to a word I said?"

"No," he confessed. There were times when a little raw honesty went a lot farther than finesse.

Surprise registered on her face. "Oh. I was talking about the chance of rain this afternoon, but I suppose I bore you, too. I didn't mean—"

Rafael interrupted her by placing his hand on her shoulder. "I'm not bored." *I'm turned on.* "I'm…preoccupied."

She looked at him warily. "Are you coming on to me?"

That made him smile. "I'm trying."

"We're in public," she reminded him.

"I know." He stepped closer. "Believe me, I know."

"Rafael." She pressed her hands to his chest. "I told you this morning—"

"You don't think this is a good idea. Neither do I," he admitted.

"Then what are you doing?"

"Surrendering. Because I don't want to fight it."

Her breathing had quickened and, behind her glasses, her eyes looked slightly out of focus. "Not here," she said, her voice so soft he barely heard it. "Not now."

Laughter and the ring of childish voices relentlessly reminded him of their audience. He took a slow step backward. "Soon, Cora." When she trembled, he nodded. "Very, very soon."

THE REST OF THE DAY passed in relative calm. The girls played in the water and the sand until their hair was salty, their skin was wrinkled and their cheeks flushed from the heat. Cora sat beneath a beach umbrella watching while Rafael entertained them. And, she thought dryly as she noted the admiring glances thrown his way, he managed to entertain the rest of the women on the beach merely by looking like some Greek god sporting black swim trunks and an eye patch.

Occasionally someone recognized him and stopped to talk. He signed a few autographs, but seemed to take the attention in stride. Even when the attention-giver appeared far more interested in his physique than his research.

Not that Cora blamed them. His skin was deliciously bronzed from the Mediterranean sun, and his flat, muscled belly and chest were to die for. Heretofore, she could not remember a time when simply staring at a man's body had brought such undiluted pleasure, but then, she also couldn't remember a time when she had such a nice body to stare at.

As for her nieces, they also seemed to find the man fascinating. Cora had to suppress a twinge of envy as she realized how easily he related to them—and they to him. Rafael bought them hot dogs and snow cones for lunch. When Molly spilled hers on her suit, he laughed good-naturedly and surrendered his own. A few moments in the water, he'd promised, would take care of the stain. He seemed to have formed an instant bond with her nieces, one that she'd very much wanted since their arrival and had somehow been unable to build.

The notion, when she dwelled on it, depressed her. Determinedly she buried her thoughts in the novel she'd brought and tuned out the shrieks and giggles from the beach. By the time the sun began to set, the girls had the look of utter, but pleasant exhaustion that followed a day of high-spirited play. Rafael helped her bundle the girls into the back seat, and almost the moment she pulled out of the parking lot, the three of them were sleeping peacefully. By unspoken agreement, Cora and Rafael made the trip home in silence.

They carried the girls upstairs. He'd left her alone and Cora managed to keep the girls awake long enough for a quick shower. She had them tucked in and sleeping fifteen minutes after they walked in the door.

Taking a deep breath, she used the brief moment of solitude to lean against the wall outside Kaitlin's room. Today it had felt more like family and less like tactical warfare. And she had Rafael to thank. Rafael, who even now sat in her living room, waiting for her. Waiting with that heated look in his eye and that sensual expression on his full mouth.

The thought had anticipatory goose bumps tickling her flesh. She stopped by her upstairs office to retrieve her preliminary work on the Conrad diaries.

She found him seated on the couch with a bottle of soda dangling casually from his fingers and his feet propped on the coffee table. He was barefoot. The realization, oddly, made her heart skip a beat. "I see you made yourself comfortable," she said.

He looked at her. "I didn't hear you come down."

She moved toward the couch slowly. He watched her progress with a renewed surge of hunger. She indicated the papers in her hand. "I thought you might like to look at these tonight," she said, avoiding his gaze. "It's some of my preliminary work on Abigail's diaries." She set the stack on the coffee table, then seemed to fidget as she looked nervously around the room.

With a soft laugh he reached for her hand and tugged until she tumbled onto the couch next to him. "Sit with me, Cora. We don't have to unravel the entire story in one night."

"I know." She still hadn't met his gaze.

He twined a tendril of hair on his finger. He was beginning to love the satiny feel of it—and the image of what it would feel like when it touched other parts of his flesh. "It was a good day, wasn't it?"

That caught her attention. She gave him a sheepish look. "Even if I was boring?"

Smiling softly, he shook his head. "Don't be so hard on yourself."

"The girls really like you. I'm glad."

His fingers settled at her nape. "They really like you, too."

She shrugged. "I'm trying."

"It takes time," he assured her. "From what you've told me about your sister, I can understand why they might have trouble trusting you."

With a heavy sigh Cora leaned back against the couch. He used the opportunity to caress the line of flesh where her sleeveless shirt ended at her shoulder. Her hands clenched in her lap. "Lauren frustrates me to death, and I'm afraid I let it show too much." She looked at him. "I know Kaitlin realizes it, and I just hope she understands that it's her mother and not her that gets me so irritated."

"Where is Lauren, anyway?" he prompted.

"Somewhere in Florida with her married lover." She rolled her head to the side so she could meet his gaze. "I probably wouldn't be so annoyed if this weren't her third true and everlasting love of the year." Her voice held an unmistakable note of bitterness. "Not to mention the fact that she hasn't bothered to call and give me a phone number or address."

"What if something happened to the girls?"

"Good question."

"Has she always been that way?"

Cora turned so one knee was propped on the sofa cushions. He let his hand drift down her back. "Mostly," she responded. "Look, if you don't mind, I'd rather not talk…"

He shook his head as he applied a gentle pressure to her back, urging her closer. "I don't mind."

"Rafael…" The breathless sound of her voice swirled in his head.

"Let me kiss you, Cora," he said. "I've been waiting all day."

Her hand came to his chest, exerted the slightest pressure, then slid around his neck in surrender. "Me, too," she admitted.

He claimed her mouth, that sweet, kissable, alluring mouth that tempted and taunted him even in his sleep. His hand caressed her face. Her fingers slid into the weight of his hair. She sighed. He heard it and felt his body temperature spike. Shifting slightly, he levered her against him so her chest was pressed firmly to his. Increasing the pressure of his kiss, he angled his head until hers was against his shoulder and she lay half on top of him.

The feeling was indescribable. He ran his callused fingertips over the satin-soft skin of her cheek, down the arch of her neck, along the neckline of her shirt. Finding the spot at her throat where her pulse beat madly, he pressed his thumb to it, savoring, drowning in the heady feel of her response to him. At last he tore his mouth away and buried his face in her neck. "Ah, Cora," he said, inhaling great breaths of her scent, "can you imagine how much I want you?"

She shuddered. "Rafael, I—"

He pressed his fingers to her moist, swollen lips. "Don't say anything." Rubbing his fingertips along the curve of her mouth, he continued, "Not tonight. When we make love, you'll want it as much as I do."

Her eyes widened, and because he couldn't resist, he pressed a kiss to the corner of her mouth. "I promise."

Cora eased away from him then and stood. She brushed her hands over her clothes as if she could brush away the imprint of his body. "I, um, have class tomorrow," she said. "I need to get some rest."

He nodded, but said nothing. She met his gaze. "Do you think you'll be all right with the girls tomorrow?"

"We'll do fine." He could almost feel the current of energy coming from her. It crackled between them.

She rubbed her hand on her forearm. "Did you have a chance to check your room yet? Is it all right?"

"I went up there while you were getting them ready for bed. It's fine. Thanks for the sheets." He couldn't resist the slight taunt. Her skin blushed a gorgeous shade of peach, and he fell a little deeper under her spell. "I like the color."

Her lips parted and she wet them with the tip of her pink tongue. He felt the tug all the way to his gut. "Oh, uh, good. I didn't think you'd have any—" She stopped and shook her head. "This is ridiculous. I'm twittering like a moron."

Another layer, he mused, of this fascinating woman who had him in her thrall. "Am I making you nervous?"

Her slight smile knocked him off guard. "Of course you're making me nervous," she said with a laugh. "You're stretched out on my sofa looking like every woman's fantasy lover, and you keep baiting me with—"

He held up a hand. "I'm not baiting."

"You're very nonchalant about all this."

"About the fact that I want to make love to you?"

She fingered the collar of her shirt. "No, it's…" Her face twisted into an adorable expression as she searched for words. "You're seducing me," she finally said.

"I'm sure as hell trying."

Cora shook her head. "You don't get it, do you. What's making me nervous is this…this persona." She waved a hand at him. "You, international superstar, renowned scientist, sexiest man on the face of the planet—and you're trying to seduce me. One part of my brain keeps screaming yes, yes, yes, while the other part—which, quite frankly, is the part I listen to most often—keeps telling me this can't be for real.''

While the idea and sound of her saying yes was quickly working its way through his blood and having a predictable effect on his libido, the sincerity of her doubt rang through. Simultaneously surprised and frustrated, he surged from the sofa and crossed to her. ''Why not?''

Her frown deepened. ''Are you kidding? My God. You could have any woman in the world.''

''There's only one I want at the moment.''

Her frustrated sigh ruffled her bangs. ''See, there it is. Why would you say something like that?''

''Why do I want you? Are you serious?''

''Of course I'm serious.''

''Cora.'' He placed his hands on her shoulders. ''Baby, did some jerk convince you—''

She rolled her eyes. ''Oh, stop. I am not a walking cliché. That's not what I mean. I'm a reasonably attractive, educated woman. I'm not wallowing in a pit of low self-esteem. I'm just saying that I have a very healthy perspective on who I am and what I am, and I can't quite figure out why ordinary Cora Prescott has got extraordinary Rafael Adriano in hot pursuit.''

His lips curved into a smile. ''I'm one of those men,'' he said, ''who really likes women.'' At her raised eyebrows, he laughed and ran his hands along her shoulders. ''I mean, likes their company, not just their other, er—''

''Move on,'' she said.

He rubbed his thumbs in the shallow depressions beneath her ears. The gentle caress made her skin flush. ''There was a time in my life when the physical package was the whole deal. I was more selfish then, and I chose lovers who attracted me physically and looked the part.''

Her gaze narrowed. ''What's changed?''

His thumb found the corner of her mouth. He pressed. ''I have. My tastes are refined. I'm not satisfied anymore with a woman who doesn't challenge my mind.''

''I think this is the first time a man's told me he wants me for my brain.''

He chuckled. ''Believe me, I'm not complaining about the packaging. What I'm saying is, there are lots of reasons you have me in your thrall.'' Sliding one hand down her arm, he intertwined their fingers. ''It's the sound of your voice when you talk about Abigail. It's the passion I see in your eyes for your nieces and your students.'' He raised their joined hands and kissed her knuckles. ''It's the way you move and the way you smell.'' Ducking his head, he pressed a kiss to her throat. ''It's the way your skin flushes when I touch you. Watching you laugh, watching you live.'' He shook his head to clear the fog of desire settling on his brain. ''It's like a fire in my blood.''

A fine tremor was traveling through her body. He felt it when she laid her hand on his chest. She raised her eyes to his, and he saw a smoky haze in them that made him wonder what she'd look like when he was inside her. Her lips parted and she said, ''No wonder.''

Sweeping his thumb along the swell of her bottom lip, he raised an eyebrow in silent query. Cora used her free hand to gently tug his hand down. ''No wonder,'' she clarified, ''that I can't seem to think straight around you. My father always said that adolescents can't be trusted to make wise decisions because their hormones are taking up too much of their brain space.'' A smile flitted across her lips. ''To be honest, I never really knew what he was talking about. Evidently I'm a bit of a late bloomer.'' Her expression turned sheepish. "I get it now."

Arousal spiraled through him. He had a sneaking suspicion that if he got any hotter, if she made him any harder, he might petrify. "Do you know that you drive me completely crazy?"

"Feeling's mutual."

He used the soft confession as an excuse to kiss her again—an easier kiss that still managed to convey a wealth of want. When he raised his head and looked at her, he nearly tossed resolve out the window. Maybe it was selfish, but he wanted her to want him just as much as he wanted her. Still, with surrender written in her slightly dazed expression, temptation nearly overcame him. He pushed the thought aside with a vision of what she'd look like when willing desire replaced the bewildered heat he now saw in her eyes. "Then dream of me, Cora," he said, and eased her away from him. "Tonight, dream of me."

Her lips parted on a swiftly indrawn breath. He saw the momentary confusion, then the slight frown that crossed her face. "I—" She stopped, shivered, then lowered her gaze. "I'll see you in the morning."

He stayed rooted for several seconds after she fled up the stairs, taking a moment to subdue his sexual frustration. He could have had her tonight, but not on his terms. She would have surrendered. He'd seen it in the sweet parting of her lips and the sultry droop of her eyelids. But it wasn't enough, and he wasn't sure why. Still, he knew that Cora's surrender wasn't what he wanted. He wanted her unconditional partnership. He wanted her to feel the same gnawing hunger he felt, experience the dizzying heat. He wanted her to pant and demand and beg. To give orders and to cling. To set the pace and follow his lead. When he finally joined his body with hers, he wanted both of them to be so high on passion that they would fly together.

This indescribable craving shocked him somewhat. He couldn't remember the last time he felt it for anything or anyone—not even the *Isabela*. This, he realized, is what del Flores must have felt for his Abigail. This is what Rafael had left home at seventeen to find. This is what had driven him for twenty years to find del Flores's story, to know what drove the restless, independent pirate into the arms of a woman who conquered him.

Shaking his head, he scooped up the papers she'd left him. He'd read them tonight while he lay awake, warring with the clamoring needs of his body. Perhaps Abigail could give him answers.

He made his way quickly to the kitchen, where he dumped the contents of his soda down the sink, checked the lock on the back door, then headed through the creaky house, switching off lights as he went. There was something incredibly gratifying about performing the simple, domestic function, as if he'd settled so thoroughly into Cora's existence that she'd have trouble rooting him out. He could almost picture del Flores creeping through the house, risking his neck for a few moments of bliss. As he mounted the stairs two at a time, his thoughts wandered to the burgundy sheets on the bed in his third-floor room.

What wonderful delights, he thought, awaited him in the hands of this incredible woman? At the landing he gave a swift glance down the hall. A night-light burned in the hallway outside two cracked doors, which must be the girls' rooms. Light streamed from beneath a third door. Cora's bedroom. As he strode down the hall toward the back stairs, he found himself straining for a sound, a whisper, anything coming from behind her door. He was two steps from her room when he heard the soft *snick* of the lock as she turned it. Abruptly he stopped and stared at the door. He could picture her on the other side, her fingers on the lock, her other hand pressed flat against the door as she waited for him to pass. Was she locking him out, he wondered, or locking herself in? Perhaps a little of both.

Chapter Six

Five days adrift, with the wind so even the gulls refuse to fly. We've been taking on water and are badly in need of repairs, yet even if the wind should carry us there, we dare not sail into a hostile port. We are vulnerable here and though I know my thoughts should be of my crew and their safety, my mind is drawn to her. In her courage, I have found the will to press on. I shall not leave her like this. I gave her my word.

Juan Rodriguez del Flores
Captain's Log, 12 July 1861

"You didn't tell us," Kaitlin accused, giving Cora an angry stare, "that he was going to be our baby-sitter."

Cora took a sip of her coffee. A brief glance at the overhead clock told her she had another fifteen minutes before she had to leave for her Tuesday a.m. seminar class. She had hoped for a continuation of the tentative peace accord they seemed to have struck. Evidently it wasn't to be. Tired and cranky after another mostly sleepless night—the man was going to be the death of her—she was quickly losing her patience. She had a ten-o'clock class this morning and would have to leave the girls with Rafael whether they acceded gracefully or not.

"Why can't we go with you?" Molly whined.

"Because she doesn't want us to," Kaitlin said.

Cora shook her head. "That's not true. If I didn't know you'd be bored sitting in my classroom, I'd be delighted to have you."

"We could wait in your office," Liza suggested.

"No," Cora said patiently. "I'm not going to leave you alone."

Kaitlin frowned. "I'm not a baby, you know. I look after Molly and Liza all the time at home."

"She does," Molly agreed. "Kaitlin even cooks for us sometimes."

No surprise there, Cora thought as she kept her expression deliberately bland. "The rules are different in my house than they are at your mother's." She shrugged. "Sorry, but that's the way it is, ladies."

Liza wriggled out of her chair and rounded the table to lay her head on Cora's lap. She still clutched Benedict Bunny. "I want to go with you, Aunt Cora. I don't want to stay here."

Cora stroked Liza's downy-soft brown curls, still warm and tousled from sleep. "You'll have fun today," she promised. "Rafael has promised to take you somewhere."

"Where?" Molly asked.

Kaitlin shook her head. "I'm sure it's someplace boring. Like the library or the grocery store or something."

Cora shook her head. "No, it's not."

"I don't like the library," Molly argued. "It's cold."

"And scary," Liza added.

Molly concurred. "And that woman with the glasses is mean."

"He's not taking you to the library," Cora assured them.

"Then where are we going?" Molly pressed.

She opened her mouth to respond when Rafael's brisk knock sounded at the back door. This time, he'd used the outside stairs, she thought, unlike last night when he'd hesitated at her bedroom door until she'd almost succumbed and yanked it open.

"I'll get it," Liza announced, and leaped up to hurry through the kitchen to the mudroom.

Cora made one more attempt with Kaitlin. "Kaitlin," she said quietly, "it'll be different this time. He's not going to be like the other sitters you've had."

The girl gave her a frosty look, then turned her head to stare out the window. Molly looked at Cora anxiously. "Aunt Cora?"

"What, Mol?"

"I like him."

She wasn't the only one, Cora thought as she steeled herself to look at him, knowing the same jolt of sexual energy would shake her when she did.

Rafael strode into the kitchen carrying Liza. Still barefoot, Cora noted. She was beginning to think she had some kind of weird fixation with the man's footwear, or lack of it.

His smile warmed the room. "Good morning."

Molly gave him a half wave. "Hi."

He glanced at Kaitlin, then gave Cora an inquiring look. She ducked his gaze and headed for the sink. "They're all yours," she told him. "I've got class in twenty minutes."

"Women's literature?" he asked.

"Nope." She dumped the contents of her mug into the sink. "History of feminist thought."

At his groan, she gave him a wry look. She was relatively pleased when her stomach flipped, but her heart kept a steady rhythm. Progress. "Care to stop in and guest lecture?"

"I'm not crazy, you know."

Liza was patting his chest. Cora suppressed a burst of envy. "Aunt Cora says you're taking us out," Liza announced. "Can Benedict Bunny go?"

"Of course," he said. "We might run into that reporter, and we'd need Benedict Bunny to defend us."

Cora picked up her briefcase, stooped to kiss Molly, then ruffled Kaitlin's hair. At least the girl didn't pull away from her. "Have a good time today," she said to no one in particular.

Molly nodded. "We'll be really good, Aunt Cora, I promise."

"I'm sure you will."

She turned to press a kiss to Liza's cheek, but the child ducked the instant before, and Rafael tipped his head in a move so perfectly timed she'd have sworn the two had rehearsed it. His lips covered hers in a brief, but intense kiss that had Molly and Liza giggling.

"They're kissing," Liza announced.

"Eeeew." Molly added.

Rafael lifted his head and winked at Cora. "We'll see you when you get home," he told her.

She blinked. How did he do this to her? She glanced at Kaitlin, who was watching her with wary distrust. "Argh," she muttered, and walked out the back door.

CORA SAT AT THE DESK in her office later that morning and contemplated the new discovery she'd made about herself. Last night and again this morning, after Rafael had kissed her, she realized that she was suddenly aware of the feel of her clothes against her skin. It was as if every quivering cell in her body was waiting, yearning for the touch of his fingers. After they'd parted last night, it had taken hours for her flesh to cool down enough to prevent her sheets from chafing.

Haunted by images of his sensual lips and his body spread on the burgundy sheets, she'd tortured herself until the small hours of the morning, searching diligently through her mind for the voice of reason that usually gave such excellent advice.

It seemed to have fallen dormant when she most needed it. Where was the cautionary note warning her not to get in over her head? Where was the commonsense rationale that said he'd move on when the job was done—and possibly break her heart in the process? To her amazement and confusion, it seemed to be yielding to a stronger, more insistent voice that said she'd been left before and survived; and a life lived in fear is a life half-lived. When she considered the consequences of a broken heart and weighed them against the consequences of never knowing what it would be like to be his lover, a broken heart seemed a small price to pay.

She rubbed her eyes as she leaned back in her chair. Abigail Conrad had thought like that—that much was clear from her diaries. Perhaps it was the other woman's fervent descriptions of her affair that were wooing Cora to recklessness. Sometime since Rafael had arrived to tempt her with vivid images of Abigail's pirate-lover, Cora had accepted that the man Abigail wrote about with such passion was, indeed, Juan Rodriguez del Flores. Abigail had burned for him with a desire that poured out across the pages of her journals. Together, the two had made magic. The chance to taste that magic, to feel its power, danced before Cora like a seasoned seducer, making her yearn.

As a bead of sweat dripped from her forehead, Cora's eyes popped open. Damn, she thought. It was making her yearn, all right, enough to have her temperature nearing the boiling point.

She reined in her thoughts and began stuffing files into her briefcase. If she continued to let her mind spin off on flights of fancy—some of which, she admitted with a slight smile, were actually quite lurid—she'd soon be so far behind on her research and her class work that even Becky wouldn't save her. Her class had gone well at least, though her concentration was shot. Somehow she couldn't keep her attention on Sappho when a certain long-haired, barefoot swashbuckler kept intruding on her thoughts. Which, as it turned out, was just as well, since her students were a-twitter with the information that Rafael had moved into her house. She spent most of the hour and a half of class time answering questions about the Conrad diaries and dodging questions about Rafael personally. Her students had ribbed her mercilessly, but Cora felt she'd survived the experience with a decent amount of dignity intact.

Now, however, as she scooped up the thick folder of news clippings Becky had left for her, she wondered how long she'd be able to keep that dignity. Quickly she flipped through the news clippings. Evidently she and her students weren't the only ones who were preoccupied with Rafael. The entire world seemed to be fascinated.

Rafael's promise to manage the press had been more effective than she thought. She'd had only one phone call after the press conference. After that, her life had remained blissfully peaceful. She'd lulled herself into the secure feeling that he had everything under control, and that whatever statement he'd released had managed to assuage curiosity.

That hope crashed down around her ears as she scanned the thick stack of clippings. He must have spent most of that afternoon giving interviews. The major newspapers had stories. The wire service had run a blurb about his new research project. According to Becky, the networks and both major cable news shows had given them airtime. And worst of all, she thought as she studied a full-color picture, they'd made the tabloids. The headline screamed, "Brilliant Archeologist now Pirate Nanny?" The picture showed him standing next to her at the podium. Somehow she didn't remember him giving her that look that said, "Bed me"— not until this morning, anyway.

The picture left a bad taste in her mouth, as if she'd just pinned her dirty laundry out on the line for all the world to see.

A soft knock drew her attention from the photo. Expecting Becky, she glanced up to find Rafael's reporter sister, Elena Dublin—she'd found the last name on her byline—standing in her open door.

"May I come in?" Elena asked

Cora's eyebrows lifted. "Sure."

Elena crossed the small space with a confident stride that reminded Cora of Rafael's own I-own-the-world grace. Dressed more casually today in jeans and a T-shirt, she was still a striking woman. Dark hair hung loose around her shoulders, and wide, almond-shaped eyes—by far her most striking feature—gave her an exotic beauty. She smiled at Cora. "I'm Elena Dublin."

Cora shook her hand and indicated the stack of news clippings with her other. "I read your article."

Elena nodded as she took the seat across from Cora's desk. "Has Rafael told you—"

"You're his sister? Yes, he mentioned it."

"Oh, I'm glad."

"And I suppose I should apologize for the bludgeoning you took at the hands of Benedict Bunny." Cora swept the clippings aside and placed her hands on her desk.

Elena laughed. "No, no. Don't worry about it. I have eight sisters—believe me, I've had my share of beatings from stuffed animals."

The other woman's easy charm reminded Cora of Rafael. If the entire family had this kind of grace, it was a wonder they hadn't collectively taken over the world. "Still, Liza is, um…"

"Precocious?"

"That's one way of putting it," Cora said dryly.

Elena nodded, her expression sympathetic. "My sister

Margie was like that—always had an opinion about things, and always wanted to make sure the rest of us knew it."

"Is she a politician?"

"Actually she's a librarian." Elena continued with a slight smile, "I think it's a control thing for her. She has power over who gets to use all the books."

Cora leaned back in her chair, the familiar creak of the ancient leather seat comforting. "So maybe there's hope for Liza?"

"I'm sure there is. And if anything, I'm the one who should be offering the apology." Elena swept the fall of her dark hair over her shoulder. "No matter what it looked like, I didn't mean to ambush the two of you."

Cora linked her hands in her lap. "I wouldn't call it an ambush exactly," she said.

Elena winced. "It never occurred to me that Rafael wouldn't be ready for the question. It always comes up when he's doing anything remotely connected to del Flores or the *Isabela*."

"We didn't have a lot of time to prepare a statement. Henry Willers called the press conference before Rafael and I had a chance to talk about our goals for the project. We were winging it."

"I learned that too late," Elena confessed. "Although, I have to admit, I still would have asked. It is part of the story."

"You can understand why I'm concerned about bringing the shipwreck into this."

"Of course."

"And frankly, what Rafael told you is the truth. This really isn't about the *Isabela*. Your brother is interested in the diaries because it's the first chance he's had to learn anything about Abigail Conrad. He's hoping the diaries will shed some new light on the del Flores mystery, but the chances of them including anything about the shipwreck are limited.''

Elena nodded. "I'm sure. But certainly, you don't think that Rafael has released everything he knows about del Flores's ship, do you? He's hiding something. I don't know what it is, but he knows something about it that he's not telling.''

"He's not obligated to tell.''

"I know, but that doesn't mean it's not news.''

Cora studied her intent face. "Do you know what will happen," she asked quietly, "if word gets out that your brother knows where that ship is?''

Elena had the grace to look nonplussed. "I have to believe that Rafael can take care of himself. He'll be first on that ship, I guarantee it.''

"If the reported treasure were the only thing at stake, I'd be inclined to agree with you. But I don't think he cares whether there's a treasure aboard or not.''

Elena's eyes narrowed. "No?''

Cora waved her hand in exasperation. "If you think he's pursuing the wreck because of its potential financial—''

Elena held out a hand to interrupt her. "I don't. I never have. I just find it interesting that you don't, either.''

"Anyone who's talked to him about—''

"That's just it.'' Elena shook her head. "It's a lot of work to get Rafael to talk about the *Isabela*—or anything else, for that matter.''

"I've noticed," Cora said with a small smile.

"I'd like to know how you squeezed it out of him.''

"I held him down while my niece beat him into submission with Benedict Bunny.''

After a second of stunned silence, Elena laughed. "I'm glad to know my instincts about you were on target.''

Cora wasn't sure how to respond to that. "Excuse me?''

Elena checked her watch. "Look, it's close to noon. Are you free for lunch by any chance?"

Cora hesitated. "Is this personal or do you want an interview?"

Elena shook her head. "Personal, I swear. I'll even tell you up front that I want to pick your brain about my brother. He's acting…a little different."

"Oh?"

Elena sighed. "Actually weird is more like it. I just want to talk to you about it, you know—" she waved a hand between them "—girl talk."

A tremor of caution slid down Cora's spine. "I'm not sure he'd appreciate that."

That made Elena laugh again. "Are you kidding? He's got nine sisters. Our primary source of entertainment is gossiping about our brothers, and they all know it."

"Maybe. But I don't think I get sister status, if you know what I mean."

Elena's expression turned knowing. "Actually I think I know exactly what you mean. Which is why I want to talk to you."

Cora thought it over, then made a quick decision. A researcher at heart, the lure of talking to someone who knew him well was irresistible. She'd seen him as a scientist, a would-be lover and a friend to her nieces. Now she wanted to see who he was in the eyes of his family, and Elena could tell her. Carefully she said, "Do I have the right to pass on any question?"

"Absolutely."

"And it's off-the-record?"

Elena held our her hands. "No notebook. And you can check me for wires if you want."

Cora shook her head. "That's not necessary." She rose and reached for her purse. "Come on. I'll show you Cape Marr."

Two hours later, having polished off a sinfully fattening dessert, Cora set down her water glass and gave Elena a shrewd look. "Okay, we've talked about your kids and my nieces, and your husband and my job, and your brothers and sisters. When are you going tell me what this is really about?"

They were seated under the awning of a picturesque bistro in the downtown area. Today was one of those rare days when the ocean breeze and the shade protected Cape Marr from the blistering summer heat. Humidity was low, and the town was cluttered with people taking advantage of the climatic respite. Elena carefully placed her napkin on the table. "Rafael," she said softly. "He's my favorite of the four of them, you know?"

"Your brothers?"

"Yes. When you have thirteen kids in one family, you sort of form allegiances with one another. Everyone segregates into groups."

"And you picked his group?"

"More like, we were our own group." She traced her finger along the edge of her knife. "Our father left us when our youngest sister was born. Mama had to take care of all of us by herself and…things weren't easy."

"I'm sorry," Cora said gently.

Elena managed a weak smile. "I was young, and I don't think I really knew how bad things were—not like the older ones, anyway." She sighed. "But Mama couldn't take the long hours or the stress, and eventually it killed her. So, Zack was the oldest and he kept us together. I still don't know how he did it, but thanks to him, we're a very close family."

Briefly Cora thought of her own sister with a pang of bitterness. There were times when she would have given anything to feel that Lauren cared, or even wanted to care, about her the way Elena obviously cared about her siblings.

She pushed the thought aside. "It must have been difficult," she said quietly.

"You can't imagine. Social services, the government, the neighbors, everybody wanted to split us up and send us off to separate families." Elena shook her head. "But you'd have to meet Zack to understand. He was like Daniel Boone at the Alamo—he was going to keep us under one roof or die trying."

"You're lucky to have him."

"We are. I don't think any of us even realized that until we were old enough to really appreciate what he did for us." Her expression softened. "I know my husband, Danny, and I find it challenging enough to raise our three kids. Zack, well, he's my hero."

Cora nodded. "I can see why."

"But Rafael—" the sparkle was back in her eyes "—he didn't respond so well to Zack's authority."

She could only imagine. "You're kidding," Cora said sarcastically.

Elena chuckled. "So you've not noticed he's not exactly a follow-the-leader kind of guy."

Cora couldn't suppress a smile. "Yes."

"Anyway—" Elena waved her hands as she set aside the harsher memories and focused on the better ones "—Rafael and Zack didn't see eye to eye about a lot of things, and Rafael left home early."

"Seventeen. He told me."

Elena's eyebrows lifted. "He did?"

"Uh-huh. He was in college and came down here that summer. That's when he discovered the del Flores story."

"Did he tell you why he left?"

"He mentioned that he and Zack didn't get along."

"Really?"

She sounded so skeptical that Cora looked at her, surprised. "There's another reason?"

"No, no, it's not that. It's just that I'm surprised he told you."

"Oh?"

Elena nodded. "Absolutely. Here's the thing, Cora. Rafael is my brother and I love him to death, but he's the most persistently private person I've ever known in my life. He doesn't tell anyone anything personal. Not ever, as far as I can tell. That whole speech at the press conference—"

"You mean the sea is like a woman?"

"That's the one." Elena's eyes danced. "Everybody else might fall for that, but it's bull."

"So I gathered."

Elena studied her for a moment, then nodded. "You get it."

"I what?"

"You get it. That's what I thought." Elena frowned as she considered her next words. "Rafael comes across as this really together, almost arrogant guy who keeps the world on a string."

"He's not." Cora said softly.

"Not at all. What happened between him and Zack, well, it was really hard on everyone. They didn't even speak for several years. Things are a little better now, but the two of them can still rub each other the wrong way on occasion. Rafael's free spirit is just so alien to Zack."

"They were very young."

"And hotheaded, both of them. They both said things they regretted. Anyway, Rafael was old enough when our father left that he took it really hard. Then Mama died, and then he had that falling-out with Zack. To my knowledge, he's never let anyone else get that close to him ever again. Even I don't feel like I really know him sometimes."

"He cares for you a great deal."

"I know he does." Elena pinned her with a piercing look. "But you—you've gotten to him."

The simple statement had a startling impact. "Why do you say that?"

"It was obvious at the press conference. Probably not to anyone but me, but I know him well enough to see that he's different with you." Elena picked up her spoon and twirled it slowly between her fingers. "What has he told you about the *Isabela?*"

"I think that would be one of those questions I'm not going to answer."

"Which is precisely my point. That means he's told you something at least about del Flores and the ship, and why he finds the entire thing so intriguing. I'm pretty sure no one else knows. He's never told me, anyway, and we're close."

"It's not unusual," Cora said carefully, "for a scientist to single out a certain project for attention. Lots of researchers have a quest—a Holy Grail, so to speak."

"I know, but with Rafael it's different. There's something about the whole del Flores legend that gets to him. I don't understand it, but I've seen the fire in his eyes when he talks about it."

"So have I," Cora admitted.

Elena set the spoon down and pressed both her hands on the table. "And until I talked to him after the press conference, I'd never seen that fire for any other reason."

"No?" Cora asked.

"Absolutely no." Elena leaned closer. "I'm telling you, Cora, he had that same look in his eyes the other day."

"Naturally. Finding Abigail Conrad's diaries is a major discovery. We have no idea what we might learn about del Flores."

Elena shook her head. "He wasn't talking about del Flores, Cora." She paused. "He was talking about you."

LATE THAT AFTERNOON Cora let herself into the house. Melody strolled in from the living room, tail wagging, and greeted Cora with a customary nudge to her hand. "Hi, sweetie," she said, stopping to scratch the collie's chin. "Got the place to yourself?"

Melody's tail thumped the floor. The lack of noise in her home took Cora off guard. Not since Lauren had brought Kaitlin, Molly and Liza to her, she realized, had she found herself home alone. Rafael must still be out with the girls. He hadn't told her when to expect their return.

Semidarkness amplified the silence. An afternoon thunderstorm, so typical of the summer months, was rolling in off the sea. Dark clouds had masked the sun, so the old house stood in shadow. Cora could almost picture Abigail creeping along the upstairs hallway toward the back stairs, using the dimness as camouflage. She would have sneaked down the stairs and thrown the lock on the back entrance so her lover could enter later that night.

Abigail had written long and sometimes graphic descriptions of what went on in that third-floor room of the house. A woman of great passion, she had lavished it on her lover.

Cora set her briefcase down, closed her eyes and simply absorbed the feel of her home while she absently stroked Melody's silken head. "Abigail," she said softly, "what are you going to tell me tonight?"

The rising storm brought strong winds, which whistled through the shutters and eaves. *She'd probably tell me,* Cora thought, *not to lock my bedroom door just in case a pirate finds his way to my room.*

If she tried very hard, Cora was certain she could hear the sound of Abigail crying for her lover—a man of the sea. There were anguished passages in the diaries where Abigail described the summer thunderstorms and begged God to spare 'Dearest,' whose ship could so easily be caught in the gale and dashed on the rocks.

A thunderclap broke the spell, and Cora headed for the

stairs, intent on changing clothes and settling down with Abigail's diaries. She'd made little progress since her initial foray into the work, her time consumed with more pressing matters. This afternoon's respite held the promise of an uninterrupted glimpse into Abigail's life.

Three hours later, she sat at the kitchen table, deeply absorbed in Abigail's writing. The three candles she'd lit when the storm had knocked out the power, cast a golden light across the carefully preserved pages. Melody lay at her feet in blissful lassitude. The thunder had finally stopped, but rain still beat steadily down. A kink in her neck reminded her that she'd been bent over the books too long without stretching.

Cora pulled off her glasses to rub her eyes when she heard the laughter and the sound of keys jingling at the front door. With a rush of damp air, giggles, a rumbling laugh and Melody's resulting bark, Rafael, Kaitlin, Molly and Liza flooded into the room. Cora leaned back in her chair and studied the small group. Even Kaitlin, she noted, appeared to be in a decent mood.

"Aunt Cora, Aunt Cora!" Molly hurried forward clutching a lopsided ceramic mug. "Look what I made for you." She thrust the object at Cora. "We went to this place where you get to make your own stuff." She pointed a finger at the artwork on the outside of the cup. "See, I put the handle on, and painted it for you and everything. That's Melody, and that's the house."

Cora stroked her thumb over the glazed surface, the asymmetrical lines of the drawing and the blob that represented Melody. "It's beautiful, Molly."

Molly took the cup and set it on the table. "It doesn't exactly stand up straight." She rotated it a little. "But it doesn't wobble."

"Which is the most important thing," Cora assured her, and wrapped an arm around her slim waist. She pressed a kiss to the child's forehead and found the skin damp from the rain. "Thank you."

Rafael held Liza, who was squirming to get down. "I made you something, too, Aunt Cora. Lookit." She held out an amorphous lump.

Rafael met Cora's gaze as she crossed the small space to accept the gift. "It's a paperweight," he supplied.

Cora took the heavy object and ruffled Liza's hair. "Of course it's a paperweight," she said.

Liza nodded vigorously. "It's for all that stuff you got on your desk."

"Thanks." Cora hefted it in her hand. "It'll do a great job."

She glanced at Kaitlin, who stood slightly to the side, lurking in the shadows. "Did you have a good day?"

The girl shrugged, her expression unreadable. Molly pulled at the hem of Cora's T-shirt. "How come there's no lights on?"

Rafael set Liza down. "Power must be out," he said, and shot Cora a questioning look.

She nodded. "For about two hours."

"Hmm." The candle flame reflected in his eye as he looked at her. With the tiniest stretch of her imagination, she could picture del Flores looking at Abigail with that precise, hungry expression. "Dinner by candlelight," he drawled. "How charming."

She gave him a wry look. "Especially since it'll have to be pizza or cold sandwiches."

"Pizza," Liza cried. "I want pizza. Just cheese."

"I like pepperoni," Molly countered.

Rafael held Cora's gaze as he said, "Kaitlin gets to pick."

"Why?" Liza demanded.

"Because," he said, turning to look at the older girl, "she

let you and Molly ride in the front seat all day today without complaining.''

Kaitlin's face, Cora noted, registered a moment of surprise before she finally moved away from the door and into the fragile circle of light cast by the candles. ''Half and half is okay,'' she said.

Cora smiled at her. ''Did you make something today, too?''

Kaitlin showed her the bowl she held. The artwork, Cora noted, was outstanding. A band of vaguely Celtic-looking designs circled the rim, and bright swatches of color melded on the inside, giving it a Matisse look. ''The place where we went,'' Kaitlin explained, ''had lots of stuff to pick from. You could either make your own thing or pick one of theirs and just paint it.''

''Kaitlin's very talented,'' Rafael said.

Cora nodded. ''I can tell.'' She held out a hand. ''May I see it?''

''It's for Mama,'' Kaitlin warned, but placed the bowl in Cora's hand.

''I'm sure she'll love it.'' She held the bowl closer to the light and studied the artwork. ''Kaitlin, this is really good.''

''Thanks.''

''Have you taken art lessons?''

''No.''

Cora tipped the bowl to look at the outer design. Rings of geometric shapes decorated the surface. ''Would you like to?''

''I don't know. I guess.''

Cora glanced at Rafael. ''We'll see if we can find something around here this summer if you want,'' she said as she looked at Kaitlin. ''It could be fun.''

Kaitlin reached for the bowl. ''Okay. Can I go change now?''

Cora nodded. ''Everyone should.'' Their clothes were wet

from the rain, and dusty and stained from the pottery excursion. "When you get back, we'll order pizza."

The girls left the kitchen with Melody trailing behind. As the door swung shut, leaving the room in relative quiet, Rafael gave Cora a look that curled her toes. Having spent the past few hours immersed in Abigail's world, she could easily picture the woman, standing in this kitchen in her bare feet and nightdress, unlatching the door for her lover.

"What *did* you make at the pottery place?" she asked him blandly.

His smile was enigmatic. "It's for later. Ask me after the girls are in bed and I'll show you."

She decided she'd rather not know. "I'll try to remember to."

He sauntered farther into the room. "Do you think Abigail greeted her lover by candlelight like this?" he asked.

He didn't stop until he stood inches from her.

"Probably," Cora retorted, her voice raspy. Lord, she thought, the man was almost breathtaking. His dark hair, glossy and damp from the rain, was slicked away from his face. A roomy white shirt, wet enough to cling to his muscular torso, opened at the throat exposing a V of bronzed skin. Snug black jeans hugged his hips and strong legs.

For most of the afternoon, she'd been trying to dismiss Elena's assertion as a sister's wishful thinking. Elena had insisted that Rafael somehow wanted Cora with the same single-minded passion that he wanted the *Isabela*.

Cora had verbally and mentally rebuffed the idea. He wanted a physical relationship with her, yes, but Cora stubbornly reminded herself to stay focused on the fact that he'd come into her sphere because of Abigail's diaries. Soon enough, he'd be gone—no matter what his sister said. Both of them would be better off if she remembered that. *Keep your head, Cora,* she warned herself as he bore down on her.

"Have a good day?" he asked as he snaked an arm around her waist.

She placed one hand on his chest, perhaps to stop his progress, maybe just to feel the steady drum of his heart beneath his warm skin. "I did," she answered. "I saw your sister."

His eyebrow lifted. "Really?" The word was the softest of whispers as he placed his other hand on her hip and fitted her tightly against his body. Her hips slipped into the hard cradle of his with breath-stealing ease.

"Yes. We had lunch."

Rafael bent his head to nuzzle her neck. "What'd you talk about?"

Cora managed a slight laugh. Her hand was now trapped between them. The other rested lightly on his forearm. "What do you think we talked about?"

She felt his smile against her skin. "I was afraid I'd sound arrogant."

"Like that's ever—" she gasped when he nipped her earlobe "—stopped you."

He raised his head to grin at her. "I'm a swashbuckler. It's part of my charm."

A warning note sounded in her head. There was something—something important—she was supposed to remember about all this, about why it couldn't and shouldn't be, but the thought eluded her. Worry seemed very far away somehow, with the heated scent of the candles filling the room and the reassuring press of his warm body on hers. "I think we should—"

"Oh, I do, too," he murmured. "I definitely think we should." His gaze was fixed on her mouth.

"Rafael—"

He covered her lips with his thumb. "I wonder what Abigail would do at a time like this." He tilted his head to indicate the diaries on the table.

Cora shuddered. Trust him to know she'd been lost in Abigail's world and was having trouble finding her balance. "She'd probably have smacked del Flores's face and told him not to paw her in her father's kitchen."

His laugh, low and mellow, fluttered her eyelashes. "And then summarily dragged him up the back stairs." A light kiss to the bridge of her nose. "Where—" another kiss to her eyebrow "—she could have her wicked way with him." He said the final word with his lips pressed to her ear.

"I don't think Abigail had any wicked ways."

"Didn't she?" He nipped her earlobe. "Do you?"

The hiss of his breath sent shivers spiraling down her spine. Her hand crept around his neck as her world continued to spin into a heady, dizzying passion. "The girls—"

"Are upstairs." He pressed her closer with an insistent pressure at the small of her back.

"We can't." She shook her head.

"We have to." He wet his lips with the tip of his tongue.

"Rafael—"

"I'm mad for you, Cora."

She moaned softly and surrendered.

The kiss robbed her breath, her balance, her common sense. His lips moved over hers in a leisurely exploration that lacked all of yesterday's urgency and none of its heat. He bewitched her as he led the way to unknown heights. Distantly she registered the sound of a moan, wondered if it could be hers. His hands wove a spell as they trailed down her back, learning her shape, molding her against him until they were so close their heartbeats melded.

It was too much and not enough. Simultaneously untamed and gentle. Cora clung to him. She threaded her fingers into his damp hair while her other hand made the journey up his arm, over his broad shoulder and behind his neck. Trailing her fingers along the hard edge of his jaw, she returned his kiss with an ardor that some unreachable part of her mind told her she should find shocking.

She was not a woman given to great passions, mocked an inner voice. But that voice had never experienced the power of an onslaught by Rafael Adriano. Wanting more, she moved a fraction of an inch closer—close enough to feel every imprint of his hard body against her own. He growled low in his throat and deepened the kiss. It went on and on, making him spiral in and out of control until she was sure she felt the room spin. When he finally lifted his head, she experienced a jolt of longing. With a slight groan, she dropped her head to his shoulder. His hands continued to glide up and down her back as he sucked in air. "Cora," he said, his voice a husky and incredibly arousing rasp, "I want you. You have no idea how much I want you."

Her hand glided back to his chest and she wedged it between them. Her fingers, she noted, were trembling. "Actually," she said, "I think I have a very good idea."

He let her ease away from him, his gaze still intense. "Do you?"

"Mmm." She retreated a few more steps. *Dignity, Cora,* she mentally chided herself when she had a brief temptation to simply toss caution to the wind and throw herself against him. She schooled her expression to a casual curiosity. "Does it feel something like an inferno—like it's simultaneously burning and purifying your gut?"

His mouth kicked into a smile. "Something like that."

"Do you wonder if maybe you've gotten a fever or something, because there's no other explanation for the sudden sensitivity of your skin?"

That made him nod. "I'm absolutely sure I have a fever."

"And the hunger? It makes your stomach ache?"

"My stomach—" he paused "—and a few other things."

She nodded. "Then I know just what it feels like." She drew a hand through her hair. "I had rubella once, and I—"

He laughed, a full, sensuous laugh that eased some of the tension in the room. "God, I adore you."

Cora glanced away. "You might not," she said, reaching for her briefcase, "after you see what I have in here."

Propping his elbow on the counter, he regarded her with a lazy smile. "It's not a piece of sexy lingerie, is it?"

"You wish." She snapped open the case.

"Like how."

She ignored that, but felt a blush race up her face and bury itself in the roots of her hair. She retrieved the copy of the weekly scandal sheet from the folder of clippings and handed it to him. "I'm afraid that whatever your public-relations people are doing to keep the *Isabela* out of this story isn't working. I've got a two-inch stack of stuff like this. That one's the most, er, dramatic."

He took the paper and studied the picture, a serious look on his face. Cora watched him closely, trying to discern his reaction. He stared intently at the paper, his eyebrows drawn together in a frown. Was he angry? At the paper? At his public-relations firm? At her?

Gently she placed her hand on his forearm. "What do you think?"

He lifted his head and gave her a searing look. "Do you think this picture makes my butt look big?"

She spent a full second in shock before she saw the sparkle in his eye. Snatching the paper from him with an outraged curse, she swatted him across the shoulder with it. "Would you take this seriously?" she demanded, and brought the paper down against his now upraised hands. He was laughing. She smacked him again for good measure.

"Calm down," he said, lunging for the paper.

She swept it out of his reach and swung it against the flat of his belly. "I can't believe you. Do you have any idea what this means?"

He laughed harder as he fended her off. "Okay, uncle," he finally said. "Uncle."

She stopped. "I'm not kidding." Pique laced her tone.

"I know," he said, his eye still sparkling, but his expression softening. "I know, I'm sorry."

"You think this is funny, don't you."

"I think the headline is hilarious," he admitted.

"That's not what I'm talking about and you know it." She wasn't ready to give in, though his apparent unconcern was doing wonders to calm her fears.

"Honey, nobody takes this stuff seriously."

Still skeptical, she pointed to the folder. "Those are from other sources. No one's going to believe that you aren't here to find that ship."

His expression turned serious and he touched her cheek. "I'm not going to let anything happen to you, Cora. Not to you, or the girls. I promise."

She looked at him, still worried, and wanted to push for details, but the sound of footsteps broke the spell.

Liza and Molly rushed into the kitchen. "We're ready," Molly announced. She and Liza both wore their pajamas.

Rafael wiped a hand over his face and gave Cora a meaningful look. "Then let's order dinner. I'm starved."

Chapter Seven

*She knocked the breath out of me. That's all there is
to it. I never would have believed that such a slip of
a woman—I swear she wouldn't last through the first
gust of a summer gale—could have brought me so
readily to my knees. But I didn't know she had the
power to take me to paradise, either.*

Juan Rodriguez del Flores
Captain's Log, 16 June 1860

Over the next several days, they fell into a pattern that left
Rafael feeling simultaneously energized and frustrated.
Most days Cora would go to the college for her classes and
her research. He had learned that she rarely worked with
the diaries out of her house. In order to preserve the fragile
paper and keep the volumes as intact as possible, she scru-
pulously adhered to the laboratory environment. The few
pages she had at home were copies, meticulously and painstakingly duplicated by an advanced photoreproductive system. That way, Cora could study every nuance of the works,
from Abigail's handwriting and the pressure of her pen to
the paper type and source, without risking any damage to
the original copies. Early on, the project had run low on

funds, and additional duplications had become cost prohib-
itive. She'd taken to studying the books in the lab and making research notes on her computer.

As a scientist, Rafael's respect for her methods grew ex-
ponentially as he began to delve into her research notes. She
was punctilious and thorough. Her attention to detail
astounded him. She identified patterns and subtleties in Abigail's writing that a less-exacting person would have easily
missed.

Every evening she brought him her report for that day.
He would spend the next several hours in his third-floor
room poring over Cora's notes. He discovered, much to his
surprise, that Abigail's writing was actually quite erotic.
That gave almost incontrovertible proof that the well-bred
daughter of a Southern gentleman had sustained a relationship that went well beyond a simple seduction by her lover.
The affair had been extended and, evidently, quite torrid.
To his growing frustration, however, any proof that her
lover had been Juan Rodriguez del Flores remained stubbornly elusive.

His determination to find the remaining diaries heightened. Fortunately his association with the project had netted
the rewards he's hoped. Money was flowing, and he was
close to reaching the three-million-dollar goal he'd set. His
contacts in Chapel Hill kept him apprised of the situation.
They also seemed to have a handle on the media. His public-
relations rep was doing her usual spectacular job keeping
the press off his back. Except for the occasional nuisance
call and the constant prodding of his sister Elena, he'd been
blessedly free to peruse his research.

He systematically examined Cora's house for any possible place Abigail may have stashed her diaries, working his
way steadily from attic to cellar. In this, he'd found unexpected allies in Kaitlin, Molly and Liza. They seemed endlessly fascinated by the twists and turns of the old house,

and loved exploring it with him. Though he made certain the girls stayed away from anything that might be even remotely dangerous, he'd had to rescue Benedict Bunny on three separate occasions. Liza had a habit of cramming the stuffed toy through even the smallest of openings ostensibly, she told Rafael, so Benedict Bunny could report what he'd seen. Thus far, the rabbit hadn't been any more successful in finding any additional diaries than he had, but Rafael was hopeful.

And though his days were spent in arduous pursuit of his research, he spent most of his nights in an increasing haze of sexual frustration as Cora's door remained firmly locked. Twice he even heard that annoying click of her lock as he made his way through the house and up to the third floor.

He had sensed from the beginning that Cora was not the kind of woman who took sex lightly. He liked her for that. She'd come to him only when she felt prepared to bond with him in an extraordinary and intimate way. Desire alone would not be enough for her.

So he'd launched a systematic campaign to wear down her defenses, using every opportunity to heighten her need and seduce her senses. He touched her whenever possible, kissed her every chance he got. When he did, he sensed the desire in her. Yet somehow, despite their proximity, they were rarely alone. Several times he caught her looking at him with banked fire in her eyes, but she would quickly mask the emotion. And soon Rafael found himself reaching for his patience.

She had his libido running at full-throttle, and he wasn't certain how much longer he could play this game of slow and steady foreplay.

By Friday night, as the girls chattered about their day and Cora asked for a mind-numbing amount of detail, he was running through an entire battery of mental exercises just to keep his arousal in check.

"Aunt Cora," Kaitlin was saying, "did I tell you that we're going to try watercolors tomorrow in art class?"

Cora shook her head. "No, really?" She'd found a children's art class at the recreation center and enrolled her niece. Though Kaitlin had only attended two classes, she seemed to be loving the experience.

"Yes," the girl said. "I need to get some paints before class."

"Okay." Cora shot Rafael a questioning look. "Will you all have time to do that tomorrow?" she asked sweetly—too sweetly.

He leaned back in his chair and regarded her shrewdly. She'd started this pattern of slightly goading questions earlier in the week, as if she was testing the boundaries of his restraint. He refused to take the bait. "I'm sure it won't be a problem. We'll go first thing in the morning so I'll have time to study your notes on Abigail's second volume in the afternoon."

With a practiced eye, he noted her swift intake of breath. The first volume had shown a younger, more naive Abigail. She had obviously written the second volume after her love affair began. It was then that her writing took on its sensual and erotic flare.

Cora held his gaze, but her hand fluttered to her throat where it pressed against the pulse he knew was throbbing there. "Oh? I didn't realize you'd gotten that far."

He nodded. "You're very thorough." Placing his elbows on the table, he leaned forward and rested his chin on his steepled fingers. "Interesting how different the tone of her writing is now, don't you think?"

Cora reached for her water glass. "Definitely interesting."

Liza, obviously unaware of the undercurrent, joined the conversation. "Guess what we found today, Aunt Cora?"

Cora held Rafael's glance a second longer, then looked at her niece. "What, sweetie?"

"Me and Molly and Benedict Bunny were in the attic with Rafael while Kaitlin was at art. We found this big thing…"

She looked at Rafael for help.

"The wooden chest," he clarified. "Yours?"

"No," Cora answered. "It was one of the things we found when we were looking for more diaries. We went through it thoroughly, searching for hidden compartments or panels, but it didn't yield anything."

"I liked the clothes," Molly said. The chest had been filled with vintage, turn-of-the-century dresses.

Cora smiled at her. "So did I."

"I think the beads were the best," Liza chimed in.

Molly set her fork down, "When I grow up, Aunt Cora, can I have one of those dresses to wear?"

"Sure," Cora responded.

"Me, too?" Liza pressed.

"You, too." Cora looked at Kaitlin. "What about you?"

Kaitlin smiled slightly and shook her head. "I don't like fringe. It tickles."

"They didn't all have fringe," Cora said quickly, then cast a quick glance at Rafael. He saw her eyes momentarily widen. She cleared her throat. "Did they?"

His gaze narrowed. "All the ones I saw did."

"Oh." Cora took a drink of her water.

He leaned forward. "Were there others?"

She seemed to consider the question, then nodded. "Two other garments, but they weren't preserved as well as the ones you saw today." She flashed a smile at Kaitlin. "That must have been what I was thinking of when I said no fringe."

"Were they the same period?" Rafael pressed.

Cora's gaze dropped to the table. "No." She pushed her

plate away. "There were some Civil War period things."
She said the words quietly. Like a confession.

Interesting. "Oh?" he said.

"Really?" Kaitlin said, her interest having been peaked
by Rafael's stories about Abigail and del Flores. "Do you
think they might have belonged to Abigail?"

Cora shrugged. "Who knows? Maybe."

Her equivocation heightened his suspicion. As passionate
as she was about Abigail Conrad, even the idea that she'd
discovered some of the woman's possessions would have
put Cora in hot pursuit of the truth. She wouldn't be satisfied
to let anything, not even something as seemingly inconse-
quential as a ballgown, go unexamined.

Excited at the possibilities, the girls plied her with questions. Rafael tapped his fingers on his thigh as he watched
and listened. Something was eluding him. Cora talked readily with the girls, but still did not meet his gaze. His eye
narrowed as he concentrated, and he felt a familiar twitching
of the scar beneath his patch. The scar always pulled when
he focused this hard.

"Was it a pretty dress?" he heard Liza ask. "Red, like
the one we saw today?"

"No. Light green," Cora replied.

"Did it have beads on it?" Molly asked.

Cora shook her head. "They didn't use beads then, Mol.
They used something called seed pearls."

Molly frowned. "What's a seed pearl?"

"It's the tiny little sliver of an irregular pearl that they
put inside an oyster to make it grow a bigger pearl."

Rafael watched Cora with piercing intensity. She was answering their questions, but picking each word with care.
He began replaying the entire conversation in his head,
searching for the niggling detail that hid the truth.

"An oyster?" Kaitlin said in disbelief. "They stick it in
an oyster?"

"Sure," Cora told her. "That's how they get pearls. When a little piece of grit gets inside an oyster, the oyster secretes a substance to coat the grit and stop the irritation. The secretion forms a hard surface and begins to form a pearl. The longer the grit stays in there, the bigger the pearl gets."

"Eeeew," Molly said. "It's like oyster spit."

"That's gross," Kaitlin concurred.

Liza nodded emphatically. "I swallowed a marble once, and Mama made me barf it up. Is that how they get the pearls out of oysters?"

Cora laughed and shook her head. "No. They just pry open the shells."

"If I found an oyster," Kaitlin asked, "could I have a pearl?"

"Maybe. Not every oyster has a pearl in it."

Molly looked at Rafael. "Have you ever found a pearl in an oyster?"

He kept his gaze trained on Cora. "No," he said, "but it's always exciting to find something unexpected."

Cora finally looked at him again. "Isn't it?"

"What was in the trunk, Cora?" he asked softly.

Her eyelashes fluttered. "I told you—clothes."

"You said Civil War period things," he pointed out.

From the corner of his eye, he saw the girls swivel their heads to look at their aunt. "There were no diaries."

The girls looked at him. "Then what was there—besides the light-green dress with the seed pearls?"

Her color heightened, but she didn't look away. "A jacket, a sash, accessories. You know, that kind of thing."

Rafael tasted victory. "What kind of jacket?"

She frowned at him. "Oh, all right." She tossed her napkin to the table. "It was very elaborate. It almost looked like a costume, instead of a piece of clothing."

"Red, black and embroidered with gold thread?" he asked as he felt his excitement rise.

"Yes."

"Did it look Spanish?"

She gave him a disgruntled nod. "Yes."

"By any chance," he drawled, "did it look like the jacket del Flores is wearing in his portrait?"

"Yes," she admitted.

Rafael scowled. "I knew it."

"Knew what?" Molly demanded.

Kaitlin touched her arm. "Knew that Juan Rodriguez del Flores had really been in this house," she said, her tone pure excitement. Kaitlin, especially, had found the possibility of Abigail's affair with the pirate completely fascinating. "It's so romantic."

Cora frowned at Rafael. "It could be a replica. I have no way of knowing."

"What do you think?"

"It was in the trunk with those later garments. The fabric looked period, and the stitching was done by hand, not machine, but still…" She shook her head. "I couldn't be sure. I wanted to have it authenticated before I said anything."

"You could have told me," he said, struggling to tamp down a burst of irritation. He thought they'd progressed beyond her distrust.

"I didn't think about it at first." At his skeptical look, she insisted, "I didn't. We were talking about the diaries, and I just forgot about it."

"And later?"

"I don't know. I just wanted to be sure. Until now, there was no proof whatsoever that Abigail's, er—" she glanced at the girls "—boyfriend was del Flores. It could have been anyone."

"Oh, Aunt Cora," Kaitlin gushed, "it had to be. It just had to be."

"I think it was," Molly added.

"Me, too," Liza said.

Cora's expression showed her exasperation. "No one knows for sure. The only thing scholars have proved is that del Flores made two voyages to Cape Marr. He could have been here for any reason, and it would be irresponsible to jump to conclusions."

The last was delivered with the same stern note he'd heard her use with Jerry. "You should have told me," he said quietly.

"I'm sorry." She shoved her fingers through her hair. "I really am. I wasn't trying to hide anything. I just didn't plan on discussing this until I knew what I was talking about." She leaned back in her chair. "But you're right. I should have told you."

He watched her for a long second, then nodded, somewhat mollified. Stroking the line of his scar with a long finger, he carefully sifted through the options, searching for truth. "The stories about Abigail and del Flores have been around a long time," he conceded. "It's not so difficult to believe that someone might have had the jacket made as a costume for a masquerade ball."

Cora nodded. "And subsequently stored it in the trunk. During the 1920s those kinds of parties were very popular. It's extremely plausible."

"I agree," he concurred. "And I'm thankful you had the foresight to have the piece studied." He couldn't quite keep the condemnation out of his tone. She should have told him this. It quite possibly changed everything.

Cora's expression turned worried. "You know what will happen if people find out about this."

He nodded. Proof of del Flores's relationship with Abigail would bring the nightmare Cora had feared. "They won't."

"You can't keep it a secret for long," she warned him.

"Why is it a secret?" Molly asked.

"Because," Kaitlin informed her, "if people find out that del Flores was really here, they'll try to find the rest of Abigail's diaries before Aunt Cora and Rafael do." Both adults knew the stakes were considerably higher.

"But they're ours!" Molly was outraged.

"Yeah," Liza said. "They can't have 'em. They're ours."

Rafael gave them a reassuring look. "Don't worry. If they're here, we'll find them." He glanced at Cora again. "But I want to see that jacket."

"I sent it to a friend at the Daughters of the American Revolution headquarters in Washington, D.C. She's a textile expert, and she's looking at it. She said she'd have it back to me with a report by next week."

"Did you tell her what it was?"

"No, just that I needed to know the period and the possible origins of the fabric. Sheila's no dummy, though. She knows I'm working on the diaries. She'll figure it out."

"And you trust her?"

Cora's eyebrows lifted. "She wouldn't have the jacket if I didn't."

It grated him that Cora had taken someone else into her confidence, but not him. It was completely irrational of course, for he'd known the woman less than a week. Still, he couldn't keep the edge from his voice when he asked, "Does anyone else know?"

"No," she said. "I was alone when I found it."

Rafael relaxed, leaned back in his chair. "Thank God."

The children seemed to sense that the strange tension had lifted and again launched into a stream of questions about Cora's find in the attic. She described in detail the jacket, the dress and the other few items she'd removed from the trunk. She kept a wary eye, Rafael noted, on him.

He was waging a silent war with himself. The familiar rush of adrenaline he felt when he narrowed the net on del

Flores had settled on him like a mantle. Long ago he'd quit asking himself why this ship, this person, this story, were so important to him. He no longer allowed himself to wonder what it was about del Flores's relationship with Abigail and the mysteries therein that he found so addictive. A part of him suspected that he didn't want to know the answer. So this was the side of himself he kept carefully tucked away.

The intensity.

The obsession.

Even the word left a bad taste in his mouth. Since the day his brother Zack had hurled it at him in an angry accusation about irresponsibility, abandonment and self-centeredness, Rafael had carefully avoided explanations. Though his reaction to Zack's tirade had been a stream of expletives and a furious departure from his brother's control, the years since had not softened the blow.

Not when other people said it, too.

Not when he'd fallen in love for the first time because of it. At twenty he'd felt indestructible, and Jocelyn Ayres had been a professor at UNC where he was a struggling student. She'd hired him as a research assistant. He thought she'd shared his passion for del Flores and Abigail. They'd enjoyed mind-blowing sex, made all the more spectacular for him by the idea that this woman was his soul mate. He had learned, too late, that ambition and not affection had driven her to use his research to advance her own career.

When confronted, Jocelyn's response had been a laughing dismissal and a label for his problem: obsession.

And a string of frivolous relationships later, there had been Sinead. She was perhaps the one woman he'd known who had wanted him for something other than a casual affair or the challenge of taming his free spirit. Her father was one of his closest friends, a Dutch oceanographer Rafael had worked with on several expeditions. Sinead's sweetness had drawn him to her. She'd asked nothing.

And he, selfish bastard that he was, had given her nothing. By the time he realized that Sinead's heart was at stake, he had already broken it. As long as his obsession with finding del Flores held him in thrall, she'd told him in a tearful goodbye, no one could hope to compete.

He realized then that he'd become the horror his brother Zack had described. And in the years that followed, he'd carefully restricted his relationships to women who knew the game and who played on his level. He didn't take advantage of innocents.

Until now, an inner voice taunted as his gaze slid to Cora.

"You're frowning," Liza announced, breaking his concentration.

Rafael blinked, then shook off the gloomy thoughts. "Was I?"

Molly nodded. "Your eyebrow was almost touching your nose. And your scar was white. Are you mad?"

Good question, he thought, though the child referred to his temper and not his mental stability. "Of course not." He stood then and forced a smile to his lips. "I think we should go out for ice cream. Any takers?"

"HELLO?" CORA SNATCHED up the phone on the third ring. They'd made the promised trip into town for ice cream, but Rafael had retreated upstairs almost the moment they returned. She'd been unable to read his mood since her revelation at dinner.

"Hi, I'm looking for Rafael." The voice was feminine and low.

Cora frowned. He took all his personal calls on his cell phone. No one called her number but the occasional reporter who slipped past his PR rep. "Who is this?"

"This is Margie Adriano. I'm one of his sisters."

The librarian, Cora remembered from her conversation with Elena. "Oh, hello. He's here, but you might want to try his cell phone. He usually doesn't—"

"Is this Cora?" Margie cut in.

"Yes," she said carefully.

"Oh, good. Elena gave me your number. She's in Miami covering a story and wanted me to call."

"I see."

"Do you happen to know if Rafael is planning anything for his birthday next week?"

Cora didn't even know his birthday was next week. "No. Not that I know of."

"This is the first time in seventeen years he's been this close to home on his birthday. Elena and I were talking about that when she called the other day."

Seventeen years, Cora noted. Since he'd left home. "Oh?"

"Yeah, um, listen." She heard Margie shift the phone to her other ear. "I don't know what he's told you about his family…"

"Other than the fact that there are twelve more of you?"

Margie laughed. "Overwhelming, isn't it?"

"I can't imagine," Cora said wryly.

"Well, this is a little tricky if he hasn't…" She hesitated.

"I know he and his older brother haven't always been on the best of terms," Cora told her. "And that he left home seventeen years ago."

"Really?" Margie said in the same surprised and delighted tone Elena had used. "He told you that?"

"Elena was surprised, too."

"She told me you were different."

Given Rafael's much publicized relationships with the super-model/socialite segment of the female population, Cora could only imagine. "I'm not surprised."

"She also told me she thought you were really good for him."

Having no answer to that, Cora waited. Margie continued, "So I was wondering if you'd be willing to help me with a little scheme."

"What kind of scheme?"

"Most of my brothers and sisters are within reasonable driving distance of Cape Marr, and I thought if Rafael was going to be there on his birthday, we could put something together for him."

Cora hesitated, feeling like the outsider. It wasn't her right or responsibility to meddle in his life. He'd made it clear he wanted a physical relationship with her, but beyond that, he'd made no promises. "I don't know," she said. "I'm not sure he would appreciate it if I got involved in this."

"I'm not asking you to do anything behind his back," Margie assured her. "And believe me, things are much better now than they were. He and Zack don't even argue anymore—well, not much, anyway. But at least they're speaking, which is something."

"I suppose."

"All I need from you is some information about where people could stay and when to come. I'm just going to fire off an e-mail and see who's interested." Margie's soft sigh carried on the line. "We really miss him," she said gently. "And I can't help but think he wouldn't be planning to be in Cape Marr, not that close to us, if he wasn't making an overture in our direction. I'd like the chance to show him that he's still one of us."

Cora thought it over, but could already feel her resolve weakening. Her own family life had been so unfulfilling. She'd longed for a deeper relationship with her parents and her sister and never had one. "What did you have in mind?" she finally said.

Ten minutes later she walked into the living room where Liza, Molly and Kaitlin were curled on the sofa watching a video. "Kaitlin," she said, "can I see you for a minute— if you're not too involved in the movie?"

Kaitlin looked a little wary. She began to untangle herself from the blankets on the couch. "How come?"

Cora smiled at her as they walked toward the kitchen. "I need your help with something."

"ABSOLUTELY NOT," Rafael virtually snarled at Jerry the next day. Kaitlin was at her art class, and Liza and Molly were with Becky. Rafael had wanted to have this confrontation in person and alone. If his mood wasn't black enough after another night of Cora's locked door and his own conflicted thoughts, this morning's phone call from his publicist had him in a rage.

Jerry raised his hands in an unconvincing conciliatory gesture. "It wasn't my idea. Henry Willers—"

"Never would have thought this up by himself." Rafael glared at him and uttered a harsh expletive. "Have you lost your mind?"

"It's an excellent idea. The media is—"

"Too curious as it is. This isn't a high-profile project, Jerry."

"Willers wants it to be."

"Willers can go to hell." He planted his hands on Jerry's desk and loomed over him. "I control the tone, the place and the scope of my projects. I am not going to turn this into a media circus."

"You sound like Cora," Jerry grumbled.

"She's the only one around here with any sense," Rafael muttered, and dropped into a chair. "My God. What the hell were you people thinking?"

"Calm down," Jerry said in a voice that had Rafael gritting his teeth. "Just calm down."

"My publicist called this morning to inform me that you've arranged a formal reception for the end of next week to announce that Cora and I have found incontrovertible proof of del Flores's relationship with Abigail Conrad, and you expect me to calm down?"

"Well, it's true, isn't it?"

Somehow, Rafael knew, Jerry had found out about the jacket. "Who the hell cares? The point is, you had no right to release the information without Cora's consent."

"She never would have agreed."

"Damn right she wouldn't have. And neither would I."

"My first priority has to be what's best for this institution, not what's best for—"

Rafael's curse was distinct and to the point. "You don't give a damn about this college. The only thing you care about is your career. You can't stand the thought that Cora's reputation is about to eclipse yours."

Jerry's color heightened. "I am still the chairman of this department. And as such, it's my job to make decisions that will benefit the department and the college."

Rafael looked at him in utter contempt. "Who are you kidding? You're pissed off at Cora because she didn't turn the diaries over to you."

"By rights," Jerry said through clenched teeth, "those diaries belong to the college. Not to Cora Prescott."

"It's her house."

"Only after she bought it from Rawlings. We sold her the property, not exclusive rights to its historical significance."

"And you're furious because she's getting credit for the research on the diaries and not you."

Jerry leaned back in his leather chair and steepled his fingers. "I am the department head," he said again. Rafael flung another expletive at him, but Jerry merely laughed.

"Don't be naive," he said. "This kind of thing happens in academia all the time."

"Sure it does," Rafael shot back. "Talented, intelligent, capable scholars like Cora Prescott get intellectually pillaged by arrogant asses like you."

Jerry's bushy eyebrows lifted. "So you've appointed yourself as her champion, have you?"

"I'm a colleague who happens to respect her work."

"Oh, really. That wouldn't be because you happen to have gotten between her sheets, would it? Tell me, how is the ice princess in bed?"

Rafael surged to his feet and stifled the urge to slug him. "Have I told you what a bastard I think you are?"

"I believe you mentioned it, yes."

"I'm not going to let you win, Jerry."

Jerry's smile was smug and infuriating. "We'll just have to see, won't we?"

Chapter Eight

It's the miserable days like this that find me longing for her, fool that I am. It could never be, though she swears she'd leave them all for me. I cannot decide whether I am more flattered by the strength of her affection or more disgusted with myself for seducing her. Were I the noble man she thinks, I'd leave her to find a future I cannot provide. Alas, I haven't the strength of will. I must have her.

Juan Rodriguez del Flores
Captain's Log, 25 December 1860

"'How I long for the sound of your voice,'" Cora read to him that night, her tone slightly hushed. "'In the deepest part of the night, I imagine it caressing my skin until I—'" She broke off abruptly and looked at Rafael.

He lay on her couch, propped on one elbow, watching her. Her expressive face registered a deep sensitivity as she read Abigail's words from the reproduction pages. From the moment she'd walked in the door that night, he'd sensed a definite shift in the sea of their relationship. Thus far, she'd given him only a tantalizing glimpse of what that change might mean, but, he thought as he watched her fight a deepening blush, things were definitely looking up. "I what?" he prompted with a slight smile.

The tips of her ears reddened, but she held his gaze. "This part is a little...stirring."

He hoped so. Unable to shake his foul mood since his conversation with Jerry that afternoon, he still hadn't given Cora the news. She'd burst into the kitchen that evening, brimming with news about some new discovery she'd made in Abigail's diaries—something she'd promised to tell him as soon as the girls were in bed. Cora's exuberance had lent the evening a lightheartedness that he'd refused to ruin by talking about Jerry Heath.

After the girls were settled and asleep, Cora had turned to him with an unmistakable look in her eyes. A look that said she was totally aware of what he wanted—and that she wanted it, too. She'd whispered, "Follow me," and he'd thought, *Anywhere.*

Fifteen minutes later he'd found himself reclined on her sofa like the sultan in *Arabian Nights* listening to the addictive voice of his Scheherezade as Cora read to him. Stirring, indeed.

She sat cross-legged on the other end of the sofa, facing him. She wore jeans and a T-shirt and had pulled her hair back into a ponytail. The look should have been casual and unexciting, but it somehow managed to tempt him as effectively as any seductive lingerie. He ran his hand along her thigh for the sheer pleasure of feeling the worn and feather-soft denim against his skin. "Finish reading to me, Cora," he prompted in a low voice meant to tell her he wanted so much more from her than a simple recitation.

Awareness evident in her gaze, she wet her lips with the tip of her tongue. "Rafael..."

Her voice was a breathless whisper. His gut tightened and he moved his hand on her thigh to a more intimate spot. "Finish," he said again.

She swallowed, then looked back at the page. Her gaze wandered for an instant until she found her place again. "'Caressing my skin until I feel it so deep in my woman's self that I hunger for more. I can picture you so easily, here by my bed, your clothes strewn from the doorway in your haste to reach me. Your flesh pressed to mine, our hearts beating in unison as you brand me with your inner fire, I am moved beyond reason, dearest. Even now, I feel the passion stirring inside me. Were it not for these sweet remembrances, I think I would go mad.'" She looked at him, her eyes bright. "It's this next part."

He continued stroking her thigh with mesmerizing circles of his thumb. "Oh?"

Cora nodded. "I almost missed this when I read it. I couldn't believe it." She ran her finger down the page and began again. "'...sweet remembrances, I think I would go mad. You'll think me silly, dearest,'—" her voice slowed to enunciate each word "—but when my sorrow at your absence is especially piquant, I sometimes slip your garment from its hiding place and wrap myself in its warmth.'"

He sat straight up. "My God. It's the jacket." Shocked out of the slow-burning sexual hunger that had lulled him into a heated haze, he felt a new, stronger kind of need gripping him. "She's talking about the jacket."

Cora nodded. "I think so, too. Listen to this. 'Your scent still lingers on it, and I am so endlessly grateful that you left it here in your haste. I will keep it until you return, despite your warnings that I should not. If it is discovered in my possession, then no consequence could cause me greater grief than its loss. Hasten back to me, dearest, so I can take you in my arms again.' Signed, 'Abigail Conrad, 10 February 1861.'" Cora beamed at him. "I couldn't believe it."

Rafael shook his head. He felt simultaneously disoriented and elated, and in the back of his mind resounded the knowledge that this victory wouldn't hold such reward had he not shared it with Cora. "Neither can I."

"And that's not all," she said. "It gets better. I called Sheila this afternoon to see if she'd made any progress with the jacket."

His mind raced at the possibilities. "And?" He'd waited almost twenty years for this.

"She said she'd sent it to a colleague of hers at the Smithsonian. He'd finished with it and was returning it to me with his report. It should be here tomorrow."

"Did he authenticate the date?" His fingers tightened on her leg.

She laid her hand on his and squeezed gently. "Would you believe that the reason Sheila couldn't identify the fabric was because of its unusual weft? And as it turns out, that particular weft was used only in one town and by one tailor on the southern coast of Spain between 1848 and 1871?"

He closed his eyes. "Del Flores."

"He was here, Rafael. In this house with Abigail."

"I knew it."

"You were right all along."

When he looked at her, saw the genuine pleasure on her face, a gripping need spiked through him. "So were you," he said.

Cora shook her head as she lifted her hand to trace the edge of his eye patch. "It's not my victory," she murmured. "I only wanted to know Abigail better. I..." She hesitated.

He shifted closer and captured her chin in his hand. "You what?"

"I saw something of myself in her."

"I know," he whispered.

"Because you saw something of yourself in del Flores."

Had the statement come from anyone else, he would have denied it, but with Cora he didn't have to. She understood, somehow, the connection he felt to the lonely, wandering man who'd lived without home or family for most of his life. "Yes," he said simply.

Cora turned her face to kiss his fingers. "The hardened pirate and the prudish schoolmarm. Who would have thought?"

He knew without asking that she was no longer speaking of del Flores and Abigail. He reached for her hand and found her fingers trembling. "You're shivering," he said softly.

"No, I'm not."

Holding her hand up before her eyes, he showed her the fine tremors. Cora curled her fingers around his hand. "I'm not shivering. I'm shaking with anticipation and thinking that I—"

He didn't let her finish the thought. Stripping her glasses off, he tossed them to the coffee table. Without them, her eyes looked wider, more expressive. He searched them. When he found the flame, he pulled her into his arms and kissed her hungrily. "Cora." He said her name against her mouth. "Ah, Cora."

She kissed him, hard, her lips tracing his in an intoxicating rhythm that simultaneously gave and begged for more.

With his hands pressed to her spine, he molded her against him. "You are...wonderful."

She whispered his name against his lips, a heated, urgent sound that crackled along his nerve endings and bewitched him. Barriers of restraint crumbled to ruin. When had desire turned to this clawing, consuming kind of need, a need that said he'd die if he didn't have her? He wanted her so close to him that he could feel every breath, every heartbeat, every exquisite, pulsing flutter of her body. If he could, he would fully absorb her.

Cora's hands had freed his hair from the leather tie at his nape. She sifted the weight of it through her fingers and opened herself to his marauding kiss. Pillaging, he thought, had never felt so good. Returning the favor, he stripped the elastic band from her hair. Waves of gold-tipped silk tumbled over his hands. He fisted one hand in it and held her mouth locked to his. In one swift move he eased her beneath him on the long sofa.

With her body aligned with his, he used his hands to explore her. He wanted to know every secret, every sensitive spot on her body. And still, he realized, it wouldn't be enough to quench his thirst for her. Needing the exquisite feel of flesh against flesh, he thrust his hands beneath the hem of her T-shirt. Her skin was warm and supple and felt like satin beneath his fingertips.

Cora trailed a line of kisses along his jaw, down the cords of his neck and across his collarbone. The featherlight touch made him groan. ''More,'' he urged.

''Everything,'' she responded, and nipped his earlobe.

His hands tightened on her flesh as he angled his head for a better taste of her. ''Let me in,'' he growled, and took her mouth again. Cora received him with a moan of undiluted pleasure. The sound enslaved him. He could feel the top of his head lifting away as bliss streaked through his bloodstream and scared his brain. The headiness of her discovery about del Flores was quickly being eclipsed by the even more dizzying sensation of making love to her.

His hand moved to the button of her jeans. ''Be sure,'' he warned her, knowing there would be no turning back.

She nodded. ''I am.''

He began to work the fastener.

''Aunt Cora?'' The soft voice penetrated his brain like a bullet.

His head lifted swiftly. When his vision focused, he saw Kaitlin standing at the bottom of the stairs, watching them. Her expression was simultaneously wary and confused. Beneath him, he felt Cora tense. Slowly he eased his hand from under her shirt. "What's wrong?" he asked Kaitlin, not surprised at the rawness of his voice.

Cora was struggling now, so he eased to the side and allowed her to sit up. She would have pushed his hands away, but he held firm. Cora looked at Kaitlin. "Honey, are you all right?"

Kaitlin hesitated, then nodded. "I need to tell you something."

Rafael pushed his hair back from his face as he struggled for balance. The woman was absolutely wrecking him. He could not remember a time when he'd felt so thoroughly rattled by a passionate kiss and the unfulfilled promise of more. Deliberately he gentled his voice. "What's wrong?" he asked Kaitlin.

"Can I come in?" she said, still watching them, still hovering in the shadows by the stairs.

Cora moved away from Rafael to make room for her niece on the couch. "Of course." She held out a hand. "Come here."

"But you were…" Kaitlin frowned. "Mama doesn't like it if we interrupt when she's…" The child stopped again and shook her head.

He saw Cora's hand clench into a fist, so he rubbed his fingers along the back of her knuckles. "It's okay, kiddo," he assured Kaitlin, and himself.

She looked as if she wanted to flee up the stairs. "I shouldn't have come down."

Rafael shook his head. "Nobody should lie awake and be alone with their problems." He squeezed Cora's hand in a silent promise that said, *We'll finish this later.*

Cora turned her hand so she could intertwine their fingers. Her tight grip gave the only outward sign that she, too, was struggling. She beckoned to her niece. "It's all right, sweetie," she said. "Come here and tell us what's wrong."

Kaitlin slowly advanced into the room. "I couldn't

sleep." She was tugging at the hem of her nightshirt. "I didn't want to tell you, but I couldn't sleep." When she was standing in front of Cora, she crossed her feet and looked up with a worried expression. "Are you going to be mad?"

Cora took Kaitlin's hand and tugged until the child climbed onto the couch to sit between them. Guiding the child's head to her lap, Cora stroked her hair. "I'm not going to be mad. What's the matter?"

Kaitlin shivered. "This afternoon while you were gone, Rafael was outside with Liza and Molly."

Cora glanced at him over Kaitlin's head. He nodded. "Around two," he told her.

Cora continued her steady stroking of Kaitlin's pale hair. "Did something happen?"

Kaitlin traced an idle circle on Cora's knee with her index finger. "The phone rang, and I thought it might be you, so I answered it."

"Who was it?" Cora prompted.

Kaitlin sat up, her eyes filled with tears. "It was Mama. She was really mad. She said she saw your picture in the paper and that if she'd known you were going to drag us into the scandal sheets, she never would have left us here." Kaitlin started to cry in earnest.

"Shh." Cora hugged her. "Honey, it's okay."

"She was so mad. She just kept yelling and yelling and she wouldn't listen to me. She said really mean things about you, Aunt Cora, and about Rafael, and I didn't know what to do."

Cora looked at Rafael, her expression worried. He scowled. Kaitlin buried her face in Cora's neck. "She said she was coming here to get us and that I'd better make sure me and Molly and Liza were ready to leave because she wasn't going to let you get away with treating us like this."

Cora kissed the top of Kaitlin's head. "It's okay, baby. It's okay."

"Why did she say that?" Kaitlin reared back so she could look at Cora's face. "I don't even know what she's talking about. Why is she so mad at us?"

"She's not mad at you," Cora assured her.

"She wouldn't stop yelling at me."

"I know." Cora snatched a tissue from the box on the coffee table and wiped Kaitlin's cheeks. "Your mother loses her temper sometimes, and she says things she doesn't mean."

"She said you were corrupting us because Rafael lives here, and that we shouldn't be exposed to people like that. She made it sound like—" she hiccupped on a renewed sob "—she made it sound like you weren't taking care of us. I told her it was a lie, but she wouldn't listen to me, Aunt Cora. She wouldn't."

"I know," Cora told her. She handed Kaitlin a fresh tissue. "But you have to trust me, Kaitlin. It's going to be all right."

"She's going to come get us and make us go with her and George. And I don't want to," Kaitlin added on a fresh burst of tears. "I don't want to."

"Me, neither," Molly yelled from the stairs. Her small face was watching them defiantly.

Liza nodded emphatically and hugged Benedict Bunny. "Me, neither," she echoed.

Cora glanced swiftly at Rafael. He was already off the couch and striding toward the stairs. "Nobody's going anywhere," he said. "At least not tonight." He picked up one girl in each arm and walked toward the sofa. "How come you're out of bed?" he asked Liza.

"We heard Kaitlin crying," Liza said. "She kept crying and crying, and we didn't know why she was so sad."

"Kaitlin never cries," Molly added. "Only Liza."

"And you," Liza insisted.

"There's nothing wrong with crying," Rafael said. "It's

good for you sometimes.'' He set his charges down next to Cora, then leaned over to press a brief kiss to her lips. ''Sounds like a cocoa night to me,'' he said, and felt a smile twitch at the corners of his mouth. ''I'll go make some. Any preferences?''

Cora's eyes twinkled with a mixture of amusement and banked desire. ''I'll tell you later,'' she said.

''Can I have marshmallows?'' Kaitlin asked. Her voice sounded so defeated that Rafael briefly contemplated the advisability of strangling the child's mother.

He kept his voice deliberately light. ''Big ones or small ones?''

''I like small ones,'' she said, ''but Molly doesn't like any and Liza likes one big one.''

''It fizzes on my lip,'' Liza explained.

He nodded. ''And then you lick it off.''

Her eyes widened appreciatively. ''You know everything.''

Ruffling her hair, he allowed his hungry gaze to linger on Cora for a few seconds longer, then quietly whispered, ''Not yet.''

IT TOOK TWO HOURS to get the girls settled and back to sleep. They lay on the floor by the sofa in an indistinguishable tangle of arms and legs. A haphazard array of pillows— survivors of an earlier pillow fight where Rafael had taken the bulk of the blows from the giggling, squealing trio of girls—formed their makeshift bed. Fluffs of scattered popcorn littered the carpet like dandelions on a summer lawn. Discarded cocoa mugs sat on the coffee table, and the animated movie had ended, leaving a snowy blue screen on the silent television.

Rafael lay on the couch with his head propped on a pillow against the armrest and Cora tucked securely against him, spoon fashion. Her back pressed against his chest, her bottom curved into his groin. She fit perfectly, he mused. He rested his chin against the top of her head and watched the flickering blue light cast shadows in the room. He wished it was cold enough for a fire. He would like to see the subtle textures of Cora's skin in the amber glow of firelight.

Cora stirred. "You trashed my house," she accused him quietly.

He nuzzled his nose against her hair. "I sent you letters warning you this would happen."

She snorted. "I also recall promises of full restitution."

He couldn't wait to fulfill that promise, either. "Pirates always pillage and plunder," he said arrogantly. "The cleanup is someone else's problem."

Cora's chuckle warmed his blood. "Good thing I have such a great nanny. I'm sure he won't mind."

In retaliation, he nipped her earlobe. "Keep it up, Professor, and I'll never show you what's involved in a well-executed pillage."

"Liar," she chided. Her fingers caressed his forearm where it lay solidly beneath her breasts. "You were wonderful with them."

"Practice," he assured her. "It's not the first time I've stayed up late with a brokenhearted female."

"Sisters?" she probed.

"Yes. They're more prone to melodrama than brothers."

"Like mine," she muttered. "I'm glad I only had one sibling to deal with."

"That woman's a menace," he grumbled.

Cora didn't pretend not to know what he was talking about. "Lauren's always been...mercurial."

Not the word he would have used, he thought uncharitably. "Explain to me how the two of you came from the same gene pool."

Her laugh tickled his nerve endings. "Well, it's always possible that maybe we didn't."

Another layer, he thought with some amazement. Here was another layer of this incredible, complex, bewitching woman. He waited for her to explain. Cora's hands continued to stroke his arms. "My mother was just like Lauren," she finally said. "Beautiful, talented, smart and completely self-absorbed." She paused. "And terrified of being alone."

"Your father," he prompted, beginning to see a picture he didn't like.

"Distant and reserved. He was bookish and scholarly, but he came from money. He was a professor at Hollins College in Virginia."

"The women's school?"

"Yes. Mama went there for two years. They met, had an affair and got married. I think Mama married him because she thought she could control him and his money."

"He resisted?"

"Not exactly." Her hands stilled. "He was just indifferent. I never understood why he bothered to get married, unless he just got tired of fighting it. He wasn't interested in anything except his books. His ambivalence drove Mother crazy. She complained about it constantly."

"You heard them arguing?"

"A few times," she said, "But generally, no. The more she yelled, the more he withdrew. And when I was seven, my mother took Lauren and me and left."

"How old was your sister?"

"Three, so I don't think it affected her as much as it did me." She sighed. "I was sad a lot. I remember always feeling sad and not very safe, like everything familiar could just disappear."

He tipped his head to nuzzle her ear. "It's scary for a child to go through something like that."

"Elena told me," she said gently, "that your father abandoned your family."

"He did." The ease of the confession surprised him. So many things seemed easier with Cora.

"It must have hurt you deeply."

"I was angry and disappointed. I felt like he'd betrayed us—especially my mother."

"Have you ever heard from him?"

"No," he said, "and I don't want to."

Cora nodded. "I can understand that."

He smoothed her hair away from her face so he could run a fingertip along her jaw. "What about your father?"

She frowned, and the corners of her eyes crinkled. "I was so shy then, and I think that's why I had always responded better to my father than I did to my mother. He was a very quiet man, even and calm, and I wanted so desperately for him to like me."

Rafael's jaw tightened. Two of his own sisters had been that way. Quiet and reserved, they'd suffered the bone-deep wounds of their father's desertion in silence, while their siblings had volubly expressed rage at his betrayal. To this day, the two were the most compassionate and generous of his family. Shared pain, he imagined, was a bond like no other. Now he could offer Cora some meaningless platitude, the kind he'd dredged up on his sisters' behalf when he'd been younger and more naive; but it wouldn't help. "You tried hard, didn't you?"

"Yes."

He could picture it so easily. An awkward, bespectacled child silently screaming for attention and validation. "The jerk," he muttered.

Her sultry chuckle eased some of the pressure in his chest. "It's all right, you know," she said. "It hurt terribly at the time, but I don't have any lasting scars from it."

Except, he thought with startling new insight, *that you still doubt your desirability.* As a child, the most important man in her life hadn't seemed to want her. No wonder she had questioned his own motives. He slid his hand down her arm to her hip, then over her abdomen. Using a gentle pressure at the swell of her belly, he shifted their position so she could fully feel the extent of his desire. "I'm sorry," he said against her ear.

Cora shuddered. "I tried so hard. I wanted to be interested in all the things he was interested in. He liked books, so I liked books. I read newspapers and newsmagazines so I could talk to him about current events. And for a while I believed it was working."

There was a wealth of hurt in that statement. Rafael tightened his hold on her, but waited for her to continue. She kept her gaze carefully trained on the blue television screen.

"Summers were the worst," she finally said. "When we were out of school, Mama would drop us off at his house and leave for an extended vacation with her new lover. By the time I was fifteen, my mother had been married and divorced four times.

"You resented her," he guessed.

"I think she embarrassed me," Cora confessed. "I was too young to really understand how afraid she was of being alone, so I just buried everything I was feeling under a pile of indignation." A short and humorless laugh tore from her throat. "She would get so angry at me when I wouldn't respond to her. When I really pushed her too hard, she'd tell me I was just like my father—heartless, cold and incredibly boring."

Rafael flinched. Cora nodded. "It hurt," she said, "but not as much as finding out that I'd spent years cultivating what I thought was my father's dignity and reserve only to find out that he really didn't care about me at all."

"When?" he asked.

"I was sixteen. He called Mama and told her I was old enough to take care of Lauren for the summer and not to bring us to him. He'd been having an affair with one of his students—just as he had with Mama. I found out later that it was a pattern for him, and if I'd been paying attention, I probably would have noticed it before.'' She shook her head ruefully. ''Lauren and I had an inordinate number of college-age baby-sitters when we stayed with him.''

Rafael muttered a dark curse. Cora tweaked his arm. ''One particular student must have had something the others didn't, though, because he told Mama he was going to get married as soon as she graduated.''

''How old was he?''

''Um, sixty, maybe. I'm not sure. He was older than my mother when they married, but I can't remember how much.''

Several long seconds of silence passed before Cora spoke again. ''Mama was furious of course. Even though I was old enough to drive, she couldn't justify leaving Lauren and me alone for an entire month. That was the first time we got dumped on a strange relative's doorstep.''

''Who?''

''My mother's cousin. And it was awful. She didn't want us there, and she was furious with Mama. The whole thing chafed, and I kept harboring fantasies that it was obviously a terrible misunderstanding. My father would call soon and straighten everything out.''

''And he didn't?''

''Nope. He was in Aruba with his new wife. We didn't even get a postcard.''

''Ah, Cora—'' he breathed.

She snuggled closer to him. ''That was when I started to feel responsible for Lauren, and resentful of Mama. Lauren was just like her. In public, she was the life of the party. Always happy, always entertaining the crowd. She smiled all the time and she was gorgeous, even then. She had perfect hair and perfect teeth and perfect skin, and she drew boys like a magnet.''

He stroked her shoulder until he found a tense spot, then steadily rubbed it. "Where were you?" he asked.

"Standing on the sidelines, feeling awkward and uncomfortable," she admitted.

"And your mother?"

"She understood Lauren much better than she understood me. They communicated, and to her credit, it's not that she didn't try with me. She and Lauren would pressure me to go shopping with them. I hated it, and they didn't know why. Mama thought I needed more confidence, so she sent me to charm school."

He groaned. Cora patted his arm in sympathy. "It was every bit as humiliating as you think."

"I didn't know they even had charm schools anymore."

"Are you kidding? We lived in South Carolina, where old traditions never die and never, ever, go out of style."

He decided he wanted to see her face for the rest of the story, so he eased her onto her back and lay half on top of her. Gently he traced her eyebrows with his fingertips. "What kind of things do you learn in charm school?"

Her eyes twinkled. "Oh, you know. What kind of fork to use when. How to fold your napkin after dinner. How to respond when a boy asks you to dance." She threaded her hands around his neck. "And that you should never find yourself in a compromising position on a sofa with a rakish-looking male."

He laughed, a warm, deep chuckle, then kissed her tenderly. "But you survived," he said when he lifted his head.

She slanted a look at her sleeping nieces. "I did. Mama died in a car accident when I was in college. That's when I found out that I really didn't resent her like I thought I did. I just felt incredibly sorry for her. I found it sad that she'd spent her entire life trying to please other people. Hardly anyone showed up for her funeral—not even family. It was tragic."

He nodded. "I know."

She pulled in a deep breath, and her eyes took on a far-away look. "But Lauren was younger. It was harder for her. In a strange sort of way, she and Mama had become best friends. It's as if there was no one else in the world who really understood what drove them. So without Mama, Lauren felt completely lost."

"And she filled the void the same way your mother did," he guessed.

"Yes. She's been married three times. I've lost count of her affairs. Kaitlin is her daughter from her first marriage, and Molly and Liza are from her third. The second only lasted five months."

He lowered his head until it rested against her shoulder. She absently stroked his hair. For long minutes he thought about what she'd told him and the insight it had given him. The deep longings she'd had as a child for acceptance and self-worth had gone unfulfilled. As a result she doubted her own desirability. With that knowledge came the freeing realization that he could, after all, offer Cora something more than a wild physical passion. He couldn't promise her forever, but he could give her something that would last long after he'd become a distant memory.

He smiled to himself. By the time the flames died down, Cora would never again have to doubt her allure. He dragged in a contented breath. "One more question," he said softly.

"Hmm." Her voice sounded sleepy.

"According to Kaitlin, Lauren seems to think I'm having a terrible influence on you."

Cora managed a partial laugh as she wriggled closer. "I'd say she's right about that. I've obviously forgotten everything I ever learned in charm school."

He tweaked her shoulder. "Why do you think your sister is so angry?" he asked.

She yawned, "I don't know. I haven't figured that out yet."

Chapter Nine

Dearest,

You are like a fever in my blood now. Since that night you showed me the glorious power of passion, I find I cannot stop remembering the exquisite feel of your hands on my flesh, your voice in my ear, your body pressed to mine in heady passion as you took me to the stars and back. Please, please, my love, hurry back to me with all swiftness. I am praying that the winds will carry you to me, so I can burn with you again.

Abigail
2 April 1861

Cora surveyed herself in the mirror and frowned. "This is ridiculous," she muttered.

Kaitlin sat on Cora's bed, smiling. "I think you look beautiful, Aunt Cora."

A week had passed since Lauren's inflammatory phone call. To Cora's knowledge, her sister had not called again. A week had also passed, she thought ruefully, since she'd nearly made love with Rafael. And every nerve ending in her body had been on standby ever since. She was so jittery, Becky had jokingly asked her if Abigail was haunting her and keeping her up nights. She was haunted, all right, and up nights, too, but it had nothing to do with Abigail and everything to do with Rafael.

When she'd finally allowed herself to think about that night, she was forced to admit one simple truth. Despite every warning she'd issued, despite her common sense, her practicality and the sheer folly of it, she'd fallen completely and irrevocably in love with Rafael. Like Abigail Conrad, she'd ignored everything that was realistic and reasonable and thrown her heart after a man who would almost surely break it.

Rafael had a wanderer's soul—freedom gave him life. Like a rare and magnificent bird, he was born to fly high above the clouds and the bounds of earth. If she tethered him, even if he willingly allowed it, she would kill the very spirit that made him so wondrous. She couldn't live with herself if she did that. The day would come when he would resent her for it, and even if he never expressed it or even hinted at it, she would know. Just as her father had looked so resentfully at her mother, Rafael would look at her with lifeless eyes—and the part of her that had survived years of disappointment and unrequited affection from her parents could never survive it from him.

But she'd surprised herself with the admission that she did, indeed, love him—this most unsuitable of men. Once, she'd imagined that loving deeply and caring intensely would lead to nothing but bitterness and sorrow. In the wake of its admission, however, had come a strange and exhilarating sense of joy. Joy that had given her a wealth of mischievous thoughts and delicious daydreams.

Unfortunately she'd had little time to pursue either. The morning after their passionate interlude, Rafael had told her about his conversation with Jerry and about tonight's reception. With the deadline inflexible and bearing down on them, they'd both spent a frantic week trying to get the necessary research completed to avoid looking unprepared under the intense scrutiny they'd face this evening. Hours poring over reports and analyses had left her head spinning. She'd fallen, exhausted, into bed during the early hours of the morning. Cora knew that nothing would have satisfied Jerry more than to have caught her off guard. Her driving motivation, however, had been to do the best she could to properly represent Abigail. She felt like she owed it to the woman.

Becky stood by the mirror in Cora's room and surveyed her with a critical eye. "I have to admit I didn't think the color would work. But it looks good."

Cora peered down at the pale-green ballgown. "I'm wearing a hoop," she said.

Becky grinned at her. "And a corset." She braced one shoulder against the wall. "And I must say that from a feminist perspective, I think it's despicable, but as a woman, I have to concede it looks damn good."

"Becky..." Cora warned.

"Well, it does. It, er, pushes and pulls everything so nicely."

Kaitlin reached out to touch the seed pearls on the green satin. "It's so pretty—even if it is oyster spit."

Cora looked in the mirror again. With her hair piled high on her head in a period style and the dress hugging her breasts and sweeping to the floor in a graceful bell, she had to admit it felt almost sinfully indulgent. Of course, that could easily be attributed to the outrageously expensive underwear she wore, and the plans she had for it when the dress came off. "I can't believe he talked me into this."

"Make you a bet," Becky said, "that he looks almost as good as you do."

That she could well imagine, Cora thought. He'd talked her into wearing Abigail's dress when he'd finally told her about his conversation with Jerry. He'd given her twenty minutes to vent her rage, then had pointed out methodically and logically, that while she couldn't prevent Jerry and Henry Willers from trying to capitalize on her research, she could ensure that she controlled the stage. Spin them, he'd warned again, before they spin you.

She had to admit that his solution was a brilliant one. Jerry didn't know about the dress or the jacket or the report Cora had received authenticating them. Rafael's PR representative had persuaded Jerry to hold the press conference in the ballroom of Cape Marr's only grand hotel—the ballroom where a portrait of del Flores wearing the red-and-black embroidered jacket hung. When Rafael and Cora arrived wearing the garments and bearing documented evidence of their authenticity, Jerry Heath wouldn't be able to draw a crowd by yelling "Fire!" much less with his usual pompous rhetoric.

And in a weak moment, with her nieces looking at her hopefully, she'd agreed. So here she was, dressed up in Abigail's finery, feeling more like one of the ugly stepsisters than Cinderella. "This isn't going to work," she complained.

"Of course it is," Becky told her. "Just stick with Rafael and everything will be fine."

Cora shook her head and turned from the mirror. Looking at her reflection was making her too nervous. She simply wasn't the showman he was, and didn't even want to be. The thought of cameras clicking and reporters yelling questions was making her palms sweat. "Kaitlin," she said, needing something to keep her mind off the pending disaster, "we'll be back around seven-thirty. Is everything going to be ready?"

Kaitlin nodded eagerly. "Becky helped, and as soon as you're gone, we'll tell Molly and Liza what's going on. I couldn't tell them before. They would have yapped."

Cora laughed. "Probably." She still didn't know what had inspired her to pull Kaitlin into Margie's scheme for Rafael's birthday, but she was increasingly grateful for the effect the shared confidence had on her niece. Kaitlin had flown into action with the skill of a seasoned party planner. And just in time, too. Cora and Margie had scheduled the party for tonight—days before she'd known about Jerry's plans. She'd been so busy the past week preparing, checking and rechecking her reports for tonight, she'd had time for little else.

So today was Rafael's birthday, and thanks to Kaitlin, his sister's party would come off without a hitch. Cora still didn't know how Rafael would react to his family—or to her interference—but Margie had effectively calmed her fears. At last count, seven of Rafael's siblings were supposed to come, including his older brother, Zack, and his family. And just to keep life interesting, Cora thought wickedly as she adjusted the lace at her bodice, she'd made plans of her own for the evening. Plans that included burgundy sheets, a bottle of wine, a couple of candles and the lace-and-satin undergarments she was wearing. "I couldn't have done it without you, Kaitlin," Cora assured her.

Kaitlin beamed. "It was fun. Margie let me pick colors and everything."

"Wait till you see the cake, Cora," Becky said. "You won't believe it."

When Cora had identified a bakery where they used a computerized process to transfer a picture onto the icing, Kaitlin had spent hours on the design. Her art teacher had been enlisted in the process, and no one except Kaitlin, the bakery and Becky, who'd played chauffeur that afternoon, had seen the finished product. "I'm sure it's wonderful."

Kaitlin nodded. "It turned out really good."

"When's everyone getting here?"

Becky checked her watch. "Thirty minutes. So we have

to get you and Rafael out the door before they come, and them in the door before you guys get back. Make sure you stay at the reception at least an hour.''

"When do I turn into a pumpkin?" Cora quipped as she reached for the satin reticule that went with the dress.

Kaitlin rolled her eyes. "Aunt Cora—"

"I know, I know." She kissed Kaitlin on top of the head. "Just shut up and have a good time."

Becky pulled open the door. "And whatever you do, don't let Jerry win. I have a fifty-dollar bet riding on his complete humiliation."

Laughing, the three of them made their way down the wide oak staircase.

OH, MY, CORA THOUGHT a moment later when she found Rafael in the foyer with Liza and Molly. He held Liza against his chest and was waltzing with her while Molly looked on and laughed. He caught a glimpse of Cora in his peripheral vision and stopped suddenly to simply stare at her. At the full impact of his heated gaze, Cora sucked in a breath so sharp it made her corset stays tighten.

"Look, Aunt Cora!" Liza exclaimed. "Isn't he beautiful?"

He certainly is, she thought, and swallowed hard. He wore slim-fitting black trousers that disappeared into immaculate black boots. Perfectly tailored, they clung to every muscular plane with a lover's familiarity. His full white shirt accented his bronze skin, and the expertly tied sash at his waist made his chest look impossibly broad. A ceremonial saber hung at his side, and the jacket, that gold-encrusted, broad-shouldered, bolero-cut jacket. Good Lord. What it did for his physique should be criminal. Cora wet her lips and met his glittering gaze. He'd pulled his hair into a neat queue at his nape and switched his usual eye patch for a black patent-leather one.

Yes, he looked beautiful, breathtaking even. Cora gripped the handrail and took a tentative step down. He set Liza on the floor and mounted the stairs two at a time until he reached her. Distantly, she heard the sound of his saber knocking the steps and suddenly knew why Abigail had been so fond of the noise. He stopped when he was on the step below, and they stood, face-to-face, eye-to-eye. "Cora," he said in a rough whisper that sent goose bumps skittering across her flesh, "you are glorious."

She swayed slightly toward him, wondered what would happen if she simply dragged him to the upstairs room, forgot the reception, skipped the party and went straight to the part where she'd give him his birthday present.

Kaitlin stepped out from behind Cora's hoop skirt and said, "Aunt Cora thinks she looks silly, but I think she looks wonderful."

"Me, too!" Liza yelled.

Rafael lifted her hand, kissed her knuckles and whispered, "As a matter of fact, so do I."

Becky coughed, loudly and intrusively. Cora blinked and the spell was broken. Becky came down the stairs and gave them a knowing look. "You'd better get going. You wouldn't want to be late to your own reception."

RAFAEL CAST a surreptitious glance at the clock and stifled a groan. They'd have to stay at this cursed event at least another half hour before they could make a graceful exit. He polished off his glass of water and plunked it down on the table.

He usually enjoyed these things. It gave him personal satisfaction to talk about his work, and an even greater satisfaction to mold the media's opinion of what he was doing and why. But tonight he'd been seriously off his game. His PR rep had been shooting him nasty looks for most of the evening. He'd found himself unable to concentrate, constantly distracted by the site of Cora hovering just beyond his reach.

Just the way she'd been all week.

From the moment he'd seen her on the stairs tonight, he'd felt the pump of adrenaline in his blood. The short ride in the car had been torturous. Twice, he'd almost suggested they skip the event and find someplace, anyplace, private enough to exhaust the sexual tension that had been steadily building since their interrupted tryst on her sofa.

Now his appetite was whetted to a razor-sharp hunger that had his hands flexing as he fought the urge to simply drag her away with him until her protests stopped and she was demanding that he satisfy her. He reveled in the image for long seconds, knowing that Cora wouldn't allow it. She wasn't a woman to be bullied or manipulated. She held her own, and that made him want her all the more.

Squaring his shoulders, he started across the room toward her. He blatantly ignored a reporter who tried to intercept him with an asinine question about the *Isabela*. He could well imagine del Flores standing at an event similar to this one, spotting Abigail across the room, surrounded—like Cora—by a ring of admirers. The pirate wouldn't have stood for it, either.

He approached her in measured strides, savoring the moment when she first noticed him bearing down on her. She shot him a warning glance over the head of a short television anchorman Rafael recognized. The censure in her green eyes steeled his resolve. Tonight, he promised himself. Tonight he would have her.

Rafael stepped into Cora's circle of acquaintances, reporters and scholars, and staked a claim. Extending his hand to her, he said softly, "Dance with me."

A hush fell on the small group, as if they sensed the deeper meaning of the commanding invitation. Her eyebrows lifted, and for a nerve-racking moment, he thought she'd refuse. But a devilish smile played at the corners of her mouth, and she raised sparkling eyes to his. Did she, too, sense the power of this moment? he wondered. Did she know that tonight, at any rate, Abigail and del Flores were finding their way together again?

Cora slid her fingers into his outstretched hand. "I'd be delighted, sir," she said softly.

His fingers curled around hers in a rush of satisfaction. From the corner of his eye, he caught the look of near rapturous pleasure on the face of his PR rep. She was already lining photographers up and had her assistant hurrying off to speak with the director of the small orchestra.

As they walked toward the wooden dance floor, Cora gave him a wry look. "Is it your policy to always make a spectacle of yourself?" she asked in a low, sultry voice that made his gut clench.

He hesitated. They reached the center of the floor, and he spun her into his arms as the music began. He made a mental note to authorize a bonus for his PR rep when he recognized the opening chords of a rumba. "It is my policy," he said as he swept his arm around her waist, "to get what I want."

The stiff boning of her corset felt decadent beneath his fingers. He lowered his head and drew an intoxicating breath of her scent. "Do you feel it, Cora?" he whispered close to her ear as he led her in the first steps. "Do you feel how much I want you?"

Her color heightened, and her eyes took on a slightly fevered look. Her fingers tightened on his shoulder. "I'm drowning," she confessed.

His hands clenched. "I've been going crazy all week."

"Me, too."

The satin of her gown was cool beneath his fingers, but he felt her warmth seeping through the delicate fabric. "Then come with me now."

She hesitated for long, breathless seconds, and he felt as though they were teetering on the precipice of a steep cliff. "Come with me," he urged again.

Cora's eyes drifted momentarily shut. She moved with him to the music, but he sensed the conflict in her. When she finally met his gaze again, her lips were trembling. "The reporters. I shouldn't..."

An equivocation, he noted, but not a refusal. He executed a few deft steps, then brought her tightly to him. He was vaguely aware that every eye in the room was studying the musical seduction with keen interest. "You want to," he urged, "as much as I do."

"That doesn't mean—"

He lowered his head. "The singe of flesh against flesh. The heat. The passion. I want to touch you...everywhere. And I want you to touch me. I want to give you such pleasure, Cora. Everything you could want."

"Rafael—"

"Do you think," he continued, knowing he was pressing an unfair advantage and not caring, "that Abigail wavered at this same moment?"

Her eyelids fluttered. "That's not fair."

He knew how strongly Abigail's writings had affected her, how much she related to the woman whose intimate diaries had brought him here. "Do you think she did?" he asked again, ruthlessly determined to slake his unrelenting thirst for her.

Cora pressed her lips together and shook her head. "No."

He spun her in a quick series of steps. "No, I won't, or no, she didn't?"

Her deep breath made her breasts rise against the satin confines of her bodice. "No," she said softly, "she didn't."

His heart missed a beat. "And?"

Her gaze met his in a melting look of surrender. "Neither will I."

Passion spiked through him, demanding his attention and damning convention. The music had not yet ended, and he could well imagine what their avid audience would conclude from this, but he didn't give a damn. With a boldness that might have made del Flores smile, Rafael looped his fingers under Cora's elbow and headed toward the door with purposeful strides. She wasn't, he noted with broad satisfaction, struggling to keep up with him.

Energy was pumping through him in a shimmering current of heat and sensation, eating away at his self-control. He held her hand as he guided her to the car, but didn't dare touch her elsewhere. Once, she whispered his name in a low, seductive voice that made him shiver. He pressed her hand to his lips to silence her. With his restraint barely leashed and his mind entirely focused on the exquisite anticipation, he wanted to simply savor the moment, not to clutter it with explanations or superfluous comments.

Cora seemed to understand. She fell silent. They reached his car, and he yielded long enough to press a hard kiss to her lips—a promise of things to come. She fought briefly with the unnatural confines and bulk of her gown, but got into the passenger seat without undue delay. The collapsible hoop of her dress necessitated that she gather it around her knees to sit. At the generous glimpse of her lace-clad legs, he stifled a groan and slammed the car door.

What in the world, he wondered as he rounded the vehicle to the driver's side, had this woman done to him that a simple flash of a well-turned calf and ankle could have his libido on overdrive? Had del Flores felt that way when he'd lured Abigail from her father's home into his private abode? Most likely, he mused, and wiped a shaking hand through his hair.

Neither spoke on the short drive to Cora's home. Beside him, he keenly sensed her arousal. Her breath was short. Her body trembled. Her hands lay laced tightly together in her lap. He shifted down and took a corner a little too fast. Cora didn't comment.

When he finally pulled up in front of the large antebellum house, he noted absently that it looked dark. With luck, Becky had the girls in bed. He had neither the focus nor the desire to concern himself with Becky's reaction to their early return. They could use the outside back stairs to his room, he reasoned. A few more minutes... Patience.

He switched off the keys and looked at her for the first time since they'd left the reception. Her hair was somewhat mussed where his fingers had pried at her elegant chignon. Her lips were parted, her face flushed. "Cora," he murmured and cupped her face in his hand. He used his thumb to lift her chin, then lowered his head to taste her lips. "Ah, Cora."

She mumbled something and threaded her hands around his neck. He buried his mouth in hers. She sighed and took him in. In all his life, he could not remember ever feeling the sweet spike of bliss and headiness he felt when Cora traced the line of his lips with her tongue. The confines of the car and the restrictions of her dress were quickly becoming intolerable. He deepened the kiss for long seconds, then tore his mouth free. "Upstairs," he urged. "Come upstairs with me."

Her fingers fluttered at his nape as she slowly withdrew. He watched her squeeze her eyes shut as though she needed to stop the world from spinning. "I have to take this dress off," she said.

He couldn't suppress a slight laugh. "That's exactly what I was thinking."

Cora shook her head. "No, I meant..." She paused. "I can't ruin it. I need to take it off first."

She was right and he knew it. Despite the strong urge he felt to fling reason and common sense to the wind, it would be irresponsible to risk damaging the dated gown. He pressed a kiss to the furrow between her eyebrows. "Then meet me upstairs in fifteen minutes?"

"Becky—" she countered.

"Will understand."

Cora swallowed, then shook her head. "No, I have to explain—"

He headed her off by pressing his thumb to her swollen lips. "Not tonight, Cora. Don't explain anything. Just come with me."

She shivered, a delicious shuddering that tripped down her spine. "Inside—"

"Trust me," he urged, and let himself out of the car. They walked in silence to the front door. He could not stop touching her. He massaged her neck with one hand while he absently jingled his keys with the other. The porch light gleamed, as did the moon, bathing their path in a swath of blue-gray color. Cora gave him a wary look as she mounted the porch stairs. She fumbled with the door and would have pushed it open, when he decided she might need something to remember while she changed.

He caught her close and kissed her deeply, vaguely aware that the door creaked open into the foyer. A sudden blinding light from the depths of the house failed to wrest his attention, but what did grab him was the unexpected—and unwelcome sound—of voices yelling, "Surprise!"

CORA GROANED and dropped her head to his shoulder. She had no one to blame but herself for this particular humiliation. The sound of robust laughter, cheers and children's voices helped her find her equilibrium, despite the too-tight pressure of his fingers at her waist. She gave him a small smile and said softly, "Happy birthday."

His gaze narrowed for a long, hair-raising second, before his implacable smile was back in place. He released her slowly and turned to face his family. Liza was already pulling on his trouser leg. "Rafael, Rafael, lookit! Look at all these people!"

He swept Liza into his arms seconds before a tide of exuberant children engulfed him. Cora didn't even try to count the bobbing heads and high-pitched voices. Becky broke away from the crowd of adults and made her way to Cora's side. "Why don't you go change?" she said firmly. "There's an awful lot of cake and ice cream in here for you to be wearing that dress."

Cora nodded. "I will." She glanced at Rafael's family. They were trying, in vain, to corral their offspring and press toward their brother. He was talking to the children, laughing, and apparently unperturbed by the abrupt end to the web of seduction he'd been weaving around her. Inexplicably annoyed by his nonchalance when she should be grateful for his élan, Cora looked at Becky. "I'll be down in a few minutes."

Becky gave her a shrewd look. "Take your time. Kaitlin's got hostess skills that make Miss Manners look like a novice. They're having a great time."

Cora nodded and headed for the stairs. Her stomach fluttered as she struggled for emotional balance. Her blood had been singing since he'd pulled her into his arms on the dance floor. Abigail's dress made her feel reckless, but she hadn't expected to feel so intoxicated by the heady realization that tonight she would let her passionate, exotic pirate lover take her to the stars. Tonight after the party, she had decided, she would join him upstairs. He wouldn't be expecting her.

But he would stoke her courage with that lazy, seductive smile, which held such promise. She pressed a hand to her abdomen as she reached the landing. The fantasies had been spinning through her mind all evening, and now she felt strangely dizzy. "Get a grip," she muttered, as she made her way down the dim corridor.

She pressed her hand flat against the cool wood of her door and pulled in a calming breath. This tremor would stop, she promised herself, taking with it the weak feeling in her knees. She would change and join the crowd downstairs. She would not succumb to the clutching need in her belly until the time was right. Practical, trustworthy, coolheaded Cora Prescott simply did not lose control of herself.

She slipped into her room and turned the lock. ''At least not yet,'' she said with a soft smile. She walked toward her bathroom as she began undoing the long line of satin-covered buttons on the gown.

HE HAD MEANT to wait. The timing couldn't have been worse. Two of his brothers, six of his sisters and all their spouses and children awaited him downstairs. He was a man of experience, a man of patience and finesse. He knew the value of timing. And he had meant to wait.

Until he heard that annoying click of the lock on Cora's bedroom door. The sound tripped an internal trigger. For weeks he'd let that sound stand between them. For weeks he'd battled a growing irritation every time he heard her shut him out.

At the sound his frustration soared. And with it his restraint fled. Perhaps it was the keen feeling that del Flores had faced a similar choice. Perhaps it was simply the result of weeks of unfulfilled sexual hunger. Whatever the case, he felt brashness swamp and overwhelm his common sense. Damn the consequences, he thought irritably. He was not going to spend another second locked from her room or her bed.

He rapped sharply on the door with his knuckles. When it yielded no answer, he pressed his ear to the door. He could hear the faint sound of running water from her bathroom. Before he could think better of it, he stepped away from the door and kicked it sharply with his booted heel. The antique lock gave easily and wrenched away from the oak frame.

The door flew open. Rafael stood in the threshold, breathing heavily. Immediately his gaze found her. She stood near the bathroom door with the loosened gown clutched to her breasts. Her eyes were wide with surprise— and something else. Something that looked like hunger. "I was in the bathroom," she said.

He took a labored breath. "Your door was locked," he announced.

Cora's laugh was warm and sultry, and it enslaved him. "I see you didn't let it stop you."

He slammed her door shut, isolating them from the noise and inconvenient reality of the party in her living room. In four quick strides, he crossed the room. When he stood inches from her, he reached for her hands. She resisted for a moment, then let him pry them away from the bodice of her gown. The dress fell to the floor in a pool of pale-green satin. Swiftly he lifted her free of it, then spread it carefully over the chaise lounge in the corner of her room. His duty to Abigail fulfilled, he turned his attention to the woman who now held him in thrall. She still wore her white lace corset and stockings. The sight and scent of her filled his head like the most powerful of aphrodisiacs. "I've been listening to you lock that door for weeks," he muttered as he drank in the sight of her.

Her fingers trembled in his. "I've been locking myself in."

The quiet admission effectively unraveled what was left of his control. He kissed her deeply, his hands molding her to him. He wanted to touch her everywhere, to learn every secret of this bewitching woman who had captured him with a simple look from her fathomless eyes. "Cora," he breathed. "Sweet Cora."

Her hands smoothed the planes of his shoulders and back.

She pressed against him and silently insisted that he give her what she wanted. Momentarily surprised by the simple act of wordless aggression, he gladly surrendered. He had dreamed of this moment for weeks, played it out in his mind in a dozen different fantasies of how it would be for them. In every one he realized, as Cora laid claim to his mouth and his body, he'd pictured himself as the seducer. She would sweetly yield to him, and he would finally have license to unleash his desire.

But Cora, evidently, had other plans.

And belatedly, he realized, he should have known that she would never be passive about anything. The thought had his blood pressure rising as her hands threaded into his hair and clutched his head closer to her. He would be the one, it seemed, to do the surrendering. And the experience was proving to be more erotic than he'd ever experienced.

With a low oath, he swept her into his arms and carried her toward the bed. "You cannot imagine," he said as he followed her down onto the quilt-covered surface, "how much I want you."

Her fingers were shaking as she traced the lines of his face. "Yes, I can. I'm starving."

He laced his fingers through hers and pressed her hands to the pillow above her head. The exquisite feel of his body fully aligned with hers seared his nerves. "Then take me," he urged.

And Cora did.

Chapter Ten

Dearest,

Forgive me, darling. I know I'm weak, and at times you must wonder why you put up with me when I show no courage. The gossip continues, and I try so very hard to ignore it. When you were here in my arms, I could, but now, when I am left feeling empty and alone, I stumble at times. They are cruel. How I long for you. My flesh burns when I remember your hands on me. My woman's self tingles and aches for the exquisite feel of your body on mine. Oh, please, dearest, come quickly for me. I do not wish to face them again without you at my side.

Abigail
10 July 1861

Fifteen minutes later Cora found herself still struggling for balance. Rafael lay beside her, one arm flung over his head, his dark hair spread on the pillow. Like hers, his breathing was harsh. Considering the impact his lovemaking had had on her, she could barely credit that her room looked the same as it had twenty minutes ago. Except, she noted as her gaze fell on the evidence of the broken lock, her splintered door frame. Cora wiped a hand over her face and tried to stifle a giggle.

He opened his eye. "Are you giggling?"

"I never giggle," she said in her best professorial voice, something she thought was rather remarkable, given that she felt like a volcano had exploded inside her.

His eye sparkled. "Maybe not," he said, turning toward her and propping himself up on one elbow, "but you make plenty of other interesting noises." With his fingertips he traced the bodice of the corset they hadn't had time to remove. "I think we'll try it without this next time, hmm?"

The mention of "next time" made her stomach flutter. "Easy for you to say," she quipped. "It's not the easiest thing in the world to take off."

His laugh was full and rich. "I'd consider that a challenge if you didn't have a living room full of people waiting for us."

Cora groaned. "Your family—"

"And all their kids," he said. "How long have you known about this?"

"A couple of weeks. Margie called me and mentioned that it had been a while since you'd all been together. With your birthday—"

He interrupted her with a tender kiss. "I've never had a better present," he said when he lifted his head.

"I thought you'd enjoy seeing them."

Rafael rubbed his thumb along her lower lip. "I wasn't talking about seeing my family—which is nice, I admit. I was talking about you, Cora. About this." He paused to kiss her forehead. "About us."

"Oh." She had a vague feeling she should say something else, but for once in her life, seemed to have run short of words.

Rafael nuzzled the side of her neck. "Let's forget the party and stay here," he suggested.

It was tempting, especially with his lips pressed to a particularly sensitive spot beneath her ear. Briefly she marveled at the amazing effect he was having on her. She, who could not remember doing anything on impulse in her life, was contemplating ignoring his family for the sake of passion. She summoned the shreds of her self-control. "We can't— Ah!" If only he wouldn't insist on touching every hot spot on her flesh.

He smiled against her skin, then nipped the place again. "It's my birthday," he said. "I can do what I want."

Oh, so tempting. She drew a shaky breath and pushed gently at his shoulder. "No, you can't. They went to a lot of trouble."

"They expect me to be irresponsible." His hands now rested on her corseted waist.

"You are incorrigible."

"So they tell me."

He cupped her breast, and Cora squirmed. Was she supposed to have this dizzying, heated need? "Rafael?"

At the query in her voice, he lifted his head. "What, love?"

Her stomach turned over. He looked beautiful, almost unreal in the dim light of her bedside lamp. His dark hair spilled over his broad shoulders and framed the sculpted planes of his face. She traced the sharp line of his chin. "Is it always going to be like this? I wasn't expecting…"

His gaze softened. "Neither was I. You're amazing. Never doubt it."

Cora swallowed. How did he always know what she needed from him? "It's not me," she assured him. "I have it on the best of authority that I'm extremely boring."

"Cora—" he moved over her so she was pressed to the sheet by his weight "—listen to me."

"No, really." She had to head him off before he offered up some incredible compliment that would make her forget this was an affair with a passionate, amazing man whose idea of permanence was penciling in a date on his calendar. She smiled at him. "Really. I'm just having a bout of incredulity. This is…a little new to me."

"You've never pillaged a man before?" he asked, smiling.

She couldn't prevent a blush. "No," she replied softly.

His gaze narrowed and he searched her expression with unsettling intensity. "Want me to show you again how much I want you?"

Oh, how she wanted it. "No, er, yes, but not right now. Duty calls."

"Is that what that noise is?"

"No, that noise is the clamor of your family waiting for the guest of honor."

He shut his eye. "They always did have rotten timing." He dipped his head. "I still think we should blow them off."

"Kaitlin planned the entire event," she said as his lips found the hollow of her throat. "Even the cake."

He stilled and raised his head. "Really?"

Cora nodded. "Uh-huh." She brushed a wave of dark hair off his forehead. "And besides, I've been having fantasies about those burgundy sheets upstairs. If we stay here—"

He kissed her hard, then rolled away with typical decisiveness. She envied him that. He swung his legs over the side of the bed. "Tonight you can tell me what those fantasies, and I'll fulfill them." He reached for his trousers.

Cora unabashedly watched him dress. He was truly splendid, she decided as she watched his bronze skin ripple over the corded muscles that had felt like bunched satin beneath her fingers. Their joining had been so fierce and explosive that there'd been little time for finesse or tender explorations. She wondered now what it would be like to take her time mapping his hard frame and learning all the textures and sensitivities of his flesh.

With the corset still pressing against her own suddenly oversensitized flesh, she watched him pull on the full, white shirt and had a sudden image of Abigail, lying in her boudoir, watching del Flores prepare to leave. Had Abigail felt this odd combination of disappointment and utter satiation? Rafael pulled his hair back and clipped it neatly at his neck. Had del Flores, Cora wondered, overwhelmed Abigail with passion, then slipped away into the night?

Had Abigail felt this same urgency when she'd known their time was short?

The thought depressed her, so Cora deliberately pushed it aside. There'd be time enough later—time when he'd found what he'd come for in her home and in her life and let his wanderer's spirit carry him away—to ponder the irrationality of her choices.

Dressed now in his trousers, shirt and boots, he walked to her side of the bed and helped her to her knees. He stooped to kiss her, a lingering, soul-stirring kiss that held the promise of a thousand more to come. "You'd better get dressed, lass," he said in his pirate's drawl. "They'll be expecting you downstairs."

Cora kissed his chest. "I suppose I should feel embarrassed that they're all going to know what we've been doing."

"Do you?" he asked quietly.

Too quietly, she thought, as if the answer mattered more than he wanted her to know. She leaned her head back and met his gaze. "No. Not at all."

His smile sent heat skittering along her nerves. "I'm glad." He smoothed her hair away from her face, then traced the curves of her ears with his fingers. "And I'm not trying to be crass, here, but time is, er, of the essence. Do you need help getting your corset off?''

Cora laughed. "I bet you say that to all the girls."

His grin was devilish. "Let's just say that if I'd known you were going to look this sexy in it, I'd have started fantasizing about it weeks ago."

"And if you help me take it off now," she observed, "we might never get downstairs."

"Point well taken." He kissed the bridge of her nose. "I'm going to run upstairs and change. I'll come get you in five minutes."

"Do you think we should go down together?"

"I think if we don't, my family is going to grill you until you crack under pressure."

She laughed. "But I have a secret weapon." At his quizzical look, she thumped his chest. "Benedict Bunny can always create a distraction for me."

He swatted her behind. "You certainly are a cheeky thing, aren't you."

"It's you," she argued, "and that terrible influence my sister claims you're having on me."

"Well, whatever it is, you can tell me about it later when all those kids are in bed."

Cora nodded. "Deal."

He scooped up his discarded saber and del Flores's jacket, and hurried from the room. Cora's fingers found the laces of her corset. She hurried through the task as best she could and made quick work of hanging and covering the vintage gown. She hesitated a moment before pulling on a pair of jeans and a T-shirt. The ridiculously lacy underwear seemed out of place underneath such casual clothes. She almost changed to something more practical until she pictured the look in his eye when he'd first seen the lacy bra and garter belt. She won another battle with her practical side and opted to leave them on. She had the inescapable feeling that she'd need the memories later to ease the ache of his absence.

True to his word, he appeared five minutes later clad in black jeans and a denim shirt. He kissed her lingeringly. "Ready for this?" His hands rested lightly at her waist.

"Do you have any idea," she probed, reaching up to straighten her glasses, "how completely out of character this is for me?"

"I have an inkling." His eye sparkled. "And I'm totally fascinated."

"Lauren's right." She stepped away from him. "You're having a terrible influence on me."

He flung an arm around her shoulders and led her toward the stairs. "Feels great, doesn't it?"

HIS FAMILY GREETED them with exuberance and charm. Twenty minutes later Cora was struggling to remember what she'd worried about. Six of Rafael's sisters, including Margie and Elena, had made the trip. His older brother, Zack, and his younger brother, Seb, were also there. Through conversation, Cora learned that the third brother, a Navy SEAL, was at sea. His two youngest sisters were still in college and were finishing up a summer-school session. And the other missing sister, a nurse, had not been able to clear her schedule. All of them had Rafael's exotic coloring and devil-may-care attitude. Even the spouses, Cora noted, seemed to have adapted to the overwhelming force of the clan. Zack's wife, August, with her auburn hair and fair coloring, fit in readily with the women as if she'd been born to the position. Most of the children present, it turned out, were hers. Several were adopted, a couple were ones she and Zack had given birth to. August claimed she could no longer remember which were which.

The laughter was loud. The conversation often even louder. Cora found herself dazzled by the easy intimacy of

Rafael's family. Even Zack, despite the tense history between the two brothers, seemed at ease. Cora watched him
put a restraining hand on the shoulder of a young boy who
was headed for the kitchen at a dead run. The stern look he
gave the child to halt his progress faded nicely into a warm
smile and a forgiving tousle of the youngster's hair when
the silent warning was received and obeyed.

Never having experienced such undiluted warmth in her
own family, Cora felt overwhelmed, but not unpleasantly
so. And she wasn't the only one, she observed. When Kaitlin's cake was received with an appreciative round of com-
pliments and questions, the child beamed. "It was Aunt
Cora's idea," Kaitlin explained regarding the intricate drawing of the *Isabela* on top of the cake.

"Kaitlin drew it herself," Cora added.

"She's taking art classes," Rafael announced as he admired the cake. "She's extremely talented." The surety of
the statement left no doubt among the group.

So they cut the cake and ate the ice cream, and one by
one, the children began to tire. Eyelids drooped and shoulders sagged, and parents and aunts and uncles took equal
responsibility for ushering the latest bedtime casualty off to
the room that Kaitlin had decided they should set aside for
the children. The large room that had once served as Colonel
Conrad's library currently stood unfurnished. Cora had not
yet had the time or funds to renovate it, so she'd had it
painted and had installed a carpet to protect the oak floors.
Now sleeping bags lay in neat rows on the thick carpet, and
a clutter of suitcases crowded one wall.

Finally, when all the children were together—some already asleep—Rafael took responsibility for ushering the
final few into the land of Nod. He sat in the center of the
floor with Liza curled in his lap and began to spin a tale for
his avid audience. The lights were off, and the only illu-

mination came from the foyer. Cora stood in the doorway and watched as the children fell quickly under his spell.

One by one, they eased into their sleeping bags and succumbed to the lulling sound of his voice and the aftermath of the day's excitement. When the last one had nodded off, he eased Liza off his lap and into the sleeping bag with Molly.

"He's amazing, isn't he?"

Surprised, Cora looked around to find Elena watching her. "Yes," she concurred, "he is."

Elena studied her for a moment. "He's different with you, though," she said. "It's like I told you that day at lunch. He looks at you differently. He cares about you."

The words gave Cora pause. *Oh, be careful,* she warned herself. *Be very careful.*

From the corner of her eye, Cora watched Rafael pick his way over the clutter of sleeping bags and making his way toward the door. "The feeling is mutual," she assured his sister.

Elena nodded. "I'm really glad."

Rafael pulled the door shut behind him as he joined them. "Mission accomplished," he said, and put his arm around Cora's shoulders. "The munchkins are dead to the world." He kissed the top of Cora's head. "And now that I think about it, I'm feeling a little tired myself."

That made Elena laugh. "I see the art of subtlety still eludes you."

"Subtlety is for cowards," he said.

She glanced at Cora. "Sure you know what you're getting into?"

"I ask myself that at least ten times a day," Cora admitted.

Elena's expression was warm as she rose on tiptoe to kiss her brother's cheek. "I'll bail you out and make your excuses."

"As usual?" he quipped.

"Naturally." She patted his arm. "Thanks to Cora's unbelievable generosity, we're all staying here." At his groan, she pinched him. "So there's plenty of time to visit tomorrow."

He nodded. "Thanks."

Elena continued, "And thanks for being so civil with Zack. It made everything easier."

"I'm glad he came." Rafael sounded sincere. At his sister's surprised look, he laughed. "I told you that we buried the hatchet after his wedding."

"Still…"

"I know." He cupped her face. "It's all right, Elena. It'll take time, but we're working on it."

She nodded. "That's all I ask." With a natural affection, she gave Cora a quick kiss on the cheek. "Thanks for making all this possible."

"My pleasure," Cora said, and meant it.

Elena shooed them toward the stairs. "Now go, before I think better of it and change my mind."

RAFAEL AWOKE the next morning with a strange sense of disorientation. The sound of hammering had awakened him, he realized. A soft rain streaked down the window of his third-story room, obliterating the usual shaft of sunlight that served as his alarm clock. It took him several seconds to identify the likely source of the hammering. Last night, he'd asked his brother, Seb, who was a master carpenter by trade, to fix the lock on Cora's door. With his usual attention to detail, Seb had started the job near the crack of dawn. No doubt, the rest of the family was starting to stir—and if experience was any measure, no one was going to be impressed with Seb's diligence. Already, Rafael could hear the sound of children's voices rising through the house.

Still, a sense of unease followed him from his half-asleep

state to full wakefulness. The warmth at his side, he immediately recognized. Cora. She'd given him everything last night. He'd never had a lover who shared so much of herself. It shook him when he thought about it. Her undiluted selflessness demanded a response from him—one he wasn't sure he could give her.

Slowly he rubbed a hand over her rib cage. Her flesh felt supple and warm beneath his fingers, and the sensation was already having an effect on him.

He couldn't remember a time when he'd felt this incredible sense of well-being—and the undeniable urge to keep feeling it. He rarely thought in terms longer than the next project, the next find, the next discovery, but now he found himself wondering how he could look forward to anything if he knew the next day would start without Cora.

It was this realization that had created his unease. No one knew better than he that dreams about forever were just that—dreams. And dreams inevitably led to disappointment. Deliberately he pushed the uncharacteristic melancholy thoughts away. Cora was stirring next to him—and she deserved all his attention.

She turned in his arms and released a long sigh. "What time is it?"

Her disgruntled tone made him smile. Cora, he had learned in the past few weeks, was not a morning person. This particular morning, improving her mood felt like a personal, and delightfully tantalizing, challenge. "Six-thirty."

She groaned. "What's that pounding noise?"

He kissed her until she opened to him. "Seb is fixing your door," he told her.

Cora stilled for a moment, then dropped her head to his shoulder. "I suppose you told him how it got broken."

He pressed a hand to the small of her back and pulled her on top of him. "Sure. I have a reputation to protect."

She glared at him. He pressed a thumb to the corner of her mouth. "That's a joke," he said.

"Promise?" she asked, still looking disgruntled.

He laughed. "Yes, I promise. I would never besmirch your honor."

Cora relaxed against him. "Getting through the party was hard enough for me. I'm pretty sure I'm not ready to face your family this morning if everyone knows you kicked my door in. I haven't quite mastered your complete disregard for public opinion."

"They loved you."

"I liked them, too," she said. "They're, um, passionate."

He cupped her bottom and gave it a light squeeze. "They're noisy, overbearing, pushy and opinionated."

"So you come by it honestly." She tweaked his chest.

He growled at her. "I have created a monster."

That won him yet another disgruntled look. "I beg your pardon?"

"Before I met you, Jerry assured me that I'd have no trouble managing you." Her jaw dropped and she squeaked. He found the tiny noise absolutely irresistible. "Yep," he affirmed.

"The cretin."

"I should have let you slug him last night," he concurred. "It probably would have made us both feel better."

Her snort was inelegant and in stark contrast to the delightful picture of femininity she made sprawled across his chest like some golden-haired seductress. "I will admit to enjoying a certain level of satisfaction when he couldn't answer that question about how the garments were authenticated. I couldn't believe he didn't know enough about the process to babble something about textile historicity and fiber analysis."

"The part I enjoyed was watching him squirm when you wouldn't come to his rescue."

She nuzzled the underside of his chin and he felt his blood pressure soar. "Why are we talking about Jerry?" she asked him in a voice that sent his pulse to the moon.

"Beats me," he drawled.

"I think we can—"

A piercing scream interrupted her. Cora raised her head, her eyes filled with alarm. "What was that?"

"Aunt Cora!" Liza's voice trilled through the house. "Aunt Cora, come quick?"

Rafael met her gaze and they simultaneously said, "Benedict Bunny."

CORA PULLED on her clothes and hurried down the stairs with Rafael hot on her heels. As predicted, they found a distraught Liza wringing her hands in a perfect imitation of her mother. She was standing in the hallway by Cora's bedroom and had drawn a crowd with her earsplitting scream. "Aunt Cora," she wailed, "Aunt Cora, it's Benedict Bunny. He's in there." She pointed to a narrow opening in the former doorjamb of Cora's bedroom door.

One of Rafael's nephews pushed his way to the front. "What's in there?"

"Benedict Bunny," Molly supplied. "Liza's always losing him."

"I am not," Liza said indignantly. "He just gets away sometimes."

Another one of the boys spoke up. "How you gonna get him out?"

Elena's daughter dropped to her knees and peered into the narrow opening. "It's dark in there. I can't see nothing."

"Anything," her mother absently corrected. "How are you going to get that thing out of there? You didn't leave much room, Seb."

Seb shot Cora an apologetic look. "Evidently I left too

much. I was pretty sure I wouldn't be able to repair the lock without replacing the jamb, so I removed part of it.'' He tapped the top of the jamb with the butt of a screwdriver. "It's weird. It's solid up here." He tapped lower, "but hollow down here. It's no wonder the lock gave way. There was nothing to hold the screws in place."

"Great," Rafael muttered.

Seb's expression turned dry. "Maybe you didn't need to work so hard."

That won a sharp look from Zack. "Children, Seb," he warned.

"Sorry." He looked at Cora again. "So I cut out part of the jamb. I was going to head into town to get a new piece this morning."

Liza wiped her eyes with the back of her hand. "I just wanted to see," she wailed. "I didn't want him to get losted."

Rafael ruffled her hair. "Don't give it another thought, Liza. We'll get him out."

"How?" she persisted.

He winked at her. "Have I failed Benedict Bunny yet?"

Kaitlin wrapped a comforting arm around her sister. "He'll get him back, Liza. Don't worry."

"I don't know," Zack's youngest son said. "It's dark in that hole. I wouldn't stick my arm in there."

Liza turned tear-filled eyes to Rafael. "Do you think Benedict Bunny is scared in there?"

"No." He went down on one knee. "Benedict Bunny isn't scared of anything."

Elena's daughter, who still sat by the hole, pointed to the opening. "Your arm won't fit in there, Uncle Rafael. You're too big."

"Think so?" he asked, and leaned down to look in the slot.

"Yeah," his nephew assured him. "No way."

Rafael grinned at him. "Have a little faith, Chip. I'm a pro at this."

"You mean she did it before?" Chip asked, incredulous. Molly nodded. "Lots of times."

Liza pressed close to Rafael's shoulder. "How you gonna do it, Rafael? You just gotta get him out of there."

"Well—" he looked at the hole "—I think if we try the coat hanger, we might shove him farther in."

Liza caught her breath. "You can't do that."

"Yeah," Chip said. "Then you might never get him out."

"Chip," his father said.

Chip shot an apologetic look at Liza. "Uncle Rafael is smart, though. He'll figure it out."

Rafael laughed. "Thanks for your confidence."

"Sure," Chip said, and shrugged.

Elena tapped an impatient foot. "Okay, the suspense is killing me. What are we going to do?"

Rafael glanced at Seb. "Can you take the rest of the jamb off?"

"I could. I'm just not certain I can match the wood. This place is an historic landmark. I was trying to minimize the damage." He looked at Cora. "Your call."

She wiped a hand through her tangled hair. "Can you take it off *carefully?*"

He nodded. "I can try."

An anxious three minutes passed while Seb painstakingly worked at the ancient square-head nails.

The kids grew restless. Liza shifted from one foot to the other and visibly tried not to ask questions. Elena chewed on her thumbnail. Zack braced one shoulder against the wall and watched the situation unfold with a benevolence Cora found fascinating in light of Rafael's description of his un-yielding older sibling.

"Almost," Seb promised as he pried loose another nail.

"How much longer?" Liza asked.

Rafael pulled her onto his lap. "Just a few more minutes."

Seb pried at the aged wood with gentle persistence until finally it slipped free with a groan. "Got it."

Liza scrambled off Rafael's lap and hurried toward the exposed hole. "Is he in there?"

Rafael grabbed her before she put her hand inside the opening. "Easy. No telling what's in there."

"I bet its got bugs," Molly said.

Liza clutched at Rafael's arms. "Can you get him out?"

Rafael looked in the opening, then gingerly extended his arm. "I can reach him," he told her.

The crowd seemed to hold its collective breath. Rafael withdrew his arm. In his large hand, he held a dusty Benedict Bunny and a slender, leather-bound volume. He looked at Cora. "I think Benedict Bunny may be a hero, after all," he said.

Cora gasped. "My God."

"What is it?" Margie asked.

Kaitlin held one hand to her mouth. "It's another of Abigail Conrad's diaries."

Rafael nodded, then looked at the opening. "And there are more," he said. "A lot more."

Chapter Eleven

*The woman has cast her lot now, and I can only pray
I reach her in time to keep her from doing something
foolish.*

Juan Rodriguez del Flores
Captain's Log, 1 October 1862

Elena was the first to break the story. They all watched it
together that afternoon on the national news channel. Elena
had called in a camera crew and put together a hastily edited
piece that explained the significance of Rafael's find and
Cora's research.

More than twenty volumes had been stashed in the wall.
Cora and Rafael had taken them to the lab for an initial
inspection. Two of the diaries, they discovered, were dated
the same month and year of Abigail's purported death and
del Flores's disappearance. Cora felt confident that further
study would yield information confirming Rafael's suspi-
cions about the possible location of the *Isabela*. The temptation was strong, but she resisted the urge to search through
the volumes without first taking the precaution to preserve
the moisture-damaged pages. The process would take several days, she knew, so they'd left the lab to report their
discovery to his family.

With Cora's permission, Elena released the story.

Her report had a predictable effect. Rafael's PR firm had three representatives on site in Cora's home by nightfall. The phone rang constantly. Cora lost count of how many quotes she gave. Rafael, she noted, watched her carefully throughout the day, as if he was unsure how she would handle the pressure.

By midday, most of his family was making plans to leave. Cora found herself reluctant to let them go. She'd never enjoyed the support of a large family, and especially not during times of personal chaos. Their presence and their unbounded optimism bolstered her courage. She didn't have the time or energy to ask herself why. Despite her insistence that she wanted them there, they seemed determined.

Cora rubbed a knot at the back of her neck as she watched Seb toss Margie's suitcase into her car for her. "All packed," Margie told Cora with a bright smile. "That's the advantage of traveling solo. No kids and no husband to corral."

"Do you really have to leave?" Cora asked her. "You said you could stay until Monday."

Margie hesitated. Seb was striding toward them. "I think things are crazy enough around here without us around."

Cora's impatience had been steadily building since the lunchtime announcement that the Adriano clan was deserting. "It's my house, Margie. Don't I get to decide who stays and who goes?"

Margie looked at her closely. "You're just being polite."

Cora gritted her teeth. "I never do things I don't want to do just to be polite. Ask your brother."

"Cora…" Margie looked worried. Seb had reached them now, and she looked to him for support.

"I'm serious." Cora indicated the house with a sweep of her hand. "It's becoming painfully obvious that within the next several hours, there are going to be reporters and God knows who else crawling all over this place. I'd at least like to have my friends around when it happens. If nothing else, I could post one of you in all the rooms to watch my stuff.''

Seb put an arm around his sister's shoulders. He looked carefully at Cora. "With all the kids—" he shrugged "—it's too much for you to deal with. We're not leaving Cape Marr— we're just going to a hotel."

"And I have no say at all in this?"

Seb shrugged. "Zack felt—"

Cora frowned. "Zack? Zack did this?"

Margie shook her head. "You're reading this wrong, Cora. We all talked it over, and Zack pointed out that—"

She clenched her hands at her sides. "That's it," she muttered, and reached for the screen door. Maybe it was the effects of a mostly sleepless night coupled with the adrenaline surge from finding Abigail's diaries. More likely, it was the fear she'd been battling that this insane happiness she felt was slipping inexorably through her fingers. Whatever was causing her current agitation, Cora had finally found a focus for it.

She located Zack in her living room. He had a pile of luggage and was issuing quiet instructions to two of his sons. When she stormed into the room, he halted midsentence and looked at her with raised eyebrows. "Cora. Is something wrong?"

"Yes," she fumed. "Sit down."

Zack's two boys looked at her openmouthed. Zack tapped them both on the head to get their attention. "Sam, go find your mother and see if she needs help. Teddy, check on your brothers."

The two gave Cora a wide berth as they raced from the room.

"What's on your mind, Cora?" Zack asked.

He didn't sit, she noted. He was used to giving orders,

not taking them. "It was your idea to run everyone out of here today."

"You don't need us underfoot."

No wonder Raphael found him so irritating, she thought. He had an implacable calm that made her itch to penetrate it. "I'm a thirty-year-old, highly educated, self-sufficient person, thank you very much. I think I'm perfectly capable of making my own decisions."

His eyebrows lifted higher. "Cora—"

"If I wanted you to leave, I'd tell you. Where do you get off making a decision like that?"

"I didn't think—"

"No, you didn't." Her anger was gathering steam, and she wasn't sure why. "You didn't think that the next few days are going to be challenging and difficult for both your brother and for me. You didn't think that his entire professional reputation might be riding on what we discover in those books. You didn't think that depending on what we find, he could either realize his dream or become the subject of unfair ridicule by a bunch of intellectual egomaniacs who would love to take him down a notch. Do you think he wants to be alone right now? Do you think he wants to know that not even his family is willing to stand by him and see this through to the end?"

Zack dropped onto the couch. "This isn't—"

Cora made an impatient gesture with her hands. "You know, from the moment I met you, I've been trying to figure out just what it is about the two of you that makes it impossible for you to get along."

"We get along," he insisted.

"Sure. Like oil and water—you get along just fine until somebody shakes the bottle. Then both of you start struggling for distance."

"I think you're reading this the wrong way."

"Am I? Then tell me why you've issued marching orders to your entire family."

He looked stung. "I did not issue orders."

"You don't have to. All you have to do is express a preference, and everyone falls into step."

"You don't—"

"Except for Rafael. He's the only one who stands his ground, and you can't stand it, can you?"

Zack's gaze darted beyond her shoulder to the door. Contemplating escape? she wondered. "I think you're reading this the wrong way."

"Well, I don't," she said. "And you might be able to get away with this patriarchal dictatorship on your own turf, but you're not doing it on mine. Your brother deserves to know he has the support of his family, and frankly, so do I. So you can just go out there—" she jabbed an angry finger at the door "—and tell them all to get their bags back in here. Because nobody's leaving this house until I say so."

His eyes sparkled with amusement as he looked at the doorway again. "I can see why you like her."

Cora glanced at the door. Rafael stood with one shoulder propped against the frame, his expression frank and admiring. "My thoughts exactly."

"Hi," she muttered irritably.

He sauntered into the room. "Hi. What's going on?"

"Cora was just telling me that I'm behaving like an autocrat."

With a laugh, Rafael eased an arm around her waist and pulled her close. "No kidding?"

Cora frowned at Zack. "I don't think this is funny."

Rafael nuzzled her neck. "Really? I think it's hilarious."

She elbowed his ribs. "Stop. I'm serious."

Raising his head, he gave her an inquiring look. "I can see that."

She looked from one man to the other. "I just think that

the next couple of days are going to be extremely stressful for both of us. We have no idea what we're going to find in those diaries.'' She examined his expression closely. ''You realize—''

''That they could invalidate every theory I have. Sure.''

''And if that happens...''

''I'll have to deal with all the Jerry Heaths of the world who are yearning to take me down a peg or two? Honey, I know that.'' He placed his hands on her waist, then turned her to face him. ''All I ever wanted was the truth. I'd like us to find out that I've been right all along, but if we don't, we don't.''

''Aren't you worried at all?''

''Yes,'' he admitted. ''I hate to eat crow. It tastes like hell.''

She gave Zack a meaningful glance. ''It's easier to stomach if someone else eats it with you.''

Rafael caught her chin and made her look at him. ''I think he's trying to be considerate.''

''Thanks for that, at least,'' his brother drawled sarcastically.

Cora frowned. ''I don't want them to leave.''

''We're going to have reporters everywhere,'' Rafael said. ''You sure you want all this company?''

''Absolutely sure,'' she said with such conviction it surprised her. There had been a time when she couldn't imagine having to share herself with so many people. Yet Rafael's family—in stark contrast to any memory she had of her own—seemed to make burdens lighter. She didn't stop to consider why. She looked at Zack. ''Please,'' she said simply.

With a short nod he rose and started for the door. He laid a hand on his brother's shoulder as he passed. ''I'll go see if August tries to kill me when I tell her to unpack all those suitcases again.''

"Good luck," Rafael said with a chuckle.

Zack made it to the foyer when a sudden and demanding knock on the door arrested his progress. He shot Cora a quizzical look. "Expecting anyone else?"

Cora shook her head. "No."

Rafael scowled. "It's either Jerry Heath, Henry Willers or a reporter."

"Already?" Cora asked.

"Vultures start circling the minute they see blood."

Cora drew a deep breath and moved toward the door. "If it's Jerry," she warned, casting Rafael an amused look, "don't bother trying to stop me. This time, I'm slugging him."

"I'll hold him down for you," he promised.

"And if it's a reporter—" she reached for the knob "—Benedict Bunny is unavailable. So you're in charge."

She pulled open the door, then stood still in utter shock when a visibly fuming Lauren stormed into the foyer like a ship in full sail. Seb and Margie were standing on the porch where Cora had left them. They watched Cora's sister warily. Lauren, who always had reveled in playing an audience, dramatically waved a newspaper in front of Cora and announced in a shrill voice, "I have come for my children."

Zack leaned back on the sofa next to his wife. "I'm not sure what you want me to say," he told his brother.

Rafael stopped pacing and looked at him. "Are you kidding? I want you to say that since it's obviously in the best interest of those three girls to stay here with Cora, the law understands that and is on their side."

Cora held out her hand to him. "Rafael—"

"Dammit," he swore, and resumed his pacing. It had been a harrowing afternoon. Lauren's untimely appearance and melodramatic announcement had brought the children running from all over the house. At the sound of her mother's voice, Liza had raced down the stairs, clutching her bunny, exuberant at the thought of seeing Lauren again. A wary Molly and an openly hostile Kaitlin had followed. As had most of Rafael's nephews and nieces. The small crowd in the foyer witnessed an ugly and demoralizing scene where Lauren had brushed past Liza's outstretched arms to hurl angry accusations at Cora.

Within moments Liza and Molly were in tears, and Kaitlin had stepped forward to confront her mother. Rafael could still feel the impact of Cora's wounded look when Lauren had turned a venomous gaze on her and accused her of stealing the loyalty of her children. Bad turned to worse when Zack's adopted sons, several of whom bore scars of similar confrontations, had joined the fray to defend their new friends.

"Stop yelling, lady," an angry Lucas had declared. "You're scaring the kid." He'd picked up Liza, who had begun to sob.

"Yeah," added Sam, crossing to Molly's side. "You're screeching."

"It's unbecoming," Beau announced with a derisive snort.

Kaitlin had turned her teary gaze to Cora. "I don't want to go," she'd said. "Please don't make me."

Lauren looked first at Rafael, then at Cora. "I can't believe this," she yelled. "I can't believe my own sister would try to turn my children against me."

Cora shook her head. "Lauren, it's not like—"

"I leave them with you so I can enjoy a small vacation from all the stress of being a single parent, and not only do I find my private life flaunted in the pages of a scandal sheet..." She paused to histrionically wave the newspaper article Cora had shown him weeks ago. Rafael scowled. Lauren gathered steam for another barrage. "But I come back here to find that you've poisoned my children's minds. There's no telling what's been going on—"

"Shut up, Lauren," Cora snapped. She'd seemed to have lost her composure. The abrupt command left a speechless Lauren with her mouth hanging open in shock. "You don't know what you're talking about," Cora snapped as she took a step closer to her sister. "And now is not the time to discuss this."

"I'm here for my children," Lauren declared again, her voice rising even higher. "Are you going to deny my right to them?"

Rafael's patience had snapped. "No one's going anywhere right now," he announced. He took Liza from Lucas and held her against his chest. She buried her wet face against his neck. "You're upsetting them," he told Lauren.

Liza had raised teary eyes to her mother. "Don't be mad, Mama. Don't be mad."

Lauren's gaze flickered to her daughter. Rafael saw a slight softening of her features. Lauren reached for the child. Liza went willingly into her mother's arms. "It's all right, baby," Lauren muttered. "Mama's here."

"It's about time," Kaitlin had said. "It certainly took you long enough."

Lauren turned her shocked expression to Kaitlin. "Sugar—"

"No," Kaitlin said angrily. "I'm not going with you." She hurried toward the stairs. "You can't make me."

Cora held out a hand to her. "Kaitlin…" The girl was already racing up the stairs.

Lauren had glared at Cora. "I hope you're proud of yourself. What did you say to her to make her hate me?"

Cora gritted her teeth. "Stop being melodramatic, Lauren. She's angry. What did you expect after you dumped them here and didn't call for over a month?"

Lauren had the grace to look embarrassed. "I meant to..." she started.

"Like Mother always meant to and never did?" Cora pressed. "It's not enough, Lauren. They needed more from you."

Lauren had angrily shifted Liza to her hip. "How dare you tell me how to raise my children. As if you know anything about what it's like to be a parent."

Rafael had heard enough. During her mother's discourse, Molly had grabbed hold of his hand and was now clutching it so tightly, he could feel the child's pulse. He picked her up. "It's all right," he told her. "Everything's going to be all right." Looking at Lauren, he said carefully. "I think we can find a way to discuss this so it won't be so upsetting to your daughters."

Her gaze had swung to him. She resembled her sister, he noted absently, but she looked like a harsher, more worn version of Cora. Her face lacked the tender expression that made Cora so alluring. Her eyes lacked the intelligence that made Cora's sparkle. "If you think," Lauren said brusquely, "that I'm going to let a renowned playboy tell me what's best for my children—"

"He's not," Liza insisted, raising her head from her mother's shoulder. "He's not a playboy." She had no idea what the word meant, but her mother's tone had told her it wasn't complimentary. "Rafael takes care of us. Don't be mean to him."

Lauren's expression darkened. "I can't believe this."

Zack intervened. "I think Rafael's right. This discussion is best had in private."

August and Margie moved forward in automatic response and began gathering children, urging them toward the stairs. Lucas belligerently held his ground. "I'm not a little kid," he said.

Seb threw an arm around his nephew's shoulders. "Nope. So you get to help us keep order upstairs."

Lucas looked to Zack for guidance. His father inclined his head toward the stairs in a silent directive. The boy hesitated, but finally yielded. Margie took Molly from Rafael. Liza allowed August to carry her. When only Cora, Lauren, Rafael and Zack remained in the foyer, Lauren had tossed the newspaper to the floor at Cora's feet. "I can't believe you, Cora. I never thought you'd do something like this."

"Lauren, why are you so angry?"

Her sister's laugh was harsh. "Why? Why? My God, I come back here and my children are in hysterics at the thought of going home with me, and you have to ask me why?"

"Will you stop thinking about yourself for once?" Cora shot back. "Of course they're upset. You barged in here like a hurricane. You didn't expect them to react to that?"

"I didn't expect them," Lauren said with irritating sweetness, "to look at me like I'm their enemy."

"Then maybe you should have tried thinking about them often enough to at least send a postcard. The only time they heard from you was when you called and scared Kaitlin half to death."

"What did you expect?" Lauren stomped her foot like an impatient teenager. "I went out for a pack of cigarettes and saw my children's picture on the front of a scandal sheet. It never occurred to me that my self-righteous, judgmental, oh-so-superior sister would expose my children to—" she waved an angry hand at Rafael "—to this."

"Oh, please." Cora crossed her arms. "As if George the married real-estate broker and your current flavor-of-the-month is the perfect role model."

Lauren gasped. "How dare you!"

"All right." Zack stepped between the two women.

"This is going nowhere." He leveled an icy look at Lauren. "You're not doing anyone any good by throwing around rash accusations about which you clearly know nothing."

"Who the hell are you?" she demanded.

"Cora's lawyer," he said smoothly.

Lauren's expression turned pale. "Her..." She looked at Cora. "You hired a lawyer?"

Rafael had to hide a grin. "Evidently," he drawled. He ignored Cora's frown.

Zack kept his gaze trained on Lauren. "And I'm afraid I'm going to have to insist that you leave."

"I'm not leaving without my children."

He held up a hand. "Surely you can see that it'll take some time to get them packed and ready." Rafael scowled at him. Zack ignored the dark look and continued to talk to Lauren. "I'm sure you have plenty of details to take care of before you'll be ready to leave with them." He pointed meaningfully to the two-seat convertible rental car Lauren had left parked in the driveway. "You'll have to find appropriate transportation."

Lauren's forehead creased. "George is coming tonight. He'll rent something bigger."

"Good," Zack continued. He angled his body so she felt crowded. She took a couple of steps toward the door. "Then I think you can see why a solid night's rest would benefit everyone."

"I don't want—"

Zack pulled open the door. "The children will travel better if they aren't tired. Is George driving back with you?"

Lauren looked indecisive. "He hates it when they whine."

Zack nodded and put a hand on her elbow. "I'm sure he does. You'll want to discuss this with him first, naturally."

"I guess..." She had one foot on the threshold.

"What time tomorrow should we expect you?" Zack asked.

"Uh…"

"How about ten?" he suggested. "That'll give Cora plenty of time to have the girls dressed and fed before you get here." When Lauren hesitated, he added, "Or would George like to participate in the morning rituals?"

That seemed to make up Lauren's mind. She stepped onto the porch and threw a final angry look at Cora. "Have them ready when I get here, Cora. I'm taking them no matter what you say."

Zack shut the door in her face. When Cora made a choked sound, Rafael looked at her sharply. She had one hand pressed to her mouth. Her eyes brimmed with unshed tears. He pulled her into his arms. "It's all right, baby," he said into her hair. "It's all right."

She clung to him. That was his first clue that she was losing a battle with despair. He rubbed her back as he looked at his older brother. "Shh. Don't cry. We'll fix it," he promised. "I swear we'll fix it."

That had been two hours ago. Cora had been unable to stop the tears. By unspoken consent, Seb, Margie and the rest of his family had taken all the children to the beach for a much-needed break from the tension in the house. Kaitlin, Molly and Liza had begged to stay with Cora, but she'd finally persuaded them to go. Rafael's PR representatives were using Cora's office at the university as their base. All the calls had been diverted to them, and Cora had taken her own phone off the hook. Now, when only August, Zack, Rafael and Cora were in the large house, it seemed unnaturally quiet. Rafael rotated his tense shoulders. "This is intolerable."

Cora stood and walked to him. "You don't have to do this," she said softly.

August nodded. "Zack's right, Rafael. You can't stop

Lauren from taking the girls with her. Your energy is better invested in helping them accept that.''

He ground his teeth in frustration as he looked at Cora. ''How can you just accept this? You know what she'll do to them.''

Cora looked stung. ''She won't hurt them,'' she said. ''She's self-centered, but she's not a terrible parent.''

''She ignored them all summer.''

Zack's hand rested on his wife's knee. ''But she brought them somewhere that she knew they'd be cared for and safe. It's not like she abandoned them, Rafael.''

He scowled at his brother. ''I cannot believe that you, of all people, are taking her side.''

''I'm not taking sides,'' Zack insisted.

August covered his hand with her own. ''Rafael, the law—''

''The law sucks,'' he bit out. ''Dammit, those children are better off with Cora, and anyone in their right mind can see that.''

Cora shook her head. ''No, Rafael. That's not true. She's their mother. They need to be with her.''

''How the hell can you say that? What's going to happen when George decides he's tired of them? Or your sister wants another vacation from motherhood? Then what?''

''Then they'll come here, and I'll love them,'' she said softly. He could hear the hint of tears in her voice.

''Cora—''

''It's okay,'' she assured him. ''It's really okay.''

''The hell it is,'' he muttered. He didn't like that desolate look he saw in her eyes. He looked at Zack. ''You're a lawyer, dammit. Do something.''

''Rafael,'' Zack said, his tone pure frustration, ''you don't honestly think that those girls would be better off having to choose sides during a court battle, do you?''

''In the long run—''

"No," Zack said. "It's too much stress for them and you know it. Cora is absolutely right. The best thing she can do for them is let them know that they always have a safe place—a place where someone loves them."

Cora wasn't looking at him now. She'd turned to stare out the window. Frustration clawed at his guts. He felt powerless and he hated it. The emotional roller coaster they'd been on for the past few days was having a definite effect on her. Finding the diaries this morning should have been one of the greatest moments of Cora's life, but she'd been steadily withdrawing from him ever since. Despite her vehement defense of him to Zack, he could practically feel her pulling away. He crossed the room and put his hands on her shoulders. When she tensed, but didn't face him, fear surged inside him. "What do you want me to do?" he asked her quietly.

Cora shrugged and pressed her fist to her mouth. "There's nothing we can do."

"Cora..."

She shook her head. "I don't want to be upset when they get back," she said. "It'll make it harder for them."

Instinct told him to press her for details, but he didn't heed it. Instead, he pressed a kiss to the top her head. "I'm here for you," he promised. "Whatever you need from me, I'm here for you."

She didn't respond.

And that scared him most of all.

Chapter Twelve

Dearest,

My minutes pass like hours now. I wait anxiously and pace my room praying that you are well, longing for your voice, trusting that you will come for me—just as you promised. Hasten, dearest. Oh, please hasten.

Abigail
5 November 1862

When the time finally came, Cora fought for the strength to break the news to her nieces without losing her composure. Rafael's family had brought the children back to the house late in the afternoon, and Cora and Rafael sat with the three girls and explained, as best they could, what had transpired. Liza sat very still on Cora's bed, her eyes wide with confusion, her hands maintaining a stranglehold on Benedict Bunny. Molly's anxious gaze darted from her older sister to Cora and back again throughout the discourse. Kaitlin watched Cora, her expression indecipherable, her hands folded in her lap. When Cora finished telling them that Lauren would come for them in the morning, no one spoke for long, tense moments.

Finally Molly raised pleading eyes to Cora. "Do you want us to leave, Aunt Cora?"

Cora caught her breath. "Oh, Mol. No, I don't want you to leave. Goodbyes are always hard, but you miss your mother, don't you?"

Molly hesitated, then nodded. Liza chimed in, "I miss Mama. I miss my bed."

"Me, too," Molly said.

Rafael took Cora's hand in his large one. She welcomed his warmth and his strength. "I'll miss you like crazy," Cora told the girls. She managed a smile for Liza. "What am I going to do without Benedict Bunny around?"

Liza's eyes widened as if that possibility was too much to even contemplate. Cora ruffled her hair. "I'm glad he'll be around to take care of you."

"Me, too," the child whispered.

Rafael winked at her. "Just be careful where you put him. Somebody else might not be as good at fishing him out of dark spots as I am."

Liza's lips trembled and she shook her head. "George wouldn't get him. I know he wouldn't."

Molly patted Liza's leg in a surprisingly adult gesture. "It's okay, Liza. Kaitlin and me'll help you keep up with him better. He won't get lost." She looked to her older sister for confirmation. "Won't we?"

Kaitlin nodded, but still didn't speak. Cora studied her oldest niece and felt her heart break. "Kaitlin," she prompted. "Sweetie, are you all right?"

Kaitlin's forehead creased. "I guess so."

"You're sure?" Cora prompted.

The child frowned. "What's going to happen next time?" she asked softly, so softly that Cora wasn't sure she'd heard her correctly.

"What?"

"Next time," Kaitlin said, her voice stronger. "What's

going to happen to us the next time Mama wants to go somewhere without us?''

''She'll leave us,'' Molly wailed. ''Where will she leave us?''

Kaitlin grabbed Molly's hand. ''I won't let anything happen to you,'' she told her younger sister.

''Oh, girls...'' Cora moved from her chair to sit with them on the bed. Liza climbed into her lap. Molly and Kaitlin curled against her side. ''Listen to me.'' She smoothed their hair away from their flushed, teary faces. ''You can always come to me. All you have to do is call me, and I'll come get you. Anywhere.''

''Even Florida?'' Molly asked as if she thought of it as the most remote place on earth.

Cora smiled at her. ''Even Florida, Mol. Wherever you are. I will not let you be alone. Not ever.''

Liza sniffed. ''What if you got other people here?''

''It wouldn't matter,'' Cora said.

Molly picked up the thread. ''But what if you're gone away somewhere and we can't find you?''

''I'll check my messages every day,'' Cora promised. ''If you call, I'll know.''

''But what if,'' Molly went on, ''you can't get there and we have to stay with someone really mean?''

''Then I'll break the door down and take you away with me.''

Molly stared at her, wide-eyed. ''Really?''

Cora shot Rafael a quick glance. ''Really. Rafael promised to teach me how.''

Kaitlin looked at Rafael. ''I think you and Aunt Cora should get married,'' she said.

Cora choked. Rafael's eyebrows lifted. ''Oh?''

''Yes,'' the child said. ''Then she wouldn't be alone. She'll be alone without us.''

Cora's throat tightened. She pushed aside the thought. ''I

will not be alone,'' she assured the girls. ''I'll have an entire summer of memories to keep me company.''

''Memories?'' Molly looked puzzled.

''Yes.'' Cora gently caressed her cheek. ''Close your eyes, and I'll show you.''

Molly frowned, but complied. ''You, too,'' Cora told Liza. Liza dropped her head back in Cora's lap and shut her eyes. Cora glanced at Kaitlin. The older girl looked at her for long seconds, seeking something, then obediently closed her eyes. Cora stroked Liza's back. ''Now,'' she said tenderly, ''let's say that you're somewhere far, far away—''

''Like Florida?'' Molly asked.

''Like Florida,'' Cora agreed. She met Rafael's intense gaze and wondered what he was thinking. He was watching her so closely she could almost feel his scrutiny. Deliberately she returned her attention to the children. ''And you're sitting there one day,'' she continued, ''and suddenly, you remember something that happened in this house. What would you remember, Molly?''

Molly frowned in concentration, but kept her eyes shut. Then her face brightened. ''I'd remember that I like your chocolate-chip waffles.''

Liza's eyes popped open. ''I wanted to say that!''

Cora encouraged her to shut her eyes again. ''Can you think of something else, Liza?''

''Um…yes,'' Liza announced. ''I remember going to the ocean. I liked the beach.''

''Me, too,'' Molly said.

''Good,'' Cora responded. ''What else?''

Molly giggled. ''I remember the night we fought with the pillows and slept in the living room.''

''Me, too,'' Liza said. ''And Rafael made hot chocolate and mine had a big marshmallow like I like it.''

''Uh-huh,'' Cora said. ''What about the attic?''

"Oh!" Molly gushed. "I love the attic. We liked looking for stuff with you and Rafael."

Liza nodded vigorously. "Benedict Bunny liked that too."

"Aunt Cora," Molly continued, "if I think really hard, I can see you sitting on the porch in the rocking chair reading to us."

"Can you?"

"Yes. You're wearing your blue sweatshirt."

"Where are you?" Cora asked.

"On the swing," Molly responded.

"I'm on the rug," Liza said, recalling the braided rug where she would often curl up at Cora's feet.

"And Kaitlin's next to me," Molly added.

Cora glanced at Kaitlin. Her eyes were still closed, but her lips had turned up into a smile. "Good," Cora encouraged them. "Anything else?"

"Rafael," Molly said. "He's teaching Liza how to dance."

"And saving Benedict Bunny," Liza added.

Kaitlin tilted her head against Cora's shoulder. "And telling us stories about Abigail and del Flores."

Cora glanced at Rafael. His expression was intense. "Are they good stories?" she prompted, still watching him.

"Oh, yes," Kaitlin breathed. "They're wonderful.

Cora kept her gaze trained on Rafael. "I think so, too," she said. His expression didn't change. Cora held his gaze a moment longer, then looked at her nieces. "So now," she said, "all you have to do when you miss me or Rafael or you want to remember what we did here, all you have to do is close your eyes. I'll be right there in your memories waiting for you."

Molly opened her eyes and a large tear trickled down her cheek. "It won't be the same."

"I know, sweetheart," Cora said. "But you'll come back sooner than you think."

Liza sniffled and sat up. "Aunt Cora?"

"What, baby doll?"

"I love you."

Cora hugged her close and fought a fresh surge of tears. "I love you, too."

RAFAEL HELD CORA to him that night and wished she would scream or cry or lash out or something. Anything would be better than the implacable calm that had shrouded her through the evening. While his family had accomplished the Herculean task of keeping everyone's spirits afloat during dinner and the too-long evening that followed, he'd watched Cora. His nieces and nephews had risen admirably to the occasion. They'd made fervent promises of visits and e-mail and instant messaging meant to settle the fears of their new friends. Kaitlin, Molly and Liza responded with growing cheer.

But Cora, Rafael noted, appeared to have found some deeply buried reservoir of stoicism that was about to drive him mad. When the children had finally been put to bed, he had felt unaccustomedly awkward. Cora stood outside the girls' rooms for long minutes, simply staring at their sleeping forms. She had seemed completely untouchable, simultaneously strong and vulnerable—like a priceless piece of glass—able to withstand phenomenal pressure and heat, yet extremely fragile. When he'd said her name, she'd looked at him with a vacancy in her eyes that had him struggling for balance.

When, he wondered, had she become more than a passion? When had she become so necessary to him? Uncertain, he'd kissed her gently and left her at her door. He'd been pleasantly surprised when she'd climbed the stairs minutes later to enter his room. He'd held up the sheet. Without a word, she'd slipped into the bed next to him.

He had not tried to make love to her, though he wondered now if he should have. If he coaxed a physical response from her, would an emotional response follow? He wasn't sure. Her fingers were tapping a random rhythm on his chest, telling him that she was still awake.

It went against his nature to let life happen to him, he decided. He would make her respond to him, even if she killed him for it. "Cora."

"Hmm?" She sounded noncommittal.

He stroked his hand down her spine. "Tell me what you're thinking."

"I'm glad your family is here," she said.

He waited. She didn't elaborate. Frustrated, he shifted her until she lay on top of him. She raised wary eyes to his. "What?" she said.

"You know what." He smoothed her hair from her face. "Talk to me. Tell me what's going on in your head."

Cora hesitated. He saw the indecision in her gaze. Deliberately he continued to stroke her back with slow, soothing sweeps of his hand. "Unless there's something else you'd rather do," he teased her gently.

She managed a slight smile. "There might be."

"Hmm. Too bad. I want to talk."

That sent her eyebrows up. "Are you kidding?"

"Hard to believe, I know." He rubbed her lower lip with his thumb. "It's a first for me."

She dropped her head to his chest. "If I talk about it, I'll probably get hysterical."

"That's all right."

He felt her sad smile against his skin. "Are you a glutton for punishment?"

"No. I just know that you're hurting. I don't want you to think you have to do it alone."

She trembled. "They'll be all right," she said, sounding only half-convinced.

"Yes."

"They know I love them."

"Completely."

"They can count on me."

"Forever."

Her shoulders lurched on a sob. "I never felt that way," she admitted. "There was never anyone I could count on."

He swallowed. "Ah, baby, I know. I know."

She nodded. "You felt the same way, didn't you?"

He thought it over and realized that no, he hadn't felt that way. He could have counted on Zack, just like everyone else. Zack would have been there for him. Rafael was the one no one had been able to count on. He didn't answer her. She was rubbing her cheek against his chest. "I don't ever want them to feel that way," Cora said.

"They won't," he vowed. No matter what, he would never allow that.

Silence stretched between them as fathomless as a starless night sky. He resisted the urge to ask again what she was thinking. He feared too much that she might be thinking that, once again, she'd trusted someone she couldn't count on. When the time came, he wouldn't be there for her. Her silence lasted so long he thought she might have fallen asleep. "Rafael?" she finally said.

"Yes?" his voice sounded gravelly.

"Would you...would you make love to me?"

The vulnerability in her tone ripped a piece of his heart out. Gently he rolled to his side so she lay against him. He took her hand and laid it against his heart while he held her gaze. "With the greatest of pleasure, Cora," he vowed, and set about showing her, the only way he knew how, how much she had come to mean to him.

THAT HAD BEEN five days ago, Cora realized numbly as she glanced from the pile of research papers on her desk to the small calendar. It sat in a shallow tray made of brightly colored paper clips. Liza had made it with Rafael's help one rainy afternoon. The girls had called every night since their departure. They sounded happy, which helped ease the lingering ache Cora felt when she remembered the teary goodbye they'd shared the morning Lauren and George had come to get them.

Molly had been full of stories about the ride home. Liza reported that George had purchased a new outfit for Benedict Bunny. Kaitlin was taking art classes at home. Cora had finally let herself weep when she'd found the gaily painted pottery bowl that Kaitlin had made on their first outing with Rafael sitting on her bed. The note inside had simply said, "Thank you for teaching me so much. I love you, Kaitlin."

Rafael had found her clutching the note and sobbing into a pillow. Wordlessly he'd joined her on the bed and held her until the storm had passed. Cora had no reasonable explanation for the ache that had started that morning in her chest and steadily spread until it permeated every limb. But she knew that even if this unrelenting pain was the price of having loved them—her nieces and Rafael—it was better than the unemotional wasteland she'd lived in for most of her life.

Over the past few days his family had departed. The large house seemed unbearably quiet without them. Rafael alone remained. Like Cora, he stayed deeply immersed in researching the additional diaries they'd discovered. The media scrutiny was intense. There were more and more demands on his time as he and Cora released details of what they were learning from the journals. Del Flores had, it seemed, intended to sail north to Cape Marr. Abigail seemed certain he was coming for her. Her writings had grown more sporadic, shorter and less detailed. Often, she hinted that she feared someone was watching her. She would beg del Flores to hurry back. The intensity was heartrending. Cora found herself deeply moved by the woman's distress.

Yet she and Rafael never spoke of the research, as if they both felt the same sense of dishonor at intruding on something so intimate and painful. Instead, he entertained her with stories of his past expeditions, and he made love to her with such intensity that she felt her heart break every time.

He showed her what it was like to live in reckless passion, to embrace love without fear or insecurity. She could never—would never—go back again. For that, she would always love him. He had made her so much stronger than she could have been on her own.

And now, she thought, it was time to set him free.

Cora scooped up the papers on her desk and tossed them into her briefcase. Today she'd found the key to the last lock that chained him to Cape Marr. Tonight she would give it to him—because she loved him too much not to.

RAFAEL LOOKED UP, the phone still pressed to his ear, when he heard Cora enter the house. She looked tired. She'd looked tired since the day the girls had left. He'd been on the verge of calling one of his sisters to beg for advice more times than he could count, but the constant pressure of the media interviews, television appearances and academic inquiries had kept him on the run. She offered him a small smile when she heard him give a curt answer to a reporter and set her briefcase down on the counter.

Rafael listened, irritated and only half-attentive to the rambling voice on the other end of the phone line. When Cora walked across the room and put her arms around his waist, he forgot whom he was talking to. When she pressed her lips to the hollow of his throat, he simply hung up. He gathered her to him and kissed her deeply. Immediately the phone started to ring again.

Rafael jerked the cord from the wall with a sharp tug. Cora laughed, but didn't stop kissing him. In a distant part of the house, he could hear the other extension ringing. He cupped her head with his hand and held her still so he could fully taste her. She made a little mewling sound in the back of her throat that drove him wild.

He kissed her until the room spun around them. Finally he dragged his mouth away and across her cheekbone. "Cora," he breathed. Would he ever have enough of her?

She pulled at his shoulders, demanding more from him. "Rafael." The way she said his name ricocheted off his nerve endings. She moved one hand to the buttons of his shirt. "Rafael, I want you closer."

He was already shoving her suit jacket off her shoulders. She jerked her arms free of the restriction. Beneath the jacket, she wore a lacy camisole that cupped her body in a fascinating combination of shadow and light. He pressed his palm against her. She arched her back and sighed. "Closer," she murmured. "Now."

He would have taken her to bed, but Cora had other plans. She didn't let him get past the table. Intrigued and totally bewitched, he willingly surrendered.

And ten minutes later he found himself marveling again at this incredible woman who affected him so deeply. He kissed a mark on her shoulder that was already turning blue. "I hurt you," he said.

She shook her head. "No."

"You'll have bruises."

She tugged her skirt into place, then pulled the lacy camisole back over her breasts and tucked it into the waistband. "You might, too," she quipped.

Rafael froze while stepping into his jeans. He gave her a probing look. She hadn't teased him in a week. "Are you cracking a joke?"

That made her frown. "Have I been that boring lately?"

He finished pulling on his jeans, then walked barefoot across the room to take her in his arms. "Not boring," he said gently, "just sad. I've been worried."

"I miss the girls."

"Me, too."

Cora pushed her hair back from her face. "They sound happy, though. Kaitlin's enjoying her art classes."

"Yes." He tilted his head to the side. "You're sure you're all right?"

She nodded. "Yes. Sorry I've been pouting."

"You're entitled, Cora. It's been a tough week."

She shrugged. "I suppose. No tougher on me than it's been on you, though. I saw that piece in the *Times* today."

He winced. He had hoped to keep that one from her. The article, about the lack of progress on the Conrad diaries, had been a particularly blistering. The reporter had interviewed several of Rafael's most vocal critics, including a certain North Carolina legislator who frequently used the Underwater Archeology Unit's funding as a punching bag. "It wasn't so bad," he told her.

"No? Dr. Peter Rhimes questioned your effectiveness."

Rafael laughed. "Rhimes questions my effectiveness every time he gets the chance."

"If you don't find the *Isabela*, some people might say that your time here has been wasted."

She was going somewhere, and it gave him an uneasy feeling. "They might."

"You're functioning on state money, Rafael. They'll crucify you if you're wrong."

He shrugged. "Archeology isn't an exact science. We have to take risks. That's my style. Besides, we use significantly more private funding than public."

"But the pressure's on to find the ship."

"It is," he admitted. "But I'm not worried about it."

Her eyebrows lifted. "Really?"

"Really."

She looked almost disappointed. He looked at her closely. "Cora, what are you up to?"

She leaned back and crossed her arms. "I have something for you in my briefcase. Why don't you look at it?"

He could hear the blood pounding in his ears. Something told him the next several minutes would be some of the most profound of his life. He walked across the room and snapped open the locks on her briefcase. Inside lay a carefully preserved page of Abigail's diaries. He scanned the date—1862. It was one of the new volumes. Cora had highlighted a passage on the laminated page. He reached for it and realized his fingers were shaking.

"Read it," she prompted softly.

He looked at her swiftly, then held the page to the light. Abigail's firm script came into focus. "'I can hardly credit it, dearest,'" he read aloud. "'After days of fruitless search and waning hope, I stood on the widow's walk today and gazed at the sea through the glass you'd given me. I saw it then, that flash of red and blue against a white sail that told me you were coming for me—just as you promised. Father has insisted you are dead, lost at sea just a few months ago. My heart would have shattered with the news, dearest, but I knew it could not be true. You promised you would come. You promised you would find a way and that the winds would bring you to me this last time. You fly another's flag, I realize now, but the ship is yours. I could not have mistaken it, or the way my heart raced with the knowledge that very soon I will be in your arms again. Perhaps, in a few days, I will join you. My heart is full, dearest, and know that I await you with the most anxious longing for the sweetness of your presence.'"

He looked at Cora. Her eyes were shining. She smiled at him and said quietly, "You were right, all along. You were right."

He had imagined this moment for years, yet now, he felt a shocking absence of emotion. Cora crossed to him and took the paper from his hands. "Rafael," she said, "I couldn't believe it when I saw this today."

"He came for her," he said.

"Yes. And it goes on to describe an island where he'd promised to take her." Cora hugged him again. "The last entry is three days before Abigail's purported death."

"He took her with him."

"To an island he'd prepared." Cora beamed at him. "If the *Isabela* did sink, then del Flores sank it after they were safe in paradise."

He felt slightly dazzled. "You think so?"

Cora nodded. "He wouldn't have let anything happen to Abigail. I'm sure of it." She pressed against him. "He loved her." She paused. "And she loved him enough to risk everything for it."

Rafael crushed Cora to him so she wouldn't see the host of conflicting emotions on his face. She could have kept this information to herself, he knew, at least for a little while. She knew that by giving it to him, she was terminating whatever reasons he had for staying here. The administration at his office was already pressuring him to take a new assignment. Now, with evidence that del Flores's ship was, at the very least, far north of its supposed site, he could not justify remaining in Cape Marr when he should be organizing an expedition to locate it.

Cora was stroking his back and brushing featherlight kisses against his throat. Cora, he realized, who had been disappointed by so many people in her life, who had yearned for the attention of self-centered parents, who had longed for a deeper relationship with her shallow sister, who had grieved the absence of her three nieces whom she loved without reservation, had just given him license to walk out of her life. And she'd done it because she loved him. He knew that as surely as he knew his own name. Cora loved him.

The thought left him feeling shaken. Just like all the others, he would be one more deserter in a long string of people who had failed her.

Overwhelmed, he swept her into his arms and headed for the stairs. He could think of nothing except showing her how incredible, how indescribably, breathtakingly passionate and beautiful he found her. Perhaps she would forgive him then, for failing to be the man who could stay and love her.

Chapter Thirteen

There was a time when I thought I could deny what she's done to me. There was even a time when I thought I wanted to. But that time is no more. Because of her, I am better than I ever could be on my own. And soon, beloved, so soon, I will show you all the wonders of life.

Juan Rodriguez del Flores
Captain's Log, 13 June 1862

Zack frowned at his brother. "It's a little late, don't you think?" he asked. He was wearing a pair of low-slung sweatpants that suggested he'd rolled out of bed to answer the door.

Rafael frowned back. "You don't have to be rude. It took me a while to get here."

"It's two in the morning," Zack said.

Rafael gave his sister-in-law an apologetic look. "I'm sorry, August. I tried to get here earlier."

"I know," she said, and damn if she didn't look amused.

Bully for her, Rafael thought irritably. Personally he'd been in a foul mood since the morning nearly a month ago when he'd walked out of Cora's house. Technically Cora had all but thrown him out. The morning after she'd given him the page from Abigail's diary, she'd cheerily announced that he was free to leave.

In fact, she'd practically helped him pack. She'd stood in the door of his room and told him all the reasons it would be best for both of them if he hurried back to the office. She could finish the research without him, she said. He would be more effective if he went back to work and raised money for the expedition, she said. Now that the girls were gone, she didn't need him anymore, she said.

What she hadn't said, but what he'd seen written on her face, was that she wasn't about to let him disappoint her. She'd toss him out of her life before she'd stay up nights wondering how and where he was. She wanted a man she could count on—and was smart enough to know it wouldn't be him.

And his guts had been churning ever since. He shoved a hand through his hair with a sigh of exasperation, then held out an envelope to Zack. "Look, all I want is to give you this, and then I'll get out of your hair. It's for Cora."

His brother arched an eyebrow. "What do you want me to do with it?"

"I want you to look it over and make sure it's drafted correctly. I had one of the department lawyers draw it up, but I'd appreciate it if you'd review it."

Zack's expression turned curious. He reached for the envelope. "What is it?"

"It's a document stating that since Cora found the initial evidence indicating the location of the *Isabela,* then she's entitled to whatever benefits it might yield if we find it on this expedition."

August tugged her husband away from the door so that Rafael could enter their large, southern Virginia home. He was scheduled to sail out of the port at Norfolk the following day. He'd phoned ahead to tell them he was coming by that night. "How long will you be gone, Rafael?"

"I'm not sure," he said, accepting August's silent invitation and stepping into the house. "At least a month. Maybe longer."

Zack had pulled the document from the envelope and was scanning it with interest. He glanced up. "Are you going to find that damned thing this time?"

Rafael nodded. "I think so. The data looks good. And I have…a hunch." He rarely admitted things like that to his more pragmatic sibling.

Zack merely nodded and returned his gaze to the contract.

August thrust her hands into the pockets of her robe. "This is so exciting. The boys haven't stopped talking about it since we got back from Cape Marr."

Zack's lips twitched. "I think they'd rather go with you than stay here and go to school."

Rafael shook his head. "Three days of galley food and they'd change their mind."

"You mean it's not glamorous?" August asked, her eyes sparkling.

Once he'd thought so. Once, he couldn't have imagined another life beyond his vagabond existence, living from expedition to expedition. Once, he'd never imagined that a woman could make him dream of forever. "Depends on your definition, I guess."

Zack began stuffing the contract back into the envelope. "Does your definition have anything to do with an antebellum house and a certain redheaded professor?"

Rafael glanced out the window. The stars twinkled in merry derision of his melancholy. "Cora's hair is blond," he said absently.

August touched his arm. "Rafael…"

He looked at her, forcing a smile. "Your hair is red, August. Zack should know the difference."

Concern registered on August's face, but behind her, Zack's snort was derisive. "Oh, for God's sake. You sound like a wounded puppy."

August gave him a sharp look. "Zack—"

He shook his head. "He does." Zack frowned at his brother. "What the hell is the matter with you?"

Rafael could feel his temper rising. "I'm not going to explain myself to you, Zack. I just want to know if that contract's legal."

Zack tossed the envelope on the coffee table. "Sit down," he commanded.

Rafael hadn't heard that note in his brother's voice since the day he'd left home. He looked at him incredulously. "I stopped taking orders from you when I turned seventeen."

"And you've never forgiven yourself for it, have you?" Zack asked.

Rafael frowned. "What are you talking about?"

His brother sighed. "Have you at least given yourself a deadline, or are you planning to sulk forever?"

August put her hand on Zack's forearm. "Honey—"

He shook his head. "No, I want to know. It's been what? Seventeen years? Aren't you getting a little tired of carrying around all that guilt?"

Rafael narrowed his gaze. "Aren't you the one who told me that no one could count on me for anything?"

"Since when did you take my word for anything?"

"Since you accused me of leaving you alone to deal with the mess at home. What happened to all that self-righteous anger, Zack?"

"I grew out of it," Zack said, his voice gentler. "And it's time you did, too."

Rafael blinked. "Until three years ago you were barely even speaking to me."

Zack shrugged. "We were stubborn. Both of us. I said things I shouldn't have, and so did you, but for crying out loud, Rafael, we were kids. I was eighteen years old. I didn't have all the answers and neither did you."

"But you didn't leave."

"So?" Zack's laugh was self-derisive. "I screwed up plenty of other stuff. Let's not forget that I appointed myself supreme ruler of the clan. Look how well that turned out."

"You provided everything for them."

"The words *control freak* come to mind."

"You were scared."

"So were you," Zack pointed out. "I just decided I didn't have to pay for it for the rest of my life."

Rafael's chest had started to hurt. "You don't understand."

"You want her," his brother continued. "You love her. You're dying without her."

August wrapped her arms around Zack's waist. "Can't you work it out, Rafael?"

"It's complicated," he said.

Zack put one arm around August's shoulders, but kept his gaze on his brother. "Of course it's complicated. If it weren't complicated, it wouldn't be love."

"Cora deserves a man she can depend on—someone who will be there for her. Her parents never were. She won't settle for less, and I can't be that person."

"Maybe she doesn't want you to," Zack said. "Did you even bother to ask her what she wanted?"

He hadn't of course. Self-centered jerk that he was, he'd simply made the decision for her. He reached for the envelope on the coffee table. "Just tell me whether or not this thing guarantees she'll get the money if I find the *Isabela*."

"She will," Zack told him, "but I'll bet you every cent I've got that the money isn't what she wants."

Rafael swept the envelope up. "It's all I've got to give," he said. "I've got to be onboard at five-thirty tomorrow morning. Thanks for looking at this.'' And he left without another word.

CORA LIFTED her face to the sun and inhaled a great breath of the fresh, salt-laden air. Ocean spray slapped her face. The wind whipped her newly cut hair against her cheeks. There was a bite in the breeze. The Caribbean waters glimmered a clear, aqua blue beneath a cloudless sky. The afternoon sunlight reflected off the white beaches in a blinding glare. How in the world, she wondered, had she lived this long without experiencing the pure rush of adrenaline that was making her skin tingle and her pulse race?

She should have tried a little recklessness a long time ago. There was something unbelievably liberating about it. Another thing she'd have to thank Rafael for when she saw him.

Cora pulled up the zipper on her windbreaker and made her way along the teak deck of the sloop that cut across the shallow waters of the bay. A few minutes more, and she'd be face-to-face with the biggest decision of her life. It should have scared her to death. And once, it might have. But today, under an infinite canopy of azure sky, it merely increased the current of energy that hummed beneath her skin. For too long, she realized, she'd made decisions based on fear of regret. She'd wasted so much time fearing regret that she'd missed the chance to embrace everything life could offer her.

Rafael had taught her that a life lived in fear was a life half-lived. And he'd made the idea completely intolerable. She could never go back, no matter what happened in the next few hours. Besides, she thought with a smile, if he said no, she'd strip him bare and torture him with kisses until he surrendered.

Cora reached the control center where her Antiguan guide was piloting the swift sloop through the narrow channels and inlets of the cove waters. She leaned against the railing. "How much longer?"

He kept his gaze focused on the water. "Hard to say. Your man has exclusive rights to these waters. His territory is large."

Her man, she thought with a satisfied smirk. She liked the sound of that.

RAFAEL BRACED his feet apart as his ship rode the swells of the Caribbean. Above his head, wind whistled through the rigging as the canvas sails billowed. The masts creaked, and water slapped the hull. Unlike most of his colleagues, Rafael had decided long ago that he preferred a schooner to the clunky, mechanized expedition crafts. Experiencing the sea in the same type of ship as his quarry gave him an edge. Normally he found the sights and scents and feel of the sea exhilarating. Lately, however, even the thrill of knowing he was on the brink of a new discovery failed to lift his mood. In the past few days, he'd managed to alienate most of his crew. At least, he thought wryly, the crew had prior experience with him. They were giving him a wide berth, but they didn't look petrified like the two research assistants he'd hired for this expedition. This morning, he'd hesitated too long before responding to a question, and Charlie Radigan, the twenty-year-old oceanology student who was responsible for mapping the changes in the currents and water temperatures, had practically crumbled.

Now the poor kid was approaching him with a look of stark terror. Deliberately Rafael removed the scowl from his face. "What's up, Charlie? Find something?"

The young man shook his head. "No, Professor, but, uh, I thought you should know that there's a boat bearing down on us."

The scowl was back. He'd lobbied hard for exclusive rights to this cape and the tidal waters that surrounded it.

The largest craft within a five-mile radius should be no more than the occasional fishing skiff. "Where?" he snapped.

"Starboard."

Rafael shouldered past the student and stalked toward the front of the ship. Sure enough, a racing sloop was sluicing through the water at a hell-for-leather pace.

CORA CAUGHT her first glimpse of the sails, and her heart skipped a beat. She wondered if Abigail had felt this way when the *Isabela* had crested the horizon. Goose bumps skittered along the surface of her skin. Her Antiguan captain gave her a toothless grin as he pointed to Rafael's ship. "There it is, lady. We'll have trouble catching it if he doesn't pull in his sails."

Cora moved to the prow and leaned forward, straining her eyes for a glimpse of Rafael on the deck of the schooner. His ship was fast, she realized, but the small sloop was faster. She drummed her fingers on the railing. Soon. Very, very soon.

RAFAEL GRITTED his teeth in frustration, then gave the order to trim the sails. It was probably a couple of tourists out for a leisurely sail. He might as well confront them before they did something stupid—like ram the hull of his multimillion-dollar floating research laboratory. "Bring me a glass, will you, Charlie?"

"Sure, sir," the young man said, racing off to fulfill the request—obviously, Rafael thought, poor Charlie couldn't wait to get away from him.

Charlie returned with the spyglass. Rafael took it without comment and held it to his good eye. What he saw made him swear so loud Charlie nearly toppled over board.

Cora was leaning across the prow of the ship, headed straight for them.

THE MINUTES DRAGGED BY until, finally her ship drew close enough to his so she could see him standing on the deck. He was glaring at her, she noted. And he looked adorable. His jeans hugged his lean hips. His shirt billowed in the breeze, and his dark hair whipped against the hard planes of his face. She ached to touch him. In the weeks since he'd left, she'd missed him more every day, but now, with him less than two hundred feet away, she felt her heart leap in sheer joy.

"WHAT THE HELL are you doing?" he bellowed as her sloop pulled alongside. Cora had the gall to grin at him.

"Hi!" she yelled. "How are you?"

Lord, the woman was insane. "I was fine until I realized you were trying to kill me. Tell your captain to pull off. We're going to collide."

Cora laughed. It lit her face and twisted his guts into knots. "Sorry, can't do that," she called back. She was running along the deck toward the low point on the railing. "But I am coming over," she announced.

He was sure he hadn't heard her correctly. Whatever Cora was doing here in the middle of the Caribbean, she wasn't stupid enough to... He saw her begin to prepare the ropes and hooks that would link her craft to his and felt the blood drain from his face. Rafael stalked toward her, torn between incredulity and undiluted terror. "Cora," he said, holding out a hand. "Just hold on."

The schooner and sloop were so close now he considered grabbing the sloop's railing. Briefly he contemplated the possibility of vaulting himself across the expanse. Cora gave him a bright smile and shook her head. "You're not talking me out of this."

Most of his crew, he noted absently, was gathering on the deck to watch the evolving spectacle. He glowered at the man behind the wheel of her sloop. "Pull away," he shouted. "Now."

The man didn't respond. Cora had most of the ropes uncoiled. "It's no use," she told him. "I paid him well enough to make sure you wouldn't intimidate him."

"Dammit, Cora!"

She shook her head and started making knots in the end of the rope that belonged in the Girl Guide hall of fame. She tossed the first grappling hook onto his deck. When one of his crew hurried to secure it, Rafael glared at him. Cora tossed another rope. "You're not talking me out of this," she said. "I'm coming over."

He swore. "Are you out of your mind?"

"No. I'm trying to get your attention." The only other crew member on her ship—a lanky fifteen-year-old who was obviously too besotted with Cora to know she was about to get herself killed—started to extend the bracketed gangplank across the railings. He lashed Cora's side in place, then waited for Rafael's crew to secure the other end.

Cora took a step toward the makeshift bridge, and Rafael's knees nearly buckled. "Cora, dammit, will you listen to me?"

"For the rest of my life," she assured him. "All you have to do is catch me first."

He might have sworn at her. He wasn't sure. All he knew was that he'd never felt anything even remotely like the stark terror that ripped through him when Cora levered herself onto the rail of that ship and started across the gangplank. He clenched his hands into fists. "I swear, if you don't go back—"

"Oh, stop. You wouldn't let me fall and you know it." She gave him a knowing look, then started across. When she was standing above the water, with both crafts moving swiftly, he realized he had stopped breathing. His last thought before she collided with him was that if she survived this fool stunt, he was going to strangle her.

The force of the impact sent them both tumbling into a pile of life jackets. He felt the breath leave his lungs in a rush. He couldn't decide whether the laughter and applause of his crew was louder than the hammering of his heart, but he crushed her to him and closed his eyes to blot out the nightmare.

Cora was struggling to breathe. The impact had knocked the breath from her, and he was holding her so tightly she thought he might have cracked one of her ribs. When she tried to free herself, an unexpected set of twinges and aches made her wince. Rafael was swearing at her, but the severity of the words was completely overshadowed by the rough yet tender way his hands were running over her body. "What's broken?" he demanded.

She laid her head on his chest. "Well, for a while, I thought it was my heart."

"Then we're even," he muttered. His voice sounded gravelly. "Because I think you just gave me my first coronary."

She choked out a laugh. His hold tightened.

"Hey, Rafael," yelled one of his crew, "you gonna lie around all day, or are we gonna find the *Isabela?*"

"We're drawing a crowd," Cora told him.

He groaned and rolled to his side. Reaching for her hand, he pulled her to her feet. His crew made a few ribald comments. He barked a couple of orders, which drew irreverent shouts of laughter. A glance at the railing told him his crew had already unlashed the gangplank and sent it back to the now fleeing sloop. Irritably he realized he would never have the chance to give that jerk a piece of his mind for putting Cora in that kind of danger. Tightening his grip on her fingers, he pulled her along behind him. "Come with me."

He led her belowdecks and into his cabin. He didn't stop

until he'd slammed the bolt home on the door and turned to face her. He was torn between a desire to kiss her sense-less and holler at her until she promised him she'd never do something like that again. "Are you—"

Cora interrupted him by laying a hand on his chest. "Ra-fael—"

"You could have been killed," he said harshly.

Her other hand went to the zipper of her windbreaker. "Can we talk about this later?" Her voice was sultry.

"No, we will not…" He forgot what he was going to say when she lowered the zipper. Beneath the windbreaker, she wore a black leather corset, laced over a white satin cami-sole.

"I see I have your attention," she said.

He decided he was having delusions. That was the only possible explanation for this fantasy unfolding before him. Cora shed the windbreaker and stepped into his arms. "Make love to me now," she whispered. "We'll argue later."

"What are you doing?" he choked out when she wrapped her arms around his waist.

She smiled and kissed his throat. "I'm pillaging."

An hour later, Cora rolled onto her side and eased her thigh over his. "I should have tried this a long time ago," she said.

He grunted. The sound was so primitively male, she laughed. Propping herself on one elbow, she looked down at his rugged, beautiful face. "I had no idea this pirating business was so satisfying."

He opened his eye. The heat she saw in his gaze made her shiver. "You scared me to death," he grumbled.

She traced a finger along the curve of his upper lip. "You weren't any more scared than I was."

Molding her hips with both his hands, he pulled her on

top of him. "You could have tried calling, you know. I have a cell phone."

Cora smiled and shook her head. "You wouldn't have believed me."

He frowned. "So you decided to shock me to death, instead?"

She thumped his chin. "No." She picked her way carefully into the explanation. "Rafael, I had no idea when I fell in love with you what it would do to me. I...I was so scared of what I felt for you."

"Cora..."

She shook her head. "No, really. It was...potent. It was consuming. I couldn't imagine what I was going to do when you left."

He frowned, and she smoothed the crease from his forehead with her fingertips. "So I did something stupid," she continued. "I pushed you away because I thought I could keep you from hurting me." She shook her head. "I didn't realize until it was too late that nothing in the world would hurt as much as spending the rest of my life without you in it."

"Cora." He pressed his hand over her mouth. "Stop it. You don't have to apologize for protecting yourself."

She pushed his hand away. "Rafael, do you love me?"

His gaze darkened. "More than you can imagine."

Her heart soared. "You are the most beautiful man I have ever known."

"Marry me," he said, cupping her face in both his hands. "Marry me and let me prove to you that I will always come home to you."

Cora kissed him, deeply. When she raised her head, her breathing was erratic. His hands had moved to the laces of her bustier. "If I marry you," she said as he pulled at the strings, "can I be the pirate at least half the time?"

"I'll pillage you," he said with a smile, "and you pillage me."

Epilogue

Five years later

The strange noise carried through the old house, and Cora tipped her head to listen. It was late. She glanced at the clock. After midnight.

She strained her ears. She heard the creak again. Her youngest son, Robert, hadn't been feeling well that afternoon. He might be out of bed. Her mother's ears and instincts told her no. Just as quickly, she ruled out the other children. Will, her oldest son, was a sound sleeper—he never got up in the night. Kaitlin, Molly and Liza were staying with them for the summer, but Kaitlin was spending the night with a friend, and Molly and Liza were asleep down the hall. She listened more intently. Perhaps Will had forgotten to pen Melody before he went upstairs, she thought with a frown, and began to push the covers back.

Then she heard the distinct sound of the security code being entered into the alarm system. She relaxed back against the pillows with a soft smile and a sigh of anticipation. He was home early.

Seconds later Rafael's booted feet struck the stairs as he took them two at a time. He was shedding his jacket as he entered the room. He paused long enough to kick his boots off, then he covered her body with his in a swift move that simultaneously staked a claim and fulfilled a promise. He laced his fingers through hers and pressed her hands to the pillows. He kissed her, warmly, intensely, for breathless minutes.

When he raised his head, she laughed. ''I thought you wouldn't be home until Friday.''

He kissed her throat. ''I worked hard.''

An understatement, she thought as his mouth glided over her jaw. He would have had to push himself relentlessly to be home two days early. His discovery of the *Isabela* five years ago had sent his scientific credibility skyrocketing. Each new success brought increased demands on his schedule, but Rafael always hurried home to her. ''You must be exhausted.''

His chuckle rumbled against her skin. ''I'm not that tired,'' he said.

She could feel her blood pressure rising. She wrapped her arms around his shoulders and clutched him to her. ''I'm glad. You're, ah, raising my expectations.''

He shifted against her and jerked the sheets away. ''I missed you,'' he breathed. ''I missed the kids.''

''They missed you, too.'' Their two sons had their father's dark good looks and winning smile. ''Robert will be so thrilled that you made it home for his T-ball game.''

He managed to remove the rest of his clothes and her nightshirt without breaking the kiss. After five years he could still impress her. She stroked his bare shoulders. ''I'm so glad you're here.''

He lifted his head. ''I am, too,'' he whispered. He touched her lips with his finger. ''The girls are here?''

Since that awful day when Lauren had arrived for the girls, Rafael and Cora had worked hard to ensure that Kai-

tlin, Molly and Liza would always know they had a home
with them. Lauren was on her second marriage since her
affair with George ended, but her daughters spent every
summer in Cape Marr. "They arrived last week. They're
dying to see you."

His hand had found a particularly sensitive spot. He drew
a circle on her flesh. "Me, too. How's Kaitlin?"

Cora had told him on the phone that Kaitlin had changed
more than the others in the past year. Adolescence was having its way with her. "She's dating," Cora informed him.

His fierce scowl made her laugh. "And she'll be happy
to argue with you about it tomorrow."

"She's too young."

"How old were you?"

"That's why I know she's too young," he grumbled.

Cora slid her hands down his back. The feel of his flesh
against hers was exquisite. "I love you desperately," she
told him.

His gaze softened. "What in the world did I do right in
my life to have you in it?"

Cora opened herself to him. "You showed me how to
live," she whispered.

"I love you, Cora. I love you."

She cradled her pirate in her arms, wrapped her heart
around his and softly responded, "Welcome home, dearest.
Welcome home."